Lies Hidden In Darkness

MW00946641

By D. Harvey Rawlings

My heart,
  there will *never* be a time when,
    I will not
      love you.
        Thank you for loving me forever,

  D.

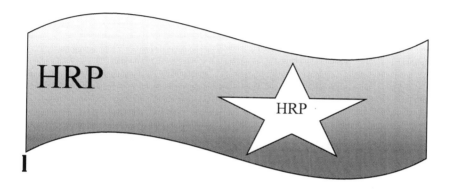

My son, may you live interesting days, in this interesting of all times,
full of laughter and fun, but most importantly of all,
        may you love,

  Dad

Prologue

The electronic door slid open and she passed through it without stopping. How she wished everything in life was so easy. Her life was easy and good at one time. However, that has all changed now. When life was good, she knew the right things to say in public. She knew the right foods to eat. She even knew the right places to be. That was all privy to her, because of how well off her parents are. However none of that matters anymore, she is forced to be estranged from them.

She was a naïve girl then living in fantasies and now, today, she's a fully grown woman with some real issues, real trauma. Some days she seemed as if she would not be able to get out of bed, burdened with the memory of it all when she could remember and when she could remember the truth. Today though, she managed to come here. Today would be a day of acceptance, accepting that she indeed has a problem and is in need of some serious help. Today she would take advantage of the beautiful skies and make the change. Today she would ask to be free from this madness, even beg if she had to.

Chicago Memorial Hospital was busy as usual, at least what she has become accustom to from her steady time here. This was her home away from home.

She thought about her last visit here and the conversation she had with Dr. Edwards. Janice, as she insisted she call her, talked to her about building her life again and moving on from the pain. She had a valid point. She did need to move on; however, there were some old scores to settle before she could, truly, move on.

All involved will have to pay she thought as she boarded the elevator and selected the number five as her floor choice. It wasn't fair that he could move on with his life. Not even that witch who made fun of the situation, when she tried to explain to him what he did to her. It made her angry then, but now it's driving her mad.

No not true remember this is not true.

Count, count, one, two, three, that's what Dr. Edwards told her to do when, the madness occurred. This would block the thoughts that weren't real and when she heard the voices in her head. The tears were building again. She always cried when she was forced to think about all this. How could she have let this happen? Didn't she see it coming?

She took herself to the pain that started all of this, too much, she thought. Could it have been different? Could she have made a difference if she had fought harder, to prevent being bound by this? It's not her fault but she blamed herself anyway, she only blamed herself.

Inside, Janice told her to focus on the good, during that time, before. What kind of good was there to remember about that night? Oh yes, the reason for being there at that time was to be with him. She wanted so much for him to forgive her for the choices she made. However, she never got her chance. Only the results remained and that was all. They will pay for all that they've done.

No. Break away. It's not the same thing. You're confused. Remember.

As she walked from the elevator to the office, she felt the wildness in her head grow intense. It was almost like trying to subdue and cage a ferocious animal, four-five-six. She felt her own rage as if it was another person inside her and she enjoyed it. It gave her the strength; she knows she will need to fulfill her plans, to be free. Part of her wanted the rage to escape but the other part knew what it was told to do, obey.

Maybe she should talk to Janice about the cynical thoughts that were trying to claim her; maybe she just needed prayer.

Whichever, the need is now.

She knew Janice was waiting on her. She is always with her, to free her and she felt safe with her. She was a comfort that she needed.

Yes, there is so much that is here that does not make sense, but you know the truth... she heard a voice in her head say. *I am always with you. I will be free.*

There it was again that quiet voice that tries to deceive her and make her weak. She shook her head and counted to shake off the intruder.

Once she entered the office she immediately went to the reception desk. The receptionist sat at the desk with no concern. It was so coldly that she didn't even look carefully to fully recognize her. She did this every time she came here, every time any patient came here. Just a little courtesy could bring her help. She should be fired or worse. However, her mission today was one of peace; she will deal with her later.

That's the reason for these visits to this Dr. Edwards, psychiatrist, is to cure her or at least to calm her down before she is forced to do something rash.

No it's to control you remember?

Ignoring the voice, she thought, it doesn't seem to be a bad idea to punish the guilty. Punish them so that they could never alter another's life the way hers has been moved. The way she pains. The way...

The door to Dr. Edwards' office opened and the doctor, stepping out quickly addressed the desk clerk.

"Vicki, hold all my appointments for tomorrow so..." She stopped in mid-sentence as she noticed her visitor. "Well you're early."

"I thought I was late."

"Come on in..."

"Dr. Edwards, your 3 o'clock cancelled," Vicki interrupted.

"Not a problem Vicki it gives me a chance to catch up with my family."

Dr. Edwards closed her door and walked over to her chair, the one that she kept close to the office chair recliner, she uses for her patients.

"Have a seat 'Karen'."

'Karen' walked in and the first place she looked at was the cherry oak stain desk. There on the desk was the gold plated letter opener that Janice's husband, Everett, bought her. Ignoring the feelings that began to rise just seeing it she sat down on the leather recliner and leaned back.

"Well, have you considered what we talked about the last time you were here?"

"I'm not sure if I understand what I'm supposed to do, I'm still angry."

"'Karen', in the process of moving forward, the anger that you feel, you must embrace it because it will only help you get through this task faster."

As she thought about what Dr. Edwards was saying and if she has decided on anything it was that she did not like to be called 'Karen'. That was after all not her name. She at least knew that. It was a pseudonym that psychiatrists sometimes used to protect the identity of their clients. But that was on their files.

If she didn't need her so much she would add Dr. Edwards to her list of people she would eventually have to kill.

No, don't think like that, once more the voice pleaded. *Don't let it be like this. Try to get some other help. Don't talk to Dr. Edwards, talk to Janice.* In her mind again she counted one, two, three.

"I know Dr. Edwards, I'm trying. I'm not sleeping at all during the night; will you be able to prescribe something more for me?"

"Yes 'Karen', but lets start into how all this is affecting you today. What did we discuss the last time you were here, do you remember?"

"That I still love him and now I can't be what he wants, because so much has happened?"

The doctor nodded.

"I wished he would return my calls but he doesn't want to see me. I know what I did caused him pain but I can't believe that the result is that he doesn't love me anymore."

"'Karen', that's perfect. That is what we discussed. Do you remember who we discussed whose fault it was?"

"I know it's, his."

"No, mistakes were made, that why it is hard to accuse just one individual. They all must…"

"He did it," 'Karen' shouted and Dr. Edwards smiled. "Didn't he do it? He left me to take the punishment for it. Then she mocked me for it. She has always mocked me all this time. Even the time when she was with him, lying in his arms; when she took my place. I remember that night as if it was happening right now. The two of them were so embroiled in their sexual display in his office and I walked in on them. I got real close to them…"

"'Karen' let's get this right. The last time we spoke you said you caught them in their public display, in a large room. What you're saying now is that you were in the room with them, right?"

"Yes that's what I meant to say, in a room."

"Okay go on, what next?"

"I was close enough to touch him. I have been watching them for years."

"Him? You mean them, right? I don't understand, where were you, tell me?" Dr. Edwards was eyeing her with great curiosity and it seemed like concern.

Fearing that she has already said too much, 'Karen' paused. She has to bring herself back to focus or else she might say too much and that will cause problems. She cannot know that she is remembering independently. She may force her tell her the true plan.

Yes, don't reveal the plan.

She would then have to do something to Dr. Edwards to keep her silent and she didn't want that to happen. More blood on her hands.

No, no violence. You didn't do that. You know it was her fault. She's the one that mocks you. She took him from you.

She can't tell her how close she has been to him lately. She has gotten this far and she's about to get even closer to tell him the truth. Before she realizes what has hit her, she will have already struck and she will be so happy; she would be free of her.

'Karen' shook her head. She reached in deep in her mind to stop the malevolent thoughts that gathered there. They confused her greatly.

Yes, you know the truth. Listen to Janice, she's your friend, the voice in her head reasoned with her. *Move on from this. Break free of this hold.*

"She has even mocked me when I called him."

Dr. Edwards didn't want to upset her any more than she was already. The last few times their sessions were very heated, almost incensed. She wanted to maintain control of this session, so she didn't let on to her that she was aware that 'Karen' changed the subject.

"You never told me you tried to contact him. What happen with that and please, please try to remain, calm?" Dr. Edwards asked.

She was trying to remain even, in spite of every fiber in her being, wanting to lash out at her. She avoided trying to rouse 'Karen' up. She has become so volatile lately that most of their sessions become heated.

'Karen' took another the silent moment to compose, within herself.

"And I didn't mean to tell you this time. Very well then, yes, yes I called him. I called him to tell him what I was going through, the hell he put me, through. She was there with him lying in his bed and I wanted to..."

"Go on 'Karen', you wanted to what?"

"I wanted them to...feel what I feel? Is that it? To know what I know..."

The doctor nodded, motioning her to continue.

She couldn't let the doctor onto everything she was feeling. She still wasn't quite sure she could fully trust that the doctor would not have total control, especially with that information, not yet. It just wasn't clear when it came to her. If she told her, Dr. Edwards would most likely have her committed or worst, jailed, for having such thoughts. But it's the truth.

Yes the truth.

It might get to a point where she would be kept sedated and comatose. Then all that she has worked for would be for not.

It was best to leave it alone, until she was sure what action she wants to take. She couldn't tell her that right at this moment in time because she wanted those that hurt her to die. Anybody that happens to stand in her way, well they had better beware.

I'm too tired to keep these thoughts from you. You must not let them control you.

It would be like the start of a nuclear war. In any war there is collateral damage, the so called innocent. But are they truly innocent or just those who ignore the chaos that is surrounding them?

'Karen' believed that there was no innocence left. Everything around her was evil, so full of despair and she would have to take care of it. She had her ways before all this, aristocratic ways.

Surely no one will believe that she was innocent, that's why she became a victim and never saw this coming. A victim to love, to hate and to all the scary things that goes bump in the night.

For years she has carried this burden, this load. It seemed like a bundle of a hundred pieces of bricks, perched centrally high up on her back. One by one the bricks would have to be removed.

Yes, that's what Janice has been trying to do all this time, remove them.

It's time that Karen' destroys them permanently one by one so that there can never be a chance that the bricks will pile on her again.

"So 'Karen' I feel that we are ready to move forward to further healing are you ready? You are aware of what we have to do to heal you right."

It was a fair question she thought as she reclined back into the comforts of the plush soft chair she was sitting in. She had a chance to beat her at her own game and be free. She will fight her at every move.

"Yes doctor, I am."

****

Exactly two hour and thirty-five minutes went by and she emerged from the elevator onto the lobby floor. As she began to exit the lobby of Chicago Memorial Hospital, renewed, she never flinched as the staff hurried about her. She wondered, were they coming after her. After all Dr. Edwards could hardly breathe when she left her office at the close of the session, actually, she had another ten minutes left on her appointment.

All the good doctor could do was nod in shock of what she had done, when she said she was leaving. She was happy now and she felt she had the strength to carry on the direction that she wanted to go in; not where Dr. Edwards wanted to take her.

Poor lady, she thought as the electronic door magically opened up for her, this time as if it was just for her. She never knew what hit her as the session took an ugly turn.

It wasn't her fault, it was this 'Karen' that the doctor insisted on calling her. She took over and the doctor never had a chance. Nevertheless, when the session got heated again, 'Karen' said all that she couldn't say. She did all that she would not do; she embodied all that she is.

How dare Dr. Edwards raise her voice as if she was appalled by what she felt? Is she or is she not supposed to understand all that she is going through? This is her doing. Isn't this what she's known all this time? She insulted her and for that she had to pay.

The session was going smoothly they were able to iron out a lot of pain that still existed from the time when *he* decided that she was not the right one for him and walked away. Dr. Edwards told her that it was selfishness that brought him to his decision and that she should be thankful that he did leave.

That somehow made sense. Why would she want a man who couldn't be there through sickness and health, until death do we part? At the first sign of trouble, he would be gone. It was true and 'Karen' agreed with her.

Lies.

As they continued the session, she came up with other points that were well, taken. By then Dr. Edwards was sitting across from her at her desk. She had 'Karen' feeling as if she was on top of the world and that nothing could hurt her, anymore.

Not until the doctor made the ultimate mistake. She suggested to her that she should forgive the man that caused her pain and 'Karen's' mind stopped to register what she said.

In 'Karen's' silence the doctor continued to drive the point of why it was so important for her to release him from her emotional prison. When the time came to respond it was 'Karen'. The 'Karen' that the doctor would regret creating. The 'Karen' she would regret meeting.

The two of them started to raise their voices at each other. Dr. Edwards apologized repeatedly about losing her professional composure, but 'Karen' didn't want to hear any of that.

Almost immediately, her eyes went again to the doctor's desk, like before. She saw the gold plated letter opener that was given as that special gift of love. It meant so much to Janice.

Her late husband, Everett, brought all the office décor and fancy statuettes around the room, he had expensive taste. She was especially fond of the antique gold painted statue that sat on the desk right beside the letter opener and Everett's framed picture.

She sat there with anger mounting from Dr. Edwards' words. She concentrated on the letter opener, eyeing it and caressing it gently with her mind. Then she felt it in her hands. Next, she felt herself lunged forward toward the doctor, plunging the tip of the letter opener into her throat, to the base.

As Dr. Edwards, responded in astonishment, she grabbed the handle of the letter opener and pulled it out. She could not breathe as she stood up and 'Karen' saw what she had done.

Looking back on all that had happened; she wished that she had handled the session differently. Even as she cradled the picture of the Janice's beloved dead husband in arms, she wished she had calmed herself before this ungodly outburst.

It was not necessary to hurt her in the way that she did. But she was blaming her for what happen, she really was. All she was trying to do was cure herself of a sickness that would one day envelope her in a corner so dark that she will never come out of it.

If only she could tell her, tell Janice how sorry that, she was not strong enough to resist being controlled. It's what drove her to this rage. 'Karen' is truly taking over.

She remembered she told Dr. Edwards that she would be back soon and all that the doctor did was nod, not taking a breath as she left the office.

When she got to her car, she felt a peevish feeling in her stomach. She realized that she hadn't eaten in two days and now that she felt released, free, she could finally eat. Where she should go, she thought, as she drove away? Where should she go?

****

Dr. Edwards slumped on the floor of her office near the letter opener and pieces of broken statue. She was near tears as she cradled the broken statuette in her arms. How could she do this? She thought she was controlling her; reasoning with her.

What could possibly be going on in her mind to want to do something like this? What can she solve by pushing her beloved present to the floor and watching it smash into many pieces? Why would she take Everett's picture?

She brought to mine the memory of her face. The look on it was horrifying. She saw a vengeful coldness in her eyes. To analyze, that one moment in time, before she push Everett's gift to her onto the floor, it was a murderous, coldness. That could raise the hair on the bravest of persons. It only lasted a moment, but it was there.

Where did that come from? It wasn't there at any of the other sessions. That was not true. It has always been there since the sessions began and even before that. But like any other time something unexpected happens in a session, Dr. Edwards, played it down. She took the seriousness from it.

She couldn't risk escalating the session any higher than it had elevated to, but she had to admit that she didn't expect her to get that angry. She just didn't think she programed that way. She shouldn't have let her leave like that. She should have reasoned her back down to a level where she felt she would be safe.

She scolded herself mentally for not staying professional during the entire session. That was something that she would work on. This was the kind of thing that got her in trouble during college, her riskiness and her inability to care for others' feeling.

Nobody's perfect.

CHAPTER 1

She followed him to the rear of the restaurant and paused as she lost sight of him. There was the old phone booths right where she remembered they would be near the restrooms. Those phone booths were antiques but they went with the décor of the restaurant. What would she say to him, because it had been years since they last saw each other? Her heart pounded in anticipation to finally look into his eyes, the eyes that have been eluding her for years or at least since she has been constantly thinking of him. She had made herself forget his look. That certain way that he would raise his left eyebrow when he wanted to say something witty, to make her laugh. How she would touch his nose gently when she felt herself falling further in love with him.

At least she thought she had forgotten all those little things.

It was all coming back to her now. How did it get to this? How did it end up that they were no longer building a life together? He was her match and she was his, but that was a long time ago. What would she say? They never said goodbye. Just one day she woke up firmly into her new life and it went on. Initially there were no regrets, because there were plenty of some things to keep the two of them busy and apart. One day went by, two days, three months and suddenly it's today eight years later.

What would she say? There was so much anger there too. It's all coming back to her now. She said this, he said that, and she thinks he meant this and he knows she meant that. Nevertheless, those things were never answered. As life went on, when she wanted to revisit that time she discovered that those things were never important. Those things were only used to hide the real reasons they were falling apart. What was the reason? What happened? She couldn't for the life of her remember what drove them to that day they did not even bother to say goodbye.

Somebody has the answer.

He has the answers she thought.

That's it, she thought.

She would walk right up to him and ask him to explain to her why. He would know the answers. He should have the answers, he always did. He always made things sound so simple; sometimes when it really was not. That's what balanced them, their time together. Their strengths and their weaknesses made the balance.

"Excuse me Miss," a woman startled her as she asked to get pass her. She was absolutely frozen and couldn't understand why her legs felt like weights as she moved unconsciously but politely to the side. She should have never come here, all these years of avoiding this place, their place, her place and his. This is where they fell in love. This is where they grew to depend on each other and this is where they had their last meal together. They were sitting not too far from where her husband, she and their guest were sitting this evening.

She guessed he had known that she was not going to call him anymore, but she never asked and she didn't know.

When she got up from that table that night many years ago, she never looked back. Why did she want to punish him so? He loved her and that was more to her than anything. No that's more to her than anything now, but back then there was a lot more to see and do.

Full circle, she has come full circle! The one very thing she had run from was now at her door again. Moreover, what was theirs in her heart is there once more. The ideas, the feelings, the hopes, the dreams, they were all in her heart and soul again. It was as if someone who had lost her memory suddenly finds this life that was long forgotten or better still, awakened.

What was she going to say? What was she going to say? Then the guilt hit. It hit hard and without mercy. It threatened to overwhelm her. It was her fault, she thought. It was her decision to leave. It was her choice. What choice could he possibly have if she was so unwillingly to continue with him? She bore the blame.

He doesn't want to see me she decided. I have caused too much confusion in the past, why would he? She decided she would leave. But if she left wouldn't it be like it was years ago, not giving him a chance to say his peace? It was not fair to him that she would choose for him to see for the second time the image of her walking away. She felt that for once she would see it through. See it through to the very end, to close this chapter for good. If not, for her sake for his. She tried to take her mind off the impending meeting.

She looked around the small hidden alcove that she was standing in and then out into the heart of the restaurant. La Maria was still beautiful and full of quaint atmosphere just like years ago, just like those years when they were in love. The picture that hung near the old fireplace is still there. There were rumors that the peasant woman in the picture standing next to the old well was the owner's grandmother, from Italy. She was very beautiful but he always told her that no beauty compared to hers. They were really in love and now this, their not. She smiled to herself because she did give it the old college try; to try to get her mind off the one and only man she ever loved. There now, it was to the surface. She never could admit that mistake she made, a mistake that altered her reality forever.

What was she going to say? Whatever she had to say had better come to mind quickly, because he emerged from the restroom. As his eyes met hers it was almost spiritual. Both of them froze in some conundrum of thought, almost a joke. He was thinking, like of all the places in the world to be, you are here. She had been so prepared, so contained, but his presence changed all that. He could not believe his eyes. She is here!?

"Hello Michael," she said silently never taking her eyes from his.

"Natalie, hi," Michael watched Natalie with curiosity. He took in her presence and had decided that if anything she has gotten more beautiful than years before, years, how many ago?

Automatically his mind drifted back to where all the feelings he was beginning to experience again came into focus. He went back ten years when they met and dated for two years. He drifted back to a time when both their lives made sense, when they were together and when he was in love.

"So, Michael Montgomery, how have you been?" Natalie asked breaking him from his muse and in order to prevent from saying what she really wanted to say.

What else could she really say to a man that she hasn't seen in almost eight years? Now she looks at him and wishes he would scoop her up in his arms and rescue her from the life she has chosen instead of him. But she knew he wouldn't, couldn't.

He looked at Natalie a little more intensely as if to figure her out. It wasn't that he was at any odds with her; it was really just damn good to see her.

"I've been good and how about you? You seem as if life has been good to you."

Natalie knew that Michael found it awkward to talk to her as well. The tension between the two of them was enough to carve into with a knife.

"Michael you and that charm, it never fails. My career has its rewards and I guess being around children constantly does a body good." Natalie said.

She was reluctant to tell him that she has two children of her own.

Why she felt like that she didn't know, after all in eight years a lot can happen?

It felt like the right thing considering all that has happened. If they talk again which she hopes will be real soon, she'll have to tell him.

"How's Sonja?"

Hopefully she chose the right tie tones, she thought, but she had to get that issue out of her system. Why would she start off their reunion with that sore subject? She knew the reason why. It was because it bothered her years ago when she first heard that he had married Sonja. It broke her heart. After all Sonja was her best friend at one time in college. It seemed that after the day Michael and Natalie broke up, weeks later Sonja moved out of the apartment they shared together.

Shortly after that, Sonja started to avoid her until their friendship was no more than a myth. At that time, it never donned on her because she had crammed so much of herself into her graduate school studies during that time. She never thought that Sonja could actually have been after Michael for herself. It wasn't an easy concept to accept would happen, but it happened.

A few years later, one of Michael's current friends, Mona Daniels, who went to college with them, became an outlet to the old crowd for Natalie. She was that familiar friendly face that Natalie needed over the years.

The two of them ran into each. It was during a time when the pharmaceutical company that Mona was VPO for, conducted business with Chicago Memorial. Natalie was interning there. They had lunch and caught up on each other's lives, but avoided any conversation about what happened with Michael, because there was no point. They were all there when the break up happened, Mona, Sebastian and JC, all there.

Mona had admitted this to Natalie, that she had been angry for a time with her. She said that Michael helped her get passed it. Mona and Natalie became even closer than their college years and life has moved on. Natalie knew it was hard for Mona several years ago to eventually tell her that Michael and Sonja were married. In addition, Natalie tried to react nonchalantly to the news, but that's when she felt the first tug at her heart.

That was the very first time that she took an honest look at herself. She admitted that she made the worst mistake of her life by marrying Christopher. From that point on, her life revolved around trying to figure out a way to apologize to Michael. No for her to get back to, Michael.

Mona suggested many times that she could invite Michael to dinner and have Natalie just come by. Natalie didn't have the nerve to carry on a one on one fight with Sonja; one that she knew would happen if they were to meet again. Mona was all for it she never liked the idea that Michael had married Sonja anyway. This stemmed from negative encounters the two of them had during their college years.

Now she was at the hour. He is standing in front of her and all she could do is wish he hadn't married her ex-best friend.

"Good, good," he responded and then dropped off his words.

He didn't want to get into his personal life right now, but she took it there. There was something uncomfortable about discussing his wife, who at one time was Natalie's best friend. It was something that he could never explain, not even to himself. It wasn't at all like he was trying to keep it a secret; he just didn't have a reason why he chose to be with Sonja.

He just didn't know. He guessed Sonja was there when he needed a mate and a confidant, but now he knows she was never his friend. She was just the one that was there to ease his heart of the pain he was feeling; a rebound. It was all messed up then and even worse now; and that was something that he didn't want to reveal to Natalie.

"Natalie, I'd like to stay and chat with you a little longer, but I have a business meeting to get back to."

He took her hands into his as he did that last night many years ago and Natalie thought she saw that same yearning in his eyes. The same as that night he tried to convince her to stay with him.

"It is so good to see you again."

"Same here," She felt the panic within her as he started to walk off. "Michael," she called to him and he turned quickly to face her.

"Yes."

"This is my office number, we should catch up more." She held a business card outstretched in her hand.

"Natalie, I…"

"Michael, *call* me."

He took the card from her hand, nodded as he left the small alcove and she sighed with relief, she did it.

As she stood alone, reality began to sink in. She suddenly remembered that she left her husband Christopher and his fellow board director, Stephen Hartford and his wife Suzann; at the dinner table. She hesitantly returned to the table and she sat down with their dinner guest.

"…and this is what Chicago Memorial needs to continue to prosper in revenue, as the Chief of Staff I will see it done."

Natalie felt the interrogation from Christopher as he probed her with his eyes. Everything has to have a time limit.

Quite naturally later, when they are alone he will ask her what kept her so long to return from the restroom. However he would never let on in public that he was the least bit interested in trivial things; such as timing on his wife.

To the Hartfords, his expression was harmless, but she knew what was developing from behind it. His world was so perfect, so planned. Nothing was going to interfere with the day-to-day operations of his life, not even her.

What was the interest that drew her to Dr. Christopher Robert Bower, candidate for Chief of Staff at Chicago Memorial? How many times has she heard him quote that title to her? If she looked back on their time together he has always been like this, self-involved.

At first it was great that he was so driven, just like Michael was, to establish her career as well as his, but Christopher his taken it to another level. Instead now it is neither her nor her career that drives him to her.

She tried to keep her composure stable as she listens with false interest to what Christopher was saying.

"Honey, would you like to comment?"

She almost lost it in that brief moment. Someone else almost took over for a brief second, someone she was sure he wouldn't like. She quickly gathered herself.

"How so dear?" Was all she could say?

Natalie wanted to get up from the table and flee. She wanted to go find Michael in the restaurant before he leaves. She would go to his table, excuse his company and then share an intimate evening with him. Just as she, has yearned for these past several years.

"Well I thought you might have an idea as to where the hospital should..."

Christopher's voice drifted from her mind. She shut him out, as she has done many times before. He was driving her crazy slowly. As usual, a few moments later, Christopher gave up his mission of charity to include her in his conversation and dominated the conversation again. Natalie didn't even bother to check into see if it was safe to exclude her own self from the talks, she knew Christopher well.

She hoped that Michael calls her tomorrow. What was she after? What did she hope to accomplish from this phone call. She pondered it awhile and realized that it was important to her that Michael forgives her for her mistake. She was willing to do anything to make amends and she hopes that Michael takes her up on the offer.

As floods of thoughts pounded in her head, she had to get up from the table again and flee; before she told Christopher what she really thought.

"Excuse me, please. I don't know what's wrong with me,"

"Do you need me dear?"

"No, I'll be alright."

She wanted to tell the asshole that she wanted to go from him, to be free, that he is what's wrong. Instead she simply slipped away from her husband and their guest as they look on.

Seconds later, somewhere in the restaurant Michael continued his meeting with his associate and their guest at his table. 'Karen' stood behind one of the pillars peering at him. She wanted to reach out to him but her mind told her no, not now, in due time.

****

"Sebastian what the hell is going on over there?" Michael yelled through the phone to Sebastian.

"Mic, I've gotta call you back, Abigail is tripping again."

"Okay, but call me, I gotta tell you who I've seen tonight. I'll be at the studio till two in the morning."

"Sebastian, hang up that damn phone, Michael is not going to help you this time," Michael heard Sebastian's wife, Abigail say. "I'm through with you and your selfishness."

He heard the phone dial tone on the other end and knew Sebastian was in big trouble again at home. Sebastian Black and Michael have been friends since freshman year at college, so he wasn't too shock that Abigail finally let loose on Se, again. He tried to warn him about giving out his cell phone number to all these females that he's messing around, with. One of them was bound to call out of the timeline that Se had arranged them in.

It's the nature of women to cause a conflict whenever they got tired of being the other one. Abigail is no fool and definitely not as naïve as she once was when they were all in college. She stuck by Sebastian throughout the entire time that he played the field and married him.

Sebastian never could come up with a reason why he felt he had to marry Abigail, when he still wanted to play the singles game. He hopes that Abigail doesn't do too much bodily harm to his buddy.

Michael really wanted to get meeting Natalie off his chest before he went home to Sonja. Of all the people to run into in Chicago, he had to run into her. This city has always been big enough for the two of them, what happened? But it was bound to happen sooner or later. After all Mona is his friend as well as hers.

It was something that two hours ago the woman that broke his heart over eight years ago is back. But there was something pleasant about the way Natalie seemed almost desperate to talk to him. It was funny that the wall he built primarily for her lost some strength today. He made a mental note that yes he was definitely going to call Ms. Natalie Vincent.

Switching gears in his mind, Michael just went back to viewing the latest taping of his cable show 'Life Talk with Deena Williams'. He hopes that this will be his ticket to the big time and that Deena Williams will take him there.

This is what he dreamed about all his life; what he went to college for film, video, television production and communications. All these studies worked for him. Then it was the internship at his current career at Local Cable KXITV. This is where he spent time pitching ideas and honing his craft to become executive producer for what is upon him now.

His dinner meeting with Tyler Scott, an executive from Warner Bros. Television and his staff went very well he thought. The monetary numbers that he bantered about exceeded Michael's expectations. Tyler assured him that *Deena* was definitely going to be a national hit. She was already killing the ratings in Illinois and the surrounding areas, beating out the local competition here, so it was inevitable that *Deena* would go nationally syndicated.

He thought again about Natalie. She would appreciate hearing this news. She was always supportive of his dreams. Of all the places to meet again for the first time, why did it have to be their place? That place. He wished that he could have taken more time to stay and talk to her. It was after all their first meeting since that night eight years ago, when she decided that her career was much more important than their love.

She is still so beautiful to him, he thought. But he couldn't let that interfere with what was going on with him now. He gave her so much before and she didn't take it then. He wasn't thinking this out of malice. He just felt that now is his chance to think about his career and his dreams. He was already dealing with Sonja and her lack of interest in what is mostly important to him, he wasn't stopping now.

But Natalie sure tugged at his heart again.

****

Sebastian was sure that the neighbors, two houses over on the street of their cul-de-sac, could hear Abigail's screams. She was going for the gold this time. She's been going at it for two hours straight and doesn't seem to be letting up. This is the maddest he has ever seen her and felt scared that something has changed this time around.

Abigail looked at him with so much intensity that he could feel at least in his mind the burn of her disappoint, what has happened? Did one of his side activities, what he likes to refer to his extra women as, call her?

Rachel, Pamela and Maris all know not to call his home and besides they only have access to his cell phone number. He's covered all the basics like not getting a cell phone bill at home, not having online access to view his cell phone bill. Even if the bill comes there it doesn't show any calls.

Sebastian has always remembered to cross all his Ts and dot all his Is. He has to admit it to himself as he gloated silently, that he lives in his perfect world. If she has anything, he will simply punch holes all through her logic.

Once again Miss Conservative Dressing Never Do Anything But Lay There And Make Him Do All The Work Abigail Black will be tamed and begging him to forgive her. He will do it, he will forgive her, but only if she agreed to his new terms and he can come up with that now...

"Do you hear me, Sebastian?" Abigail broke through his concentration.

"Abigail, I hear you. Everyone can hear you, but I don't understand you. What's the problem?"

"I have had it up to here with your cheating. I can't take it anymore."

"I don't know what you are talking about..."

"Oh you don't huh?"

Abigail exited the bedroom and Sebastian heard her stomping heavily down the stairs. He mentally followed her footsteps to the kitchen or so he imagined she was going. He thought that he should leave, because she could be going to get a knife or something. His wife was not herself and new behavior tends to breed different response.

Immediately, as if out of nowhere, Abigail appeared in the doorway of their huge bedroom. Sebastian felt a streak of fear rationalizing that she stealthily returned upstairs. He realized she was holding a large gift box, not wielding a knife.

A gift she wants to give me a gift he thought?

"I want you to see this stupid shit."

"Honey, you didn't have to get me anything. I've done nothing to disserve it."

"Sebastian," she screamed. "Wake the hell up. I didn't buy this, it came through the mail. I presume it's from one of those trashy sluts you been running around with."

Abigail threw the box on the floor and it fell open on its side. From out of the box, dead, black spray roses splattered around the opening. Beneath the flowers and partially out of the box, facedown, a small baby doll.

"What the hell?" Sebastian said genuinely shocked.

"You know what it is. One of your whores has decided to end your fling, probably because you promise her something you couldn't deliver. Humph, I know about that."

"What are you talking about baby?"

"You know Sebastian, I've always admired you for the way you could turn things around and make me believe that I am the one that's wrong. I let you do it because I loved you so much, that I wouldn't let myself believe you could actually do me this way. I realize I can be a little clingy at times, but you are my husband and as my husband you're supposed to be my best friend. I never shared myself with any other man but you. You were my first and only and this is the thanks, I get from you. What is she number twenty-two or two hundred twenty-two? Did you ever really love me or was I just the right one to start a family? Well the jokes on you right because, I haven't been able to get pregnant, now. Is that the reason why you're punishing me?"

Abigail didn't wait for an answer; she simply left the room because she didn't have any strength left in her to hear his response.

As she ran to the room which was designated as a baby's nursery, she looked at all the items that she has collected over the years waiting on a miracle, her miracle baby.

The doctors told her that it was nothing wrong with her, nothing wrong with Sebastian, just that there had been some scarring from her last procedure. Then why was God not allowing her the one thing that would make her happy? What could possibly be the great design?

She sat in the corner where the rocking chair was, placed. This is where she would have sat and bonded with her child, her baby. She wondered to herself whether Sebastian had any idea what was going on with her. Is he as upset as she is, that they couldn't have this dream that they both said they wanted.

The gift through the mail was just another way to remind her of her pain. Could it be one of Sebastian's whores trying to taunt her. Did Sebastian discuss their problem with them? She thought about it for a while. The more she drifted into this depression and carried a burden of responsibility the more it hurt her. Sebastian acts like he isn't married, then she was going to do the same. She decided just then that she is going to bring this room another look and she is going to give herself a different outlook.

Fourteen years of being with him. Eight years married to Sebastian and all that she can show for it is a large, pictorial home. A home with empty souls to, occupy each of the empty rooms. She is going to have some fun, so much fun that the hollow feeling that she has in her heart won't even be noticed.

She will go back to work at the publishing company that she use to work at. That was before Sebastian became the famous 'Mr. Sebastian the Morning Lover', radio personality for the number one radio station in all of Chicago, and convinced her to quit her career to start a family; big joke. He never considers her, but she's always putting him first, well never no more.

****

"You feel so good to me," Mona heard Jackson say to her as they made love.

He was everything to her right now. To hear him return the affection helped to smooth over the reality of their relationship. It was the fact that he's married and she's his thing on the side. Of course as Jackson would say, it won't be too long before they were together permanently. All she has to do is be patient. It's been almost a year, but it's been worth it.

Jackson Crane has shown her more in their short months together than she's allowed herself to experience in all her adult life. The expensive outings, trips, jewelry, gifts were all extra added attractions to this fling, the trappings.

Of course she didn't need these things from him because she could get them on her own. It's the lifestyle that befits the Vice President of Operations at one of Chicago's major pharmaceutical companies, Cultrax. But what woman doesn't want to see her man do his best to charm her?

Being the other woman, is nothing new to Mona. He's just one more thing she has, to avoid the reality of settling down with someone herself. In the past, all she would have to do is tolerate her men friends up until the time they go home or wherever the hell they go.

She's lied before when one of her married men called himself telling her that he was going to leave his wife, to be with her.

She had responded with something very unbelievable, like not being able to sleep until their together again; or he's the only one to get her off. Mona lied to him and the others because she knew they were lying to her, but she didn't care men are pigs. However, Jackson was becoming something totally different.

She lay embraced within Jackson's hold, she felt special, like he really seemed to care about her. He kissed her like a man in love, as Mona tasted his tongue's wetness. She felt his passion.

Jackson had to admit to himself that Mona is worth the time. The things that she did to him sexual, his wife, Leanne couldn't or would never do. It was almost tempting to leave his wife right now for Mona, if it was always going to be like this.

"You wear me out, baby," Jackson said as he collapsed on the bed beside her.

Mona just laid motionless, enveloped still in the feeling of Jackson. He was truly her best lover all right.

She reminisced back on the first night she met Jackson. Sebastian of all people was the catalyst. He had convinced Mona to go with him to one of these online swing parties, like the ones they talk about on Twitter and Facebook. At first she did her usual protests, but Sebastian has always been able to charm her and most recently charmed her panties off.

This happened shortly after Sebastian had married Abigail, Mona made her move. Through the years she teased him more and more. He was one of her best friends but the attraction was always between them, even in college. Like always, Mona got what she set out to get, no matter what the cost or how it affected Abigail.

Sebastian paid Mona's membership fee and they were off thick as thieves into the wild side of life. After the two of them had sex together that night, Mona then met Jackson.

They turned each other inside out. They continued to see each other doing freaky things together, since. It didn't bother Mona the least bit two weeks after they met that he turned out to be married.

"Well I guess I'll go."

"Do you have to go, it's still early?"

"Mona, it won't be long. I just need to close out a few things and I will tell Leanne that I'm leaving her."

It was almost funny to hear him say that even though she wanted it to be true, it couldn't, so cliché'. Jackson was convincing though, convincing enough to convince her. But what would she do, Mona thought as he left her apartment, if he was being for real? She's not going to let herself fall for him that's for sure. Jackson Crane may hit the G-spot, but that's not going to do it for her. But what will?

Moments later as Jackson got into his car, he smiled to himself. The memory of his night with Mona made him want her again. This is definitely a bonus plus. This was far from what he set out to do with Mona. If he didn't watch it he would accidently, fall for her and that would complicate his plans.

It has taken too long to get this close to her. However plans aside she's everything he's been searching for in a bed partner. She is so willing to explore anything that he feels fit to impose on her, and he has a lot in mind. Why not have a little fun while, conducting business?

Leanne could use a few pointers from her. He doesn't know what happened to her but she is surely different than when they first met. She first met him that night at the swing party; the same night that he met Mona. She encouraged him to approach her. Their relationship now at best is an arrangement. It means little to nothing. She has her agenda and he has hers, but she promised him excitement.

He thought that she was just as exuberant and scorching as Mona but she is not. No matter it's a means to an end. It will be fun to see how far the sex games with Mona will go while implementing his major plan.

Mona watched him from her window, kittenishly. She wondered if he was thinking of her. She was being silly but it is what it is. Her phone rang and she picked it up to answer it hoping it was Jackson calling.

"Hello," she said too sexily. "Uh, hello, Ms. Daniels, this is Craig McNair."

"Oh hi Craig, what's up?" She hoped she didn't sound too disappointed to the assistant lab technician from Cultrax. It wasn't that she was surprised by the call but in her heart she wanted it to be Jackson.

"We were just getting ready to wrap things up for the night and Dr. Monarch wanted me to tell you that the project is moving along swimmingly. We should reach our deadline ahead of time by 3 weeks. That's good news right?"

"It certainly is. Tell Paul that I will be in tomorrow at 11 and we can go over the specifics."

"Will do Ms. Daniels, oh yes I may be late tomorrow too, because I'm going out to celebrate."

"Well don't get into any one-night-stands, I'll need you communicable for our noon meeting."

"Just going to have a few drinks, I'm not going to fall for any fast girls tonight."

"Then I am going to sleep well. See ya." Mona cooed silently as she hung up the phone.

Other than men, the most important thing to Mona was her career, which she took very seriously and never allows anyone to interfere with it. Her position at Cultrax as the VPO gave her the perks, the finance and the power she so much craved.

****

It was getting late as John 'JC' Carpenter watched the sexy shapely female from slide down the iron pole, for the umpteenth time. He had been here, at the strip club too long, waiting for Desiree. He was sure that, this was one of the nights, when she worked.

JC was hooked on this stripper and he knows she knew it. But she wasn't connecting with him. How could she not know? For the last month he's always requested Desiree to come to his table after her set, but she always goes to another patron.

What was it about him that turned her away? He considered himself average and he makes very good money but he wanted excitement, like Sebastian and Mona. He's always been behind the scenes and under the radar.

He's made a good career in Real Estate, being a top seller at the company that he works at. Chicago has been good to him even in this economic climate, but not with love.

Single and thirty JC, just started to take his life seriously. How many times was he close to being married, but didn't have enough personality for the women to move forward with him. How he always envied Sebastian and the way he controlled all his situations.

Sebastian is this big major radio deejay personality as all the Chicago papers is always referring to him as. He's also just as much a one major womanizer. He does anything he wants to do and the women just seem to throw themselves at him with no hesitation. Even in college, he had women parading in and through his dorm and apartment.

Years' being his friend and JC has not even measured up to him, at least in JC's eyes. Maybe that's the reason why he turned to drugs in college. The drugs helped him feel good about being a loser. Sebastian knew this. When it got out of control, Michael was a big help to him getting him off his drug of choice, Methamphetamine. It took him years to shake that off but he's off it now and never going back.

As he chugalugged his beer, he caught a glimpse of Desiree standing behind him. She was in the crowd that, gathered at the bar for drinks, through the mirrors on the stage. She was sitting on the corner of the bar peering at him.

To JC she didn't look like she belonged in a place like The Exterior or any strip club. Not that he is thinking that exotic dancers were some lower form of life. She had class about her that some of the white collar women he worked with have. But they lacked the mystery that Désiree projected and he wanted to know her secrets.

As he stared at her through the mirror, she brought her focus to meet his gazed. For one brief moment, JC decided that now was the time to empty out all the money in his bank account and give it to Desiree. She winked at him and he returned the greeting with a nod.

She mouthed the question, '*would you like some company*' and JC noticed it and nodded again. He almost thought he had a science to it now. All he had to do now was keep it cool and she may not recognize that he was not at all like the ladies' man, Sebastian Black. He knew he over idolized Sebastian. He knew that and couldn't do anything about it. Sebastian was his safety net.

Desiree moved slowly to the table and sat down in the chair closest to him.

"Are you sure this is what you want?" she said. "What do I want?"

"Me."

CHAPTER 2

When Michael returned home, it was late, but earlier than he had told Sebastian. He just didn't want to stay at the station that long. Seeing Natalie really blew his mind and he couldn't think. She wants him to call her tomorrow and even though he wanted to do that desperately, he wasn't sure. He wasn't sure that he could face her again after seeing her tonight. Wow, it really has been over eight years since that night. That last night they shared together at La Maria and it still cuts into him like a knife. For two years prior to that last night they were together full of the love they had for each other, all the time. Then all of a sudden it ended.

He had loved her so much. Back then, all he could do was put that love in a bottle, cork it and place it on a shelf. Now the bottle is about to crash down and spill out over now. If it does what will happen? Why does Natalie want to see him?

As he climbed out of his car, he noticed the gray Mercedes strangely parked again a half a block up the street as usual. It's been parked standing there for the last few months at least twice a week and lately it's been more frequently. It just sits there with the parking lights on, that's how Michael could identify it as a Mercedes, but not one he has seen in his neighborhood before.

He always thought of his neighborhood as being quiet and safe, that's why he hasn't thought anything about it. But why does it seem that the car is watching him, waiting on him somehow.

Could it be Natalie, sitting in the car? It would make sense now that she has contacted him. Michael thought about it some more and decided to walk up the street to confront the person in the car. The Brands live up there and if anything Michael could always fake like he's going to visit them.

Michael moved five steps on the sidewalk towards the car and instantly the Mercedes headlights came on. Almost simultaneously, the Mercedes backed up quickly and disappeared, screeching around the corner of the block, it was sitting at.

Well no doubt the car relates to him. Relieved in a way, Michael turned around and headed back towards his home. His body shook slightly from the chill that invaded his body. The summer air did nothing to comfort the eerie feeling that he had. If that is Natalie, why was she reacting like this? What if it isn't her than who?

He opened the door and walked into the house. It was after ten so he knew Taylor was sleep already and he hoped that Sonja was sleep as well. He noticed the kitchen lights on and moved towards it through the door. Please God, let Sonja be gone to bed, he thought.

He was not ready for yet another confrontation with her that he knew would happen if they talk tonight. Unfortunately as walked into the kitchen he heard the first cruel laughter from fate in his mind. He saw Sonja sitting in her regular spot at the kitchen isle, eating that damn dietary ice cream she seems to purchase by the truckloads. She never finishes it and usually the ice cream just goes spoil. She doesn't even need to be on a diet she's in perfect frame.

Sonja looked up at Michael, watched him go to the refrigerator, and pull out a bottle of tomato juice.

"And hello to you too. Your mail's over on the baker's rack."

Opening the top he sipped slowly on the tomato juice. He wished secretly that the juice would last forever so he didn't have to converse with her.

"Another late night at the cable station Michael? I thought I asked you to come home early so that Mrs. Berman didn't have to watch Taylor, pass her normal sitting time."

Michael took the bottle from his lips as he look into Sonja eyes. How cold those eyes have gotten over the years and how calculating. Every since Taylor was born, Sonja's control over him has grown. Simple parental duties became a contest and when she started the Craft Store business, she considered herself just as busy as he is.

Taylor is his darling, the one good thing out of this marriage. When she put her tiny heart into his hands, he vowed that he would never let her exist in this world without knowing that he loves her and that he would always be there for her. She is the most lovable six-year old a father could hope to have. She believed in him and he really felt it. If only her mother could realize it.

Michael offered Sonja a love at first and she rejected it. She always seemed to hold back and never truly let herself love or trust Michael. Why was she so afraid? He would be romantic with her and it was as if Sonja wasn't there.

This reason was, as the years went by Michael just unleashed that love he's had for Natalie to sustain him. It was easy to relive that passion with Natalie because it never fulfilled its promise. The memory of their time together saved his sanity. But Sonja never seemed to fit into that love.

"If you remember, I told you that I had a meeting with one of the business execs from Warner."

"Sure. Whatever."

"I'm going to bed Sonja."

"Michael we have to talk. This thing that we're doing is getting out of hand."

"How is it getting out of hand, we're not cutting each other's throats."

"Yet."

"Yet, what's the problem Sonja; you didn't make enough money today at the craft store? Where is this argument going, because I'm tired?"

"I'm not stopping you."

Michael tossed the bottle in the trash and walked out. He didn't even bother to mention the mysterious car to her. It was clear that she had she some steam to blow off and Michael was the target.

Sonja didn't know herself where she was taking the argument, that's why she backed away from it. This was a first though and should have been a milestone in favor of their relationship. Most of the time, it would be words bantering back and forth. What happened to them she thought? How cliché does that sound. It was obvious that they were growing apart.

That's why the craft store has been so important to her, almost like an obsession; 'Sonja's Favorite Crafts'. For the last 2 years, it has served as her sanctuary, her home away from home. Michael seems like he doesn't mind anyway, all because she was never her.

As much as she has tried, she feels she has never been able to fill that void that Natalie Vincent has left. It was almost an insult for him make love to her the way that he used to make love to Natalie. Then to know, that it was Natalie that he really wanted to make love to. Michael didn't even have the nerve to be original with her just replaying some dead memory.

In college, when she used to share a dorm room with Natalie she would secretly watch them making love, wishing that it was her. She would dream that he was hers. When she finally got the chance to be with him, all she wanted was her chance; not be second best.

He promised her when they got together that he was through loving Natalie, but he had lied. He punished her for Natalie's crimes or was he just angry with her for being the one he didn't want.

It wasn't her fault that she loved Michael the moment she laid eyes on him. The anticipation of finally meeting the man that was converting her sorority sister from a bookworm into a love sick slave was almost like thirsting for water; and he was worth it too.

She wanted him. He had a presence, drive. He belonged to Natalie, but she didn't appreciate a man as strong as Michael and she certainty, didn't disserve him. He disserved to be, loved, as Sonja knew she could love him. That's why she worked to dissolve their relationship. It seemed so easy.

She began working her schemes on Natalie by breaking into her computer and deleting or altering her classwork. That put her behind in her work until it became overwhelming and stressful. She made sure that she was everywhere they were. She had a guy call Natalie's mother pretending to be a professor complaining of her daughters falling fledging GPA.

How gullible Natalie's mother was. She believed that a college professor would waste his time to call the parent of one of his students; in regards to her class performance. It was college after all, not high school. That con was too sweet.

Even erasing all the phone messages left by her mother was giving the little spoil brat what she disserved. But the kick off was the risky conversation that Sonja had with Natalie's mother 'in confidence' letting her know that her precious, bookworm daughter was in over her head with a no good player like Michael. She insisted that the Michael that was introduced to them was not the man at all.

After Sonja finished telling her of Michael's fictional exploits with other women her mother agreed to slowly separate the two of them with mother's love. She kept Sonja's anonymity and it worked.

Once the pressure was on Natalie and she was out of the picture that's when she was able to make her move. In the weeks after Natalie broke up with Michael, Sonja made sure she'd bump into him outside the same cable station where he works at even today. She wore her hottest clothes. She became his confidant consoling him and then finally several months later, letting him make love to her.

She cured his aching heart and she became Mrs. Michael Montgomery in return. This is what she wanted. She never really considered herself as being Natalie's friend, so there was never any reason to feel guilty about stealing him. Actually she didn't steal him, he was given to her.

Sonja turned the kitchen light out. The shimmering light from the full moon outside illuminated to guide her way through the house; until she was at the top of the stairs. She looked into Taylor's room. She was asleep. She looked into the spare bedroom, the one before her own bedroom.

The silhouettes of her ceramic dolls she kept there, made the small collection look huge, but they were still, peaceful and waiting. She went to her bedroom door, opened it and walked in. Michael lay motionless as she approached the bed, but she knew he was he was awake.

What happened to them? Every time she searches for answer at the bottom of her thoughts would come the only answer, Natalie.

****

The next day, Natalie sat in the Starbuck's coffee staff lounge at the hospital. She sipped her coffee with little to no consciousness, as thoughts of Michael flooded her mind. It was pass noon and he hadn't called like she asked him to.

What did she expect? What did she think he would do? After he had a chance to sleep on it, he probably decided that he wasn't going to take himself through all that again.

How she hoped she could turn back the hands of time and love him as he loved her then. It was no point in brooding over it, today. Just like all the other years before it was just something she would have to deal with. *No*, not this time, she was going to find an end to this madness before it consumed her and finally destroy her.

"Hi Natalie, I'm glad I caught up with you." Natalie turned sharply to face the voice behind her. It was her friend, Dr. Janice Edwards.

"Hello Janice, I…"

"I know, I know, you were too busy to come to see me. But you know I always have time to talk you, no matter what."

"I know but I've got some heavy things on my mind and I just wanted to be under the radar today."

"But that's my specialty," Janice said as she sat down at Natalie's table. "Things, that is on peoples' minds."

"I don't need professional help on this one Janice, I just need a friend."

"All jokes aside, I'm here for you if you need to talk, you know how we close we are."

Natalie nodded to Janice in acknowledgment. It was good to know that Janice was so concerned about her well-being. But this thing with Michael is not something she would want to see get out. Natalie was thinking on the line of Mona when she said she needed a friend.

Janice with all her good intents and purposes is really somewhat of a blabbermouth. It's a wonder that any of her patients haven't sued her on confidentiality issues. She's been like this since meeting her years ago, during her intern here.

No she wasn't really like this at first. Before, she was so full of life, vibrant, sophisticated and professional. You couldn't get her to discuss her job. They become fast friends then.

It was after her husband died and she was gone for nearly a year. That's when the change happened. When she returned, it was as if she was a new person, subdued, almost non-caring and aristocratic. Not even looking like the same person. Death does that to people she guessed.

Natalie, herself has heard more than her fair share of these sessions over the last pass years as lunchtime gossip. She surely doesn't want her troubles to be the next thing on the talk circuit menu.

"What you should do is tell Dr. Christopher Bower where to go. It's enough to be second to his work, but to be his prisoner as well."

"Janice, please be discreet. I don't want you to be overheard by one of his nurse's fan club members. It's enough to live under that kind of suspicion at home, so working under it is not on my Christmas to do list."

"I hear you."

Dr. Edwards looked at her with subtle concern. Something was happening with Natalie Bower. The solution was puzzling her even more as the seconds passed. She's hiding something. It was more than the usual conflicts going on in Natalie's marriage; something else is pulling at her.

She has been friends with Natalie for almost four years now. She made sure they became fast friends to re-establish what was. Since then she has always analyzed her, like she did all that crossed her path. It just goes with the territory.

This change in behavior that Natalie is exhibiting is that of a woman torn. There's a decision that is about to be made. By the looks of things, it will irrevocably change Natalie's life forever. The fear is written all over her face.

"Natalie, I know that in the past, I have treated information from my sessions with little regards. If you want to talk, it's just between you and me. I have always respected our friendship. It's not like the patient that I have now who is filling with so much rage that she is becoming unstable. Oops there I go again. I promised you I wouldn't talk about those things in public."

Natalie looked into Janice's sincere face and started to cry. After a brief second, she caught herself realizing where the two of them were. She quickly and sharply got up from the table and bolted from the canteen, leaving Janice sitting in shock.

This is too good to let go of. She didn't realize how very close to the edge, Natalie really is. She's up to something, she was sure of it. Even though outwardly she had to be concerned about her friend, she couldn't resist smiling to herself. She knew her trade well and that fact made her proud, that even in the sincerest of moments, she can still accurately diagnosis a patient.

Her disbelieving cousin told her, she should move on from this profession before someone got hurt. She knew she had what it takes.

****

Natalie returned to her office and hurriedly went inside. She was very upset. Kelly was not at her usual spot at the front desk. Then she remembered it was still into her lunch hour. The door was not locked. Then suddenly to the right of her she saw the figure move. How long was the figure sitting there watching her, where the patients waited to be seen sits?

Natalie cursed herself, because she knew better than to walk into a deserted area and not be on alert. Why would she feel fear in this public place is beyond her? But that's how she's been feeling lately, like something or someone was after her. Slowly she turned to face the figure.

"Natalie is you okay? I didn't mean to startle you."

It was that voice. She's never forgotten that voice. It was Michael's voice.

"Michael? What are you doing here?"

"I told Kelly that I was Mona's brother, coming to see you. I figured that Mona spends a lot of time here, so I thought that would work better than trying to tell her I was an old friend. That was okay right?"

Michael watched every move Natalie made as if to commit her to memory. It was good to be close to her again.

"Of course, I won't fire her this time, since it's you. What are you doing here?"

She didn't know herself why she kept asking that question, but she was in shock.

How do I look? She questioned herself. *Damn you Michael Montgomery, you caught me of guard, like I did you.*

"So, this is you in your natural habitat, good, good. Instead of calling you and playing phone tag for the next two weeks, I decided I'd settled on the direct approach. I was trying to get here before noon, but you know traffic in Chicago this time of day."

"Well, can you stay awhile?"

"The question is do you have time for me with your schedule?"

"All day," she joked.

That was a catchphrase that Michael would playfully use in those days when they were together. He always meant it to let her know that there was no other place he'd rather be than with her at any time.

He paused as he realized she has changed and he could feel it. She had to be careful with how she handled this meeting with him. After all, it's not like the two of them are single and able to pick up where they just left off, if at all.

"I mean, I have a clear schedule today. I guess all my little patients are healthy."

"Must, be that TLC, Dr. Vincent."

Michael wished he hadn't called her by her maiden name. He was painfully aware that Natalie is married with two children.

When he found out from Sebastian, who, found out from Mona; it was like a knife in the heart. He hadn't felt that much pain since the night Natalie walked away from him. Even though he knew her life was not on hold, it still bothered him.

It was awkward enough to share the same friend with Natalie. He made sure never to interrogated Mona and just let it go. He felt he had to. It was good just too secretly check in on her whenever he could, just to see if she was okay.

Mona tried to interest Michael in a friendship with Natalie at one point. He couldn't go back to being just friends with the only woman that could actually stop his heart from beating. He died when Natalie left him and it was by the grace of God that he was able to move forward again.

That night eight years ago when Natalie left him alone at the table at La Maria, Michael drank so much wine. Samantha, the owner, had to convince him to call Sebastian to come pick him up; before she would let him leave the restaurant. He stayed in bed for almost a week before he could get back to his senses and then just so.

He began to feel that pain again now, almost as if it was that night again. As he followed Natalie into her office, he backed away from her a bit. She turned around and noticed his hesitation. So she took his hand and the pain instantly went away.

"Have a seat Michael." Natalie motioned to the plush loveseat nearest to her desk.

Michael did not sit down immediately. He simply stood in front of Natalie and look deeply into her eyes. He was caught in a void of emotions which is something that he experienced a lot lately.

He reached out for her and stroked her cheek. She didn't move. It was almost as if he was reminiscing and even he could not explain it. He slid the palm of his hand around to back of her neck and intertwine his fingers playfully into her long hair. Michael noticed earlier, that she still keeps her hair long. That was one of her magical attractions, which he loved about her.

She tilted the side of her cheek to relax her face against Michael's forearm. She closed her eyes. He slowly pulled her close to him and brought his other arm up around her. This is what he's wanted to do, what he's been dreaming of doing since the day he lost her, just her hold to.

Natalie lost herself in the dream of the embrace. Neither of them was thinking about that one little fact that the two of them are each married, to someone else. It never entered their thoughts. Michael pulled Natalie's face towards his. He wanted to taste her lips again. There was no denying him and Natalie didn't want to. But before his lips connected with hers, Natalie spoke in a whisper.

"Michael, I'm so sorry. I didn't mean…forgive me."

He smiled and connected his eyes to meet hers, even more intensely than before.

"I don't want to talk about that right now. I just want to do this."

He leaned into her wet lips with his. It was back where it once was with him. For Natalie, she felt the release of her guilt, at least for now.

He lingered into the kiss and she did not hesitate to receive what she felt was her reward, up until her phone rang and the intercom page came on.

"Yes Kelly," Natalie said as she broke the kiss and embrace.

"Dr. Bower, I'm back, I'm sorry I'm a little late but the traffic in this city, this time of day is crazy."

"Yes…"

"Are you okay?"

"Yes, I have a visitor…remember?"

"Oh…yes. Mr. Daniels. Sorry I buzzed."

"Okay."

"She an apologetic sort isn't she?" Michael said to break the awkward moment.

"Well, I could learn from that example."

"So is this all you're gonna do from now on, apologize? That's not why I came here."

"I messed up. I made this mistake…"

"I made plenty of them too and that's what it was a mistake. Look I'm not going to stand here and try to tell you that I haven't been pissed at you. Not going to say I never blamed you for not communicating with me, then. But I'm here now with you, again."

She was speechless. *He hasn't changed. He is still that understanding person.*

I don't disserve his understanding right now. I need him to be angry with me, she thought.

"I'm not going to give you what you want. You want me to waste time asking you why and I already know why. I was there remember? It's been roughly eight years since I last seen you last. I don't want to waste another minute dwelling on something that we can't change. I've already had to learn to live in a world without you and I don't like it."

"That's all we can do is, dwell on the past. I'm married, you're married and to my ex-best friend. What is there?"

"Well when you saw me at the restaurant what did you want?"

"Your forgiveness..."

"You always had that and so much more. I'm not going to play around with you Natalie, you need to know...?"

"Michael, wait, not now..."

"I'm not going to wait. I don't care what you do with the information you are about to hear. It's yours to process how you feel, but you need to know that I have never stopped loving you and I have been in pain since the day you left. I've always felt that you are my soul mate. I will never love another woman the way that I love you. I don't understand it. I don't have any answers, but I've been waiting to tell you this for a long time and it's for real."

Natalie went back to her desk and sat in the comfort of the high back plush chair that goes with it. She couldn't even look at him to tell him what she felt. She didn't have the strength. He looked at her with concern. Maybe this was too much, too soon, but this was always his way. It was devastating though, because what was going to happen now?

Natalie was right, she is married and so is he. What good is going to come out of telling her the truth? Michael turned towards the door strong and upright, opened it and walked out. He waited until he reached the men's restroom and went inside. That's when he gave the slightest indication that he was a man who has just felt his heart ripped away. It was his soul a second time and this time hurt more than the last. He just lowered his head and splashed water on his face.

CHAPTER 3

'Karen' sat at the dresser mirror of her bedroom. She was flipping through her to do list. She didn't want to take this revenge lightly. She wanted to make sure that she followed everything down to the letter. This is the way it will have to be. She still felt bad about scaring Dr. Edwards, a week ago. It wasn't that she meant to do her any harm but the doctor pissed her off. How dare she make her feel bad about her own thoughts? She knew the truth and so did the doctor.

She looked at the pictures she had surrounding her mirror. As cliché' as it was like something out of a psychotic thriller, she knew she was every bit far from being crazy. She was only angry and she was doing this out of revenge and control. There's nothing demented about sweet revenge.

"*Yes it is,*" she heard the voice.

She continued to scan the pictures with resentment until she reached his picture. She stared intensely into his eyes as if she was trying to communicate with him. What is he going to say? Was he smiling because he approved of all that she was doing or was he telling her that she should just forget all of this to come be with him again?

But he lied to her and betrayed her by being with her.

This is so confusing.

She wasn't sure of anything anymore. All she was sure of was the way she felt about these two as she glared at the pictures. What she was made to feel.

Moreover, as 'Karen' glared, she felt something inside of her weld up. This murderous rage exploded within, as she hurled the heavy jewelry box that was sitting on the dresser at the mirror. The mirror shattered and the jewelry box fell open onto the floor.

While open, the box began to play a baby's lullaby, that caught 'Karen's' attention. It calmed her as well as the baby that was crying, which seemed first to be in the back of her mind. Then she realized it was coming from the other room.

"Mommy's coming precious." She said as she got up from her seat. She shouldn't have let these thoughts control her, she thought. It scared the baby.

As she ran to the other her room, there inside was a baby's crib and many, many dolls, surrounding the room.

"Mommy's here baby. Did the bad people scare you? Mommy tried to destroy them, but I'm not sure it worked."

'Karen' reached into the crib and cradled the baby in her arms but the baby was motionless. It felt cold and hard to her like plastic.

"There, there now, you've frightened yourself stiff. I'll tell you what, let's go call daddy and make him listen to you. Mommy has been trying to get through to him, but he won't listen. He loves you but he doesn't love mommy. When I'm through, he'll wish we had never met and then we can be with your real father."

'Karen' walked back into her bedroom with the baby cradled to her breast. As she sat down on the side of her bed, she felt a strange presence within her and then the voice faintly whispered.

'What are you doing? It's not real. None of this is real. Why don't you stop this? You have the power. You are in control, remember. This...'

"Enough! Get out before I take a knife and carve you out. All you are doing is trying to confuse me, like he did and like she does. You were too weak to be there to stop all this, now get out! I'm trying to make a private call and you don't need to be here in my affairs. Get out!"

'Karen' waited a moment and realized that she had won. This is just what Dr. Edwards told her to do every time she heard the other voices. Why was she always talking to her from the other room? It was her, the other, she knew that, but she didn't need to be in her business like that. Dr. Edwards said that the other would eventually try to contact her. Attempt to control her to do the unspeakable weak things that did not fit into their plans.

She reached for the phone on the nightstand and it rang wildly before she could touch it. It startled her as she drew back quickly from it. She was a little bother by the intrusion, because she had some things to do.

"Hello," she said as she answered it. She almost wants to say 'flick off'.

"Oh hi," her voice changed into a sort of singsong tone. "Yes I'll be there. You want me to come and sit with you or are you going to be with some friends...baby you know I'm all about you. Isn't that what I told you, can you say the same...the music, the lullaby, that's my roommate trying to get her baby to sleep? I told her when she let that no good guy get her pregnant that she was going to have problems...It is a problem when you're raising a baby on your own, that's why I can't, don't, don't have any...I don't know if you'd make a good father. There's some guys you know that are not good for women to be around you know...Because I can tell, anyway you know what they say about you men nowadays...So you're telling me that you're totally different huh? Well we will see baby, we will see...Okay I'll see you tonight, bye."

She held the phone to her ear as she listened deeply to the dial tone. The humming sound the earpiece made was very soothing to her and serves to keep her focused. She hesitated for a minute;

actually thinking clear now and then suddenly the madness emerged again. She dialed a set of numbers on the base. 'Karen' got up from the bed and went over to where the jewelry box laid on the floor.

Over to the left of the box was the picture of the man that changed her life forever. She pushed him from her mind as she continued with the call. It's really interesting what kind of information a person can get when they put their mind, body and soul into it.

She listened to him chant 'hello' repeatedly. She reveled in the pleasure of taunting him. Then she pulled out the tape recorder and pushed play button. The sounds of a baby crying uncontrollably were deafening to her, but it was more important to hear the response she was getting from him. He pleaded to her to tell him what she wanted. She heard his inquiries as to who was it on the line.

He was calling out different women's names. Names, no doubt are of some of his other victims. They were victims all right. She knew they were because she was told they were. They were women that he couldn't possibly have a meaningful relationship with because he can't be trusted. Everybody knew that, especially his wife.

He finally went silent on the other end and then the phone line went dead. 'Karen' felt the satisfaction of his pleads. This is what she said would happened when she heard him the satisfaction. She was able to go to work now. She needed the boost because of what she had to deal with at work. It was a living. It was, all that she could do now without worrying about making a living.

'No not you. This is not you.'

She had cut off her mother and she has no relationship with her father. It was partly their fault she's like this. After all, it was their decisions that made this happen. She needed help and they didn't lift a hand to get it for her.

No call them. Their probably wondering what has happen to you.

It would be best that she gets ready for work. She had some things to take care of along the way. She'll think about meeting her man later if that's what she can call him. Maybe she should call him her pawn.

*****

Sebastian sat back on the recliner, in the den of his house. He thought about the calls he's been receiving. He wondered why in all these years, that he is no closer to knowing who it is and why they were calling. It was a good thing that Abigail was not here to hear any of this or he would be in knee-deep crap with her, again.

Just like last week with the baby doll. Abigail didn't know that this stuff had been going on since before they got married. As a matter of fact since college, while they were dating. Could it be that some broad is telling him that he has a child with her. What kind of crazy broads would waste time doing this? Why not reveal it?

Fortunately it's only once a year, during the summer that the calls and the dolls come. The years before Sebastian would somehow be able to spare Abigail from the trauma of seeing these things. This year he was not so lucky. It was as if this year something different was going on. The air was thick with something dark looming. He should call the police he thought or better yet hired a detective. A detective would be more discreet and if it is simply an angry baby's momma or a scorned ex, he could end it before it gets public.

The worst thing for his career right now is headlines reading, 'Dead Beat DJ Jock Dad Drives Mistress Over the Edge.' It would make the radio station owners run him out of town. No, he thought. This is not the time to rock the boat. In all these years, nothing has happened. Maybe this will all blow over if he just sit back and keep quiet. Nobody knows that the dolls or the calls were still coming except Michael.

Sebastian heard the front door open. He guessed Abigail. She hadn't spoken to him since last week when all that drama went down, followed by a similar phone called. She should be breaking down now. If anything, he should be worried about it being her. This is passed anything that Abigail has done. Most of their arguments end up with the two of them together, beating the sheets.

Sometimes Sebastian would purposely piss her off so that he could transform her into her raw passion. She's hot when she's so desperate to save their marriage. What has changed, though, a new man? Again, the air loomed with a dark eerie thickness and it was beginning to suffocate him.

"Abigail, baby, are you hungry? You want to go out to dinner?" he yelled out, trying to get her to reveal her location.

There was no response, just movement heading in his direction. Not again, he thought. It's on again? Sebastian thoughts were drowning in fear. Here it's about to get there again.

He didn't understand why he's held on to Abigail all these years. She's everything that he doesn't want in his woman; mousey, mothering, needy. No zest is there like the women he messes with unless he pushes her. Why is he holding on to her?

After a few moments Abigail appeared in the doorway breaking Sebastian's thoughts. Sebastian could not believe his eyes. Abigail was standing in the doorway, not dressed in the loosely fitted, church-like, clothing that he was accustom to seeing her in. This Abigail that he saw before him was wearing a tight, silk, blouse and a very from fitting skirt; with shoes on to rival any hooker.

"What are you going to do, just stare at me," Abigail asked. "What do you think?"

She twirled around a few times.

Sebastian eyed Abigail from the floor where her three inch heals started up to the short black skirt, with the split on the left thigh to the tight thin blouse she was wearing. This was something that he has never seen before and at that moment; he was aroused by her.

"What kind of joke are you playing Abigail? I don't need you to remind me of what you think my taste in women is."

"Sebastian, why do you think it's always about you anyway," she said as she spun around again.

"It's my show now, lover. I've come to the conclusion that I allowed myself to live up to your rules. You know when we're alone and lying in bed at night and you open up. I guess that's where your conscience is, in our bed, because it sure as hell's not anywhere else. Oh yeah you talk about your hopes and dreams, your ideal woman. And like a fool I became your so called ideal woman while you run around with those so called radio groupies that supposedly don't mean a thing to you. You know Sebastian you really should called Michael up and ask him if you could get a cable show based around your wonderful acting skills. You won me over. But like all shows good or bad, it's time for cancellation. It was a good run, having the mousey wife a running around for your image. The mystery being is he a player, is he faithful; can I get him? It was the perfect cover for you. Well baby all that is in the past. From now on, you are going to see a new me. Abigail Black is dead. I'm about to turn it on. I'm not going to worry about this baby deal, your infidelity or this lousy house anymore. From this point on Ambrosia is going to have herself some fun."

"Who?" Sebastian asked almost mockingly.

Even though the content to this argument is different, he has heard Abigail on her anger platform before. In about two days, she'll be back on her humble trail and begging for his forgiveness. At this point it was hard to take her serious.

"Ambrosia, don't call me anything else. Oh and by the way, I'm back working as of Wednesday. Sonja has given me a position working at the craft store until my other prospect with a publishing company comes through. So you might want to get your own meals. Or better still, cook me a meal."

"Abigail, are you feeling alright?"

"Am-bros-ia, and I'm feeling great, damn it. I just want to live like you, Mr. Morning Lover…"

Abigail left Sebastian to wonder what he just witness.

In the hallway, leading down the stairs the new Ambrosia felt a tinge of indifference. It took all of her strength to make this change and some in reserve to stand up to execute it. But this was her change of heart. But the recovery came back when she saw the look on Sebastian's face.

For the first time in her time with him, she saw fear. Part of her wanted to relish in the satisfying aspect of the emotion, but another part felt concern over his well-being. It was not as easy as she imagined, but by God there's no turning back now.

By God, No, God wouldn't approve of this fight fire with fire solution. So it'll be her on her own, then. This is what choice Sebastian has left her. She is not happy and he doesn't care. She spent years of putting up with his extra martial affairs and these threats of an illegitimate child.

She braced herself on the stair rails as she recollected the first time years ago, she got the call with the baby crying in the background. She never told Sebastian nor did she ever question him about it. She just tried like hell to get pregnant so he would never leave her.

How did she let herself come to this? Needy, insecure and fearful all the things, that men seem to hate in women. This is what she has allowed to shape her womanhood, well no more.

As Abigail reached the bottom of the stairs, she felt renewed once again. Abigail, Ambrosia was going to work. This alter ego was what she needed. Maybe she needed some more personalities to fill her mind and ease her pain. Sebastian disserves this payback and payback is what he'll get.

****

Wednesday evening Mona walked towards her condo door and saw a package. According to the shape of the long rectangle box, it was long stem roses inside. Jackson Crane is the perfect lover and full of romance, she thought. It's still too good to be true.

The two of them were just out together and he sent her these flowers. Mona picked up the box and opened the door to her condo. She felt loved by Jackson more than she'd ever felt before.

This fitted right into her risqué lifestyle. She couldn't figure whether it was just her excitement of this forbidden love affair with Jackson or was it really love. She admits she hasn't felt the feeling conjured so deep in her before Jackson, except maybe with Sebastian. She couldn't explain the new sensations but she wanted to explore them.

It was a great end to a great day. Dr. Monarch's staff conducted the last trial demonstration for the board of the new diabetes pill that will revolutionize the medical industry. Mona was going to be just a bit richer, not filthy but comfortable, once they get FDA approval. Their files and all the preparations were locked safely in her office safe. So getting this from Jackson is the cherry on her sundae.

Once inside her bedroom she laid the box on the bed and seductively slid the red ribbon over the end of the box. She amused herself almost feeling as if she was unwrapping something naughty she brought from the nearby exotic shop.

Her heart pounded with excitement because she thought this was first personal thing from Jackson aside from his sex. Mona leaned in close and thought how kittenishly, silly she must look. This is not the first time she's received flowers.

These are some of the tools that she has surmised men use for the hunt and the capture of women's heart. Well she has never been caught, not until now.

Once the lid was off the box, it took Mona not even a millisecond to draw back away from the box and stumble backwards into the wall near her dresser. As she bumped her back and head hard against the wall, she let out the most blood, curdling, scream that's ever been heard in the history of the horror cinema.

She slumped to the floor motionless for a moment trying to gather her self together. She was horrified from what she saw in the box. There were dead snakes, black dead roses and a baby doll's head with something red all over it, looking like blood. The short exposure to the horror was enough to trigger a long forgotten trauma that she experienced the day of her college graduation.

It wasn't much then other than a nasty little college prank that she felt disserved no more attention than her middle finger. But this is what, eight years later? This is something else. Could it be the same person? But most importantly why?

She brought herself to look at the box top that had falling off the box to the side. Clearly, in big bold blood red letters, read '**die bitch, like all whores do...and believe me you will** '.

Mona immediately jumped up and ran to her phone. In her haste, she was trying to discern who she should call. Should she call the police, or Jackson, maybe Sebastian, no call Michael?

Michael is the only one who remembered what happened during that day at college. Mona thought it was the sigma's that pulled the prank; mostly because she has always been verbal about her disgust for them.

"Hello," the male voice answered.

"Michael, good I thought you would be there at the studio."

"Mona hey, what's up, you sound funny?"

"I need some advice before I call the police, you got a minute."

"Yes, anything, I'm just editing today's taping that's all."

"I don't know what to think of it, but today I received a flower delivery…"

Michael listened intensely over the phone, as he reclined back in the sturdy, uncomfortable chair in the editing booth. It was not a place to get comfortable in.

As Mona told her story, Michael got up out of his seat and went over to the glass studio windows. The one peer out into the studio one level down above the audience. That's when he noticed the movements of a shadow and then quickly guided his attentions to the exit door that was just slowly closing.

"Mic, are you there, Mic?"

"Yes Mona, I'm here. I thought that I was alone, never mind. You were saying that the box lid read the same as the one back in college?"

"Yes the thing about 'die bitch'?"

Michael went to the only window that shows the outside view to the parking lot. The window was installed because the weather person kept getting the weather wrong. At least this would prevent a person from saying it was cloudy and raining when it was clearly, sunny.

This time the focus was not the weather. A gray Mercedes was slowly backing out of the parking lot. It was as if it was trying to sneak away from some deadly predator. It was the same style as the car in his neighborhood.

What is going on? The ice has been broken with Natalie so it couldn't be her. Who is afraid to talk to him or who is stalking him? Other times this has happened to him. It's been like this a few years into college.

When he would be working out at the gym on campus, late, someone would follow him into the building but would never come all the way up the stairs. They would even go into another apartment, beneath him it seemed.

At first, he thought it was Sonja. Only she always seemed to show up everywhere he was for the longest time until they started talking to each other. It just never connected then and it's even more puzzling now. Ten years or so later, these bizarre things are popping back up repeating all over again, with no meaning.

"Mona, sit tight, I'm on my way."

*****

JC knew that he was, hooked. Désiree was everything he wanted in a woman, his woman. The excitement of it all, just her name excited him. JC knew that wasn't her real name, but that only added to the intrigue.

He sat at his regular table and watched her go through her routine. She was late tonight, very late but he would have waited on her forever. In the weeks time that he has known her, his life has taken a turn to where he's never been before.

She rounded herself in a perfect seductive circle as she curved the pole and JC lost his breathe. Désiree softly put down her body onto the floor as if she wanted some sexual company. Then the lights went out. It was enough to blacken the stage.

After a few minutes as expected when the lights come back on Desiree was standing behind JC with drinks in both hands. For the past week, his has been the routine. Her set always ended like somebody carried her off into the night.

JC took the drinks from her and set them on the table.

"Did you love the show, baby," Désiree said as she leaned into him to kiss him before she sat down.

"Yes I did. I can't wait to get you home."

"I think that's all you want me for, sex. Drink your drink and I'll think about going over to your place." She stared seductively into his eyes as she licked her lips at him.

"Well I guess I can go, since I had a good night tonight. Everything fell into place."

He looked squarely into Désiree eyes. It bothered him, what she said. He couldn't figure out why, but he was on her every word. That made him realize he was really falling for her. Désiree saw the apprehensiveness in his eyes and placed her hand on his.

"Tips baby, it was a good night for tips. Now drink up."

All she has to do is breathe his way and he was as good as gone. Still he couldn't help but realize that there was more to her than meets the eye. It was all he could think of as he down his Courvoisier VSOP.

She started him on this drink. His favorite drink has always been Christian Brother's brandy. He didn't like what she had introduced to him because it always left him far more buzzed than he would like. Also it was bitter to him. But he drank it every night they were together and he loved it because it was her idea and he would do anything for her.

"Are you ready to go baby?" she asked.

JC just nodded feeling the effects of the drink already. It was weird to him that this stuff packed such a bang on the first glass. No wonder he never drank Courvoisier before, it knocks him out too close to being like Crystal Meth and he didn't like that. He was already getting to where he wanted to be on the two glasses of Brandy he drank during her set. Now it was almost as if he couldn't stand.

"Are you going to be alright, JC?" Désiree asked.

"I'm alright. It's the Courvoisier; it takes some getting use to."

"It'll be alright. All my men have gotten their best performance out of that drink."

It wasn't that JC thought that he dating a virgin, she was an exotic dancer after all. So she had to have had some sort of a sexual past. But even though he knew this, it still bothered him to hear her say it.

"So I'm temporary?" he asked.

"Well what would make you say that?"

"You just did."

"I just said that this is what all my men have gotten their best performance out of. Look around you, JC, this is a strip club, there's no virgins here." She finished.

Désiree knew that she was pushing JC's delicate buttons. There must have been some insecurity issue at one time, not very long ago. Well if he wants to roll with her, then it would be best if he suck it up and be a man about it.

Her track record wasn't very good with men lately and there are things that she is in the process of doing to make her life right. She'd be damn if she'll let him play on her sympathy and deter her from what she wants to do.

No prisoners, those are the rules. The last thing she needs is a stalker, stalking the predator. Still it would be to her best interest if she gives him a little empathy.

"JC come on let's go. You know I'm all about you. Baby, don't spoil the mood."

That was all it took. A delicate mind indeed, he was like putty. She ruled all that was going on around her and that made Desiree the stripper, exotic dancer, whatever, very happy.

****

Michael was not too far away from Mona's condo. He was delayed when the digital recorder malfunctioned right as he was just finishing the editing of last night's taping. As he made his way though the city his cell phone rang, but he didn't recognize the number on the caller it.

"Hello,"

"Michael, hi it's Natalie."

"Natalie hi," he smiled.

"Well I'm going to make this quick. Our second meeting was a little awkward. I thought the third should be charm. How would you like to meet me for lunch tomorrow, 1 o'clock at the Montague Hotel on the river front?"

Michael knew that inviting him to lunch was a hard thing for Natalie to do. Ever since they've reestablished their existence to each other, he's noticed a change in her.

The old Natalie would never make such a risky invitation, mainly because of the possible implications behind the invite. But he's noticed that the Natalie that is in the here and now acted more on her feelings, whatever the feelings. What is it that she wants from him and how far will she go to get it?

Michael didn't know too much about her husband. He only knows that he is older and some stuffy want to be Chief of the Medical Staff at the hospital Natalie works.

He could see Natalie falling for that kind of safety net. He was right up her field. Nevertheless, she wants to meet with him. Even though their meeting in her office was pretty much the same as years before, he hadn't forgotten about that, reluctantly he agreed.

"1 o'clock, I will be there Ms. Vincent."

Natalie paused; it had been far too long since someone has given her some independence from her husband's identity; Dr. Christopher Bower's wife, wife of the future Chief of Staff, Mrs. Bower or Dr. Natalie Bower. She never got a chance to establish her own career, her identity. Christopher orchestrated every move, every decision. She was his charity work to do with as he pleases and he never let her forget it.

"See you Michael."

Now that was the old Natalie, Michael noticed. He noticed she got quiet when he mistakenly called her by her maiden name. But to him time had stopped. This Dr. Bower was someone foreign to him and he didn't know her. He didn't know her, but something told Michael, that Dr. Natalie Bower has been who he has been in love with all these years. She's the one who will take risk and possible sacrifice what Natalie Vincent would not sacrifice many years ago. What does she want?

CHAPTER 4

Natalie cradled her cell phone to her heart while she sat on her bed and closed her eyes. Something was brewing inside her with each thought of Michael, each time they spoke. Did she sound desperate? That's all she was concern with about right now. Moreover, what is she doing inviting him to lunch tomorrow? Things were moving fast. It's been a week since their meeting and her world's been turned upside down. But what is strange is that Natalie is willing to be about Natalie right now, not Christopher.

"Mommy, do you hear me, Daddy is almost here?"
She turned towards her daughter.

"Tiff, yes I heard you."

She didn't really and she wished she hadn't this time. Even though Christopher's homecoming was routinely at this time, she wasn't looking forward to it. Every evening for the last seven years there would be a gut wrenching pain that formed at the bottom of her stomach each day.

It was stress and Natalie knew it. It would come whenever Christopher came within a close proximity of her? She was filling with intense anxiety and it overwhelmed her.

"Mommy do you want me to put the food on the table?"

"No Tiffany, I'm coming down."

That's when Natalie realized how much of her life belonged to someone else. Christopher caused her anxieties and Tiffany her beautiful daughter eased it. But in between she seemed lost, like she was on hold, waiting.

Tiffany and her youngest daughter Merry are her lifelines of some sort. It was magical that when they came into her life five and six years ago. She was in a place that she told Michael she was going to be later years after she established her career.

But it was Christopher he made it seemed so easy. He guided her and she followed. He gave her the security of a relationship, then a marriage and kids as well as her career.

It was well mapped out and constructed, she had everything. In her perfect would she did have everything, everything but love in her life and the love of her life. It was almost stifling like being choked by a person to death, slowly.

Natalie stepped to the bottom of the stairs and gathered her thoughts. She was in no rush because Christopher always took approximately twenty minutes to come into the house. Why, she didn't know but this has been his routine since the girls were born.

In the beginning, the girls would be waiting in the dining room with the nanny or with Natalie. They would scream with delight at the mere mention of their father's arrival. Finally, when he arrived he would bond with them for five minutes and later it would be as if the girls didn't exist.

So Natalie learned how to over compensate for his neglect. It wasn't that he was mean to them; it was the coldness that Natalie tried to block from the girls.

"Mom, may I have dinner in my room?" Merry asked her immediately when Natalie entered the room.

"Merry no, why do you always ask that and you know what I'm going to say?"

Merry looked at her mother and decided there was no further need in saying anything else. Her mother was right. She always says no.

Natalie looked at her youngest daughter and saw the repetition in her eyes. Everything and everyday was like the next and the previous. Something has to break the continuality.

"Merry, how about if you and your sister take your dinner in to the family room."

"Are you serious mommy?"

"Yes Tiffany."

The girls didn't hesitate any longer. They got up and disappeared into the next room.

Christopher came through the kitchen door and into the dining room. He noticed the girls was not there waiting for him and started to show concern. When he spotted Natalie, he wiped the concern from his face. It was all right for the girls to be away tonight because he was tired. He needed a peaceful night.

Natalie observed her husband. She took in his sudden coldness. She knew in his mind that the girls' absent from the dining room was running through his mind. He wants to know where they are but he will not ask, because that would mean that he is not in control. Natalie should tell him, anticipating his every question. This time however, he will just have to ask. She was tired of catering to his every whim, anticipating and getting nothing in return.

"Dinner, Christopher?"

Where are the girls? He thought.

"No I ate at the hospital. I'm going to the den to read. Don't wait up."

"What do you mean you ate at the hospital? Did it ever occur to you to give me a call so I wouldn't keep the girls waiting for you before they can eat?"

Christopher passed at the sudden abruptness of his wife. He hadn't heard her talk like this in years. He thought he had gotten rid of her old way of thinking. How could they be a success if they constantly thinking in two different directions?

He'll make it to the Chief of Staff position because of his drive and decisions. Natalie lacked the cohesiveness needed to reach his goals. He had to work with her to get to his level and she should appreciate his input into her life, he thought.

She was a timid, med student when they met, with no direction needing a rescuer and she enjoyed his passion for medicine. She was excited for his ideas and it was clear that she wanted to be a part of his fantastic world. She needed someone to take her mind off Michael.

It's okay that she's eight years younger than he is, because she adapted well to the age difference. She has become the perfect Chief of Staff, wife.

So what is going on tonight? Is she unraveling out of pressure from all of the training he has bestowed upon her? This is a perfect vehicle that the two of them have the perfect life, two children, perfect little, girls. What is her problem?

Christopher's subconscious beckon to him to calm down and show no outwardly signs of concern. She must not see you as anything else but calm. You are the leader, he remind himself.

"I didn't know I had to check in with you. You know of my whereabouts and how busy I am during the course of the, day. I don't have time to alert you to every minute change in my schedule."

Natalie just stared at him and before she could respond, he spoke.

"I don't care to discuss this any longer. Like I said, I'll be in the den, reading."

"And like I said, did it ever occur to you to call so that the girls and I aren't just sitting around here waiting for you to come home. Our lives are not on hold for you. Next time just use common courtesy for a change."

"I'm not sure Natalie where you are going with this, but this is not you. I suggest that you stay focus on all that you have and discontinue the aggression that I hear in your voice. It will not solve anything and I don't care to hear it."

He began to walk away, stopped and turned to face her.

"Maybe you should speak to that friend of yours Janice Edwards; she's a counselor or something like that right, such as she is."

Natalie stared at Christopher, of all the egotistical things to say. He has the nerve to act as if her friends were beneath his notice.

He has known Janice for over five years now. In all of that time he should know what profession she is in, considering that she is under staff at he same hospital he is wants to be Chief of Staff at. What a bastard.

"Tell the girls when they get home that I will see them in the morning."

"The girls are home in the family room had you bothered to ask before."

"You should have just volunteered the information, it saves time." Christopher exited the room.

She couldn't believe that she is married to that asshole. What did she ever see in him and what kind of nightmare is she in. The thoughts were enough to make her scream.

Natalie stifled the emotion for the sake of her girls. Instead, she went into the kitchen and slipped out the back door to purge herself.

****

After Michael arrived at Mona's and went into her bedroom, he looked at the nasty message on the rose box top that lay on Mona's bed. She changed her mind and decided not to call the police. Against his better judgment, he agreed to it. It was only after she agreed to stay at his house for a few days. He would call Sonja in a few minutes at home to let her know Mona was coming by.

Then he remembered it was Wednesday the night that Sonja stayed the latest at the craft store. Since Abigail has been working there for a week, Sonja has been pretty calm and understanding. It was at first seeming as if she had given up on his dreams and grew less tolerable of them. It was almost as if she believes that he didn't need to put in the time that he does to grow.

It started when she stopped being a housewife and started the craft store. The change was gradual but it seemed as if she was competing with his career. Was it that Sonja didn't believe in her own self worth and made it difficult for him to grow in his career?

"Michael you should call Sonja before we leave. I don't want to just be at your spot when she gets home. You know the two of us don't get along that well. She only tolerates me because of you and only just so."

"Mona that's not true."

Michael laughed in his mind because he knew that Mona was correct. Ever since Mona and Sonja had that last falling out several months after Michael and Sonja got together, the two ladies have been at odds. Still they never really got along, even in college.

As he dialed the number to the craft store he pondered whether it was a good idea to invite Mona to stay. But what choice did he have. They were not alerting the police.

Sebastian's marriage was already strained with Abigail's new persona so he couldn't help. JC is all in love with a woman no one has met. Natalie, well Mona didn't give him the impression that she was as close with the husband as she is with Natalie.

There was so much secrecy going on Michael felt. Or was it just privacy. Ever one is entitled to live a private life separate from their friends. But no one seems to talk like they use to. Even lately when they get together on Thursday nights to play poker like they have since they were sophomores in college, it all seems so forced like everyone wanted to be somewhere else.

"Michael," he heard Sonja on the other end of the phone. "Why are you calling me at Mona's? Why aren't you at home? I told you that Mrs. Berman has a life too. What the hell is wrong with you?"

"And hello to you too. Look Mona had an emergency and I…"

"Oh here it goes again; one of your precious friends is in trouble…again. What do you want Michael?"

"Mona has run into some bad trouble at her condo, so I told her that she could stay at our place."

"And"

"Sonja I just wanted to give you heads up. What's your problem? You know, never mind, see you at home." Michael ended the call.

****

Sonja stared at the phone as if she was watching TV and Abigail stared at her. "Girl, why are you, so mean to that man."

"Abigail."

"Am-bros-ia,"

"Yeah right, I'm not mean to Michael. He just pisses me off. When am I going to come first? And he hung up the phone on me."

"Sonja, it's not a secret the way you deal with Michael."

No it wasn't a secret, thought Sonja. What has happen to Michael and her? Their relationship at best is dwindling to a few fights a week.

"You don't give Michael the benefit of the doubt. You just charge in and blow off on him like there's no tomorrow. What is wrong girl?"

"Nothing is wrong like I said I want to be first in Michael's life, not some shadow in the wake of his damn friends."

"Friends, you mean Natalie, don't you?"

Sonja stiffened and became rigid. It was always inevitable that someone would bring it up to her, but she didn't expect Abigail to be the first one. Whatever the case, she did not want to discuss Natalie Vincent.

She is all of a distant memory to her. Well no, not really, she's with her everyday, in her head. She's always living up to her; always having to feel inadequate to her.

If the opportunity ever came about to kill Natalie she'd probably do it, just so she could be free of her. Why? It's because her husband is still in love with the memory of her.

It was only two years of his life, compared to the eight years Sonja has given him. These are the best years of her life. She has given it to him, sacrificed them on his altar and all she received in the end is second best.

"And what if I do mean Natalie? After all what is he still thinking about her for anyway, after all these years?"

"Because you are not doing what you're suppose to be doing. Sonja you can say what you want to say, but you never gave Michael his fair shake with you. Lady, I've known you since college and you know I know. Because I'm married to a pitiful bastard, it leaves me time to notice other people marriages and envy them. You had Michael's heart, soul and mind, in the beginning. They were yours for the taking. But you didn't know what you wanted."

Abigail paused for a moment to let all that she just said sink into Sonja's mind. When she thought she should continue she did but with caution, she took a deep breath.

"I'm only going to say this because I need to bring this into the conversation, but when I'm finish we need never mention it again. Sonja, you stole Michael from Natalie. Because you did it that way, the anger and guilt behind all that deception is what's causing you to be angry at him. You feel like you shouldn't had to do that, but it's too late for you to feel anger behind that. You need to get over it. Michael's not your problem. The fact that you never liked Natalie has been your problem. It is causing you to lose this man, the one you worked so many strings to get. He loves you but not like Natalie, but you have his name, his child. Michael is a decent man, but yet you treated him like he was like Sebastian. There are no white picket fences, but you have parked your car right up next to one. Now tell me who has the problem?"

Sonja remained quiet to what Abigail said. It was a hard pill to swallow but she knew that everything said was correct. How did she figure it out? The confirmation came from the tears streaming down Sonja face.

It has been years since she has cried, for any reason. Her heart was like ice and nothing seemed to bother her. Even the threat of losing Michael didn't appear to affect her. But it did.

It was still hard for her to admit her wrong doing, but history has already recorded them. Try as she might she may never forget and never heal.

"You know Ambrosia, you have a point," she responded getting her self together and wiping her tears.

Abigail felt proud of herself that she was able to get through to her friend. As structured as Sonja thinks she is it's just the opposite.

"But not for one damn minute will I excuse all the things that Michael has done to me. Mona Daniels is going to be staying in my house for days. That's one right there. And you know you should be the last one to turn the other cheek, knowing that tramp whore screwed you husband."

"Sonja I don't know that and at this point I don't care, Sebastian will get his. It's all about me now, only because I don't have a choice, my husband is no good. But you gotta choice. I'm serious if you don't get off this hate campaign that you're on, Michael is going to walk."

Abigail turned to walk behind the checkout counter, leaving Sonja leaning against the counter. Before she could turn to face Sonja to continue their conversation, a loud crash of glass splattering sounded.

Abigail ducked quickly for cover as she heard Sonja scream in pure horror. Abigail heard what sounded like Sonja falling to the floor with a thump. What happened she thought? There were no gun shot sounds and what happened to Sonja?

Abigail listened a few seconds more and called out to Sonja. When Sonja didn't answer she got up slowly and peered out to the front of the store and saw all the glass and displays everywhere. When she deemed it safe she ran around to the front of the counter and saw Sonja lying on the floor.

Sonja's eyes were wide open, motionless and blood was everywhere. Abigail screamed as she quickly grabbed the counter phone from the handset and dialed 911.

****

Later, JC woke up in his bed and he was alone. He mind was groggy as he realized it wasn't morning yet. Where is Désiree he wondered? The room was still enchanted from the scent of her perfume and he breathed it in, arousing his sense.

He got up out of bed and at first he had to adjust to operating his motor skills. If he wasn't so sure that he wasn't, it seemed as if he was on Meth again, everything made him feel like that he guessed. Cognac is some strong shit. JC suddenly heard splashing in the bathroom. Desiree was in there he guessed.

When he opened the door to the bathroom, candles were lit everywhere and Desiree lay in his bathtub full of pink bubbles. He laughed at the sight of her because he thought of that last Victoria's Secret commercial with the sexy model in the tub the water just above her breast. Desiree could be his model anytime.

"Baby what cha up to?"

"I'm soaking myself. I don't know what was on your mind earlier, but you really put me through it, I could barely walk."

That's what he wants to hear Desiree thought that's what I'm going to say. JC smiled and then blushed a little dropping his eyes to the floor. On the floor he noticed her panties lying on top of her clothes and that aroused him.

She definitely brought the freak out of him, that's for sure. That's when he noticed the scrapings of what seemed like dirt on and around her clothes. As he looked over the floor he saw a light trail of it everywhere.

"Désiree baby, you've been outside or something."

Desiree stared at JC a moment before she spoke. She watched him closely as he stared down at her clothing on the floor. He was a very nosey man and that was another flaw.

"Well if you must know lover, I fell down outside in your parking lot."

"Are you all right?"

"Just my pride is bruised that's all. What I need to do is be more careful."

"You went out while I was sleep?" She nodded. "By the way what time is it?"

Ugh, more questions from this man. Doesn't he know that she doesn't give a cat's ass what men think; but just this time?

"JC, it's about two hours after we left the club. You dove into me quick. I told you that Cognac does a body good. And I'm still feeling it."

"I didn't hurt you did I?" Désiree looked at him and thought 'if you only knew'. "No lover, I like it rough from you."

JC was feeling proud of himself. This woman is with him and he has found the woman of his dreams, but he couldn't remember sleeping with her. Desiree looked intensely at him. What he saw was a sensual woman worshipping him. But Desiree was somewhere else in that moment, a place in her mind.

****

Michael and Mona got out of his car and slowly walked towards Sonja's craft store the coolness of the summer night keeping him alert. When he got the call from Abigail the tone of her made him think the worst.

As they came upon the splattered glass and damage surrounding the window it appeared as if something heavy went down here. There were a number of police around as well as emergency medical technician. One of the techs was tending to Sonja.

"I'm not going to the hospital, I'm fine," he heard Sonja scream. 'It's just a bump."

Abigail had forewarned Michael that although Sonja was not seriously injured, she was very agitated because she needed to get stitches. Once Michael was inside he saw for himself. In spite of what was going on between the two of them he was still very concern about her.

"Michael, tell them that I don't need to go to the hospital."

Michael didn't answer directly, instead he took in the, reminisce of blood that apparently someone tried to clean up. It looked pretty bad.

"Sonja, honey, you should have gone to the hospital when the ambulance arrived. Now that I've seen you, definitely you should go. You have a head injury and you've lost some blood."

Sonja stared intensely at Michael and then to Mona. Was he patronizing her, because he does that? Instead of contemplating the answer she focused all her anger at Mona. She wished she could take a blunt object and bash her head in. She causes some of the problems that Michael and she are having. If she every gets the chance...

"Are you coming with me, Michael?" Sonja said without taking her eyes off Mona.

Mona rolled her eyes, upwards and looked over at Abigail. Abigail never batted an eye as she stared back at Mona, stiffly posed waiting for a response from Michael too.

Although she never inquired about the depth of Sebastian and Mona's relationship, she's never really trusted Mona. If there is any truth to what Sonja mentioned earlier, she will kill Sebastian.

"Well, yes Sonja, but what about Taylor?"

"See what I'm talking about Abigail. I'm sitting here bleeding to death and all Michael is worried about is getting that whore to my house for safekeeping."

Time seemed to stop in that moment of seconds it took for Sonja's words to register in Mona's mind. She exploded on its impact.

"Bitch, who are you calling a whore? If your head wasn't already split, I'd do the honors."

Both Michael and Abigail jumped between the two of them as Sonja and Mona moved toward each other.

"Sonja your head injury," Abigail declared.

"Mona the police," Michael warned.

Mona and Sonja glared at each other and stood motionless. Michael didn't say anything else. He grabbed Sonja's arm and motioned her toward the front door, as everyone else looked on. Mona stood looking a Sonja departing. How she wished she could throw a piece of glass in the back of her head.

She turned to look at Abigail. She looked different to Mona. It was something about her clothing. She noticed that immediately when she and Michael had arrived. She's definitely changed since the wedding, Mona thought. Not as mousey as she has been in the past. Mona also wondered if this changed came about, from finding out that she slept with Sebastian.

Well even if not Mona made a promise that she will keep her distance from Abigail, because this new version of her bears watching. It's no telling what a woman, who wants to have children as bad as Abigail and is scorned by her husband, will do. That was always one of Sebastian's biggest fears, but yet he carries on like he does. Yes there's something to worry about behind those eyes.

"Well, I guess you'll have to catch a cab." Abigail said, causing a chill to go through Mona.

"Yes Abigail, I guess I will."

"My name is Ambrosia."

****

"Did you really need to say all that," Michael said to Sonja as they were driving to the hospital in his car.

"Oh you're talking to me now?"

"Sonja you know that wasn't right. Why did you say that about Mona?"

"It is so funny how you can be so interested in everyone else's feelings and not mine. If she had called me a whore, would you have been so alert? She called me a bitch."

"And I stepped in and I checked her, so that things wouldn't get out of hand."

"Michael things are already out of hand. Mona slept with Sebastian that's a fact and I don't like that. Abigail is my friend. How can you be friends with someone like that? On top of that she doesn't even like me and I'm the wife of her supposedly good friend."

"First of all Mona did not sleep with Sebastian. They may have flirted with each other in the past, but their just harmless friends now. One of the reasons she never liked you started in college when you and your sorority played that dirty prank on her by leaving that nasty note on graduation day. It's bad enough being snobby you, Kimberly and those others."

"I know my source is correct on the Sebastian thing. It's almost if I saw them myself. What are you talking about some note?"

"Never mind it really isn't an issue. The bottom line is that Mona and you have never tried to get along and you were looking for any excuse to keep her out of our house. Why don't we talk about what just happen tonight, that's more important anyway?"

It's all that Sonja and he do now, argue. It was stupid for him to bring up the college prank for the simple fact that if indeed it had been Sonja then, is it Sonja now? What would be the reason?

Mona should never be in Sonja thoughts and nowadays the only real time that all of his friends have together is still Thursday nights. Now JC is even missing that. His new love must be the one; but what with all the mystery? Why hasn't anyone met her? Michael thought about it and decided that he would make it his priority to meet JC's new girl, but only after he takes care of himself.

As bad as it is to think about this at this time, he looked forward to his lunch with Natalie. He looked over at Sonja and wished he had never traveled down this road. What happened tonight should have had more of an impact on him but really it didn't. It's not that he didn't care, it was the way Sonja carried it.

It's hard to feel compassion for a seemingly compassionless woman. She was growing increasingly cold and may be no way to turn it around. So why should he bother trying to make it work when clearly Sonja is not trying to do what it takes to make it work. If it blows up, it just does.

The rest of the ride was in silence. Michael let his mind drift off to thoughts of Natalie and wonder was she dealing with crazy issues as well. Maybe that's the reason why Natalie is so persistent in wanting to get together. Michael hoped that there would be no complications tomorrow because he really needed this escape, even if it is just lunch.

When he held her in his arms the other day it felt just like it was a tight glove around his fingers and hands. And he didn't have a single problem with following through with meeting her for lunch.

It no longer matter to him that he was married. It didn't matter that his wife was injured tonight. It didn't matter that tomorrow she will be recuperating at home. He probably needs to be there for her as well, but he won't. It doesn't matter that he'd rather be with Natalie right now than walking into Chicago Memorial.

****

Inside the hospital the medical staff was doing their usual thing. Michael followed Sonja into the emergency room, pass the elevators. The elevator doors opened. Dr. Edwards stepped off the elevator realizing that she had forgotten to cancel her evening appointments for tomorrow. She needed to make room for an extended session with 'Karen'.

It had been weeks since the incident with the statuette happened. It took a couple of days for her to calm down from all that chaos. She almost had her committed.

What did she say that triggered this violent reaction from 'Karen'? She thought that she had her under control. She thought that she was getting through to her and on her way to solving her problems without medicating 'Karen'.

Now she has realized that medication will be the only saving grace that she will have with 'Karen'. She will have to add more days to her visits. During their session tomorrow she will prescribe lithium, to try to manage 'Karen's' anger. The anger was an apparent residue of their sessions together.

What will 'Karen' do? Will she accept the medication or will she fly off into a murderous rage. The thought of being bludgeoned to death by her own patient, with her own personal things, made her a little bit apprehensive. Maybe she should have security in the outer office just in case.

She felt weird suggesting these things to herself, but in all the nine years of her career has it ever got to this point where she feared for her life. She was actually dreading her next appointment with 'Karen'. This was becoming real work. Something was wrong because she seems to be losing control.

She felt that she was good at what she does. Her cousin's negative comments, be damned. She was the failure not her. She is Dr. Janice Edwards. She disserved to be guided through this trauma in her life. It was not her doing and she should not have to pay the penalty for the poor judgment she used in the past or what they all did.

The greatest hope is that 'Karen' considers her a friend and allows her to trust that she needs her help. A mental note was made that she would get 'Karen' to go into depth revealing those secrets she is trying to hide. She may have to submit her to more hypnotism to get the information.

Speaking of secrets she wished that Natalie would reveal to her what it is that has been troubling her. Clearly some days Natalie is on a natural high you would think that she was falling in love. Everyone in this hospital knows that Natalie's marriage to the soon to be Chief of Staff is on hold, everyone except the hospital decision board.

There's nothing there, so she can't be falling back in love with him. Then there were days when Natalie was so close to tears that Janice almost called someone else in her department to offer help to her. She knew however that would be friendship suicide.

Natalie would never forgive her and she knows that. She has to keep her near to watch her. But what *is* going on with this woman who has become her friend of all people? She put that on the main list of things to accomplish real soon, the answer to that question.

CHAPTER 5

The next day at noon the sun beamed across the midsummer skies with an intent purpose it seemed to bring comfort to all that desired it. Natalie Vincent Bower strolled casually down the street towards the Montague Hotel. If anyone was looking any closer they would noticed that she was dripping with anticipation. She was going to see the man she loves.

Wait! She thought. *How can she think that? Where did that come from?*

Natalie was silent for a moment even in her mind. Whatever happens in those moments helps her to suddenly realize that she still was very much in love with Michael.

He has been what has helped her survive this hell that she has been living. He helped her to be open once more with her feelings. She was able, because he revealed his true feelings to her, to open this door and be confident. Now that the door is open what is going to happen now? What is going to be accomplished in establishing this reconnection? Is she going to leave Christopher?

Minutes later she entered the Montague Hotel and went over to the dining area. It was lunch time but the setting inside the dining area was moderately, lit and cozy. She had never been to this hotel. She heard some scuttlebutt about it being one of the most romantic places to eat. That's probably why she chose this place. She wanted her time spent with Michael as romantic as possible. She wanted to create a new place for them.

Again where is this going? What is the point to all this intrigue? She felt like she was following a movie script. Well what is the next line? What is the next direction? Michael sat in the corner of the dining area at an out of the way table. He waved to Natalie as she was being guided by the waiter.

"Michael, you've been waiting," she paused and smiled mischievously. "All day, huh?"

"Well Ms. Vincent not quite all day. How was your trip over here? Was it as fantasizing as mine?"

Natalie hesitated to answer Michael with truth. Suddenly she reminded herself that she was the one who arranged all this. Michael did his part; he showed up. It was up to her to lead him to the new agenda. But what was the new agenda? What is it that she wants to accomplish here, damn it what?

Why don't you admit it Natalie, she heard a voice within her thoughts. *Why don't you go on and tell him the truth? Tell him what you feel.*

"Yes Michael, I floated all the way over here, now does that sound corny or what?"

"Well," he grabbed her hand and squeezed it gently. "It would be, if I didn't believe that you were telling the truth. Besides that how I got here."

"Michael Montgomery you're too much. Do you see anything on the menu that stands out?"

"I took the liberty of ordering a bottle of wine, red, something new, not that cheap stuff we use to drink back in the day. But I also have another idea as well. How would you like to take this afternoon somewhere more private?"

Michael didn't wait for Natalie to catch up or even answer the question; he simply just laid a card room key on the table.

"Can you elaborate a bit more Mr. Montgomery?"

"Yes. How about you and I skip the meal and catch up on old times. It seems that both you and I could use a bit of reminiscing."

She couldn't believe how forward Michael is being and its obvious how much thought he put into the room key. He got a room at the Montague hotel, she couldn't believe it.

"Michael what's on your mind?"

"What's been on my mind for eight years, now? I want you back."

Natalie listened without comment.

You want this too, go for it. You need this, the voice in her head whispered again.

This is the man that she thought about for the eight years of hell that she's been in six of them wasted with Christopher, why was she playing hard to get?

She has dreamed about a second chance to be close to him and the opportunity is here. But this is wrong. This is not how she thought it would be. How they would reconnect. He is a good man and it would be too easy to get caught up in the fantasy of her past with him. But there was no other way.

She would have to decline this request and that's when the chills surrounded her; it came from inside. She saw that familiar look. It was the same look that she saw when she looked in Michael's eyes that night. The night she was supposed to leave him forever.

She saw it again. It was there waiting behind the hope that this time she moves in step with him and not give up on him. The struggle to do the right thing resonated with her mind, but she went with her heart.

"I will at least get dessert, right?"

"Oh yes."

****

Dr. Edwards stood in the doorway of her doctor's office nervously. It was a good thing for her that 'Karen' had to stop at Vicki's desk to take care of some paperwork. When 'Karen' spoke to her, her blood curled. Now she had her game face on and tried to stand erect, but she felt that she was on the verge of tilting over.

She watched 'Karen' standing at the other side of the outer office, pass Vicki's desk, with scrutiny. She looked taller to the good doctor and was a bit intimidating. She decided to focus on some of the things that made her angry about 'Karen'. This is a technique that she taught to some of her patients when they were deeply introverted and needed some backbone.

She often gathered strength herself when she was dealing with a less desirable topic or individual. She would invoke the anger. She logically put it in its proper place while all the time gathering a wall of strength from it. It will stop her from having anxieties about where 'Karen' would try to take the session.

The first wave of anger was at the arrogance of 'Karen' to be late today. Thirty minutes when Dr. Edwards had cleared her entire afternoon schedule. Then the nonchalant, non-apologetic way that, 'Karen' sauntered into the office. But the icing on the cake was that she has not forgiven her for smashing her precious statute that Everett had given her. That little bitch.

There now, it was done. Now she had it up. The wall was there. Of course 'Karen' didn't mean to do what she had done and the only recourse is to excuse her. She will not be blindsided by her again. With the newly found emotional control the doctor turned on her heels, leaving her office door open, returned to the plush comforts of her office chair; to await the challenge.

"Dr. Edwards," 'Karen' said sheepishly as she entered the office and waited for the doctor to motion for her to sit down in front of her desk. "Dr. Edwards, I have to apologize for my behavior last week. It was crazy, I went crazy. I don't know what came over me. But I want you to know that I want to work at this, to help myself."

Dr. Edwards looked intensely at 'Karen' before she spoke. This was definitely not what she anticipated going through today. She was sure that she was about to embark on the fight of her life. 'Karen' waited patiently while Dr Edwards prepared to answer her.

That was good. That sounded very sincere, 'Karen' heard the voice in her mind say.

She was at first irritated but she allowed the voice to surface because it seemed right.

This is what you do when you want to achieve the ultimate goal. If you reveal yourself again she will probably have you put away and where will you be then? How will you break free?

'Karen' understood what the voice was trying to rationalize to her. How would she be able to perform her brand of punishment on those who have hurt her if she is strap down and medicated on the fifth floor?

No you're confused.

"'Karen' I sympathize with what you're going through, but control is one of the first attempts at healing. I'm concern that you did what you did, because you don't have any control anymore." Dr. Edwards did not allow her tone to betray her feelings.

She kept her professional edge.

"I don't want to explore the reason until I prescribe you a type of medicine that will help balance your moods and aid you in calming yourself in instances when you feel heavily agitated. It will also help with times of sadness and guilt."

So this is the help that she wants to give you? Kill the bitch. Stab her through her heart with that damn letter opener on her desk, she probably never uses. It's not hers anyway. She heard her thoughts say.

She began to feel the tug at her inner thoughts as the other voice pleaded with her.

No! Listen...Janice, she's the professional. She can help you. If you take the medicine it will cure you, calm you; free you. You must not kill.

The assaults on her thoughts were going back and forth. What seemed like hours to 'Karen' were only seconds in the real world. It didn't last much longer, when Dr. Edwards finally sensing there was a problem, intervened.

"'Karen', are you okay, you seem shaken?"

"I'm fine. I have a headache, that's all." She said too seriously.

She watched 'Karen' with curiosity. She was definitely dealing with issues and is in need of help.

'I won't let her stop us.' We have plans, do you hear me? Get it together. Do you want to get to him or not? This is your chance to talk to him. Get the damn prescription and let her believe you will take the pills. I have plans for those pills.'

"Dr. Edwards thank you for your support. You're the only friend that I have so if you think that the pills will do the job, than I trust you."

She looked again into 'Karen's' eyes. There was so much darkness there that she could see nothing, but there was also calmness. It was hard to distinguish at this moment and probably a quick test would tell it all.

"'Karen' before we begin our session, I wanted to know have you really thought about what happened last session. I was asking you to forgive those who you believe are guilty. I still want you to consider that as we are moving on."

She waited for an eruption response from her but as the seconds ticked away there was nothing but silence. In 'Karen's mind she has already accomplished what she set out to do and in the process, gathered more.

Now she can more easily draw a conclusion to this punishment she's been going through and punish, not forgive those who are really guilty.

"I agree doctor, Janice, I really do."

Dr. Edward knew for sure now that she was lying but if she takes the lithium, she will be able to get through to her and eventually, under control again.

"Good, 'Karen'. So let's talk about our goals."

****

Across town, once they opened the door to the hotel suite it was on. It was a dream. One kiss lead to another and another and clothing was removed and the heat exploded within the two of them.

Moments later Natalie lay in ecstasy entangled beneath Michael. It was not in her mind, this was for real. They have crossed the line and thankfully there was no turning back. Michael was the lover that she has missed out on for years and she has missed this. She was home.

Michael gave his all to his lovemaking. This woman has been the missing part of his soul and he long for this as well. Neither one of them thought of the ramifications as they swayed rhythmically in the sweat of their union.

It was unholy, but it was out of love. Was it wrong to give into the rekindling of their love, a love that insolubly may have been sabotaged, even by fate? There was no logical reason why Michael and Natalie's love did not workout.

As Michael caressed her and moved his hands down the outline of her body. He didn't want it to end but he knew that it would be more to come. He thought about Sonja briefly. It was the only time that he allowed himself the displeasure.

It wasn't that he hated the thought of Sonja; it was just that thinking about her caused a complication that he didn't really want to deal with right now.

It is sure to be hard to leave the comfort of this room and return to his reality that included his loveless life with Sonja. Also it felt weird being with Natalie and being married to her ex-best friend. It reeked of a dirty Lifetime movie.

"Natalie, I'm sorry I…you know, Sonja."

"Michael, if the two of us are to have any kind of relationship, you have to be able to talk to me. I am here now and I want to listen. I know how it feels to want to share something, but not have anyone to trust, or better still, that would know exactly how you feel."

"Natalie I don't want to talk about Sonja with you. Part of me will never bring myself to understand how I let that happen. I didn't come to get you, knowing how much I love you. Remember you talked about forgiveness and forgiven you? Well you see now why I don't hold anything over you? I have made mistakes too."

"Really it's okay. I don't have a problem with hearing what you have on your mind. Above anything that this is, I'm your friend."

"Yeah well I know these two people who are in a similar situation like ours and all they do, all the time is talk about the ills of their marriages and nothing else is the focus. It just recently started to turn around to something else, but the strong focus of their entire being together is still the ills of their marriages. I don't want that to be us. I want us to be together. I love you. I never stopped."

"But they're getting better those two, like you said."

"I don't know I just made that up, so I could tell you again that I love you."

"Michael Montgomery, I don't know what goes on in your mind. Sometimes I think you give too much and you don't think that I feel the same, but I do. You don't have to carry this love by yourself."

"I give credit to what I know is right. I know that we are meant to be together, somehow and I have always believed that. I know that you are my woman."

"Okay, this is deeper than I have time for today. You keep this up and I might not want to leave this room. I thought you were going to talk to me about Sonja?"

Reluctantly, Michael drew in a deep breath. He was uncomfortable about this triangle that he has created, but Natalie did say she didn't mind listening to him. Although he didn't agree that he would talk to her about Sonja, he needed a friend right now.

"Last night someone threw a stone cinder block through the Craft store window that Sonja owns. She was startled, fell back against the checkout counter and got a nasty gash in the back of her head. When I got there, I was with Mona and all Sonja seemed to do the whole time was complain. Of course Mona and Sonja got into it and I looked like the bad guy as usual. I'm sure Mona has told you about the cold war the two of them have over the years. It's almost second nature. I'm so use to it. At the hospital, she and I got into it, right in the emergency room and I walked out. I left her there and Abigail picked her up. I guess when she got home she was so zonked out from the pain medicine she got that she skipped arguing with me and went to bed. I left early this morning because I'm so freaking tired of the continuous arguments. I'm constantly thinking about leaving her. It's so funny that the whole time I should have be thinking about Sonja and her well-being, I was wondering how you were doing and waiting on this time with you."

She should have appeared judgmental to him, but she was far from that. She understood exactly what he was talking about. She didn't care a thing about Sonja either and she felt that exact same way when Christopher came home last night. She only she wished that he would have disappeared from the face of the earth.

He looked at her as he lay next to her and wondered what she was thinking right this minute. Was she as relaxed as he was and as scared.

The two of them have entered into this affair for survival. He was already feeling refreshed. There was so much clarity that he was building on and amidst the clarity was chaos waiting to kick off.

Natalie was also relaxed in her world, because in her world Michael now existed again. Hearing about Sonja's dirty deeds only made being with him more attractive. She wanted to hold him tight to her and comfort him. She was with her soul mate again. The gap that was there before is now filled more ways that can be imagined.

Now, what to do about Christopher? Can she go back to letting him touch her? Even though there is not much sexual contact between them, they do have sex. Most of the time, it's very impersonal, a few quick thrust and she's left holding the bag. She was left laying there without the pleasure of an orgasm or even the concern from Christopher.

Now she was freed. She was freed to explore her unreleased passion. She strongly remembered the passion Michael could ignite in her. *But this was wrong.*

Natalie looked over at the antique clock that decorated the fancy mantelpiece. They had time for one more round of dessert she thought. It was an affair she had to remember this. But does she care? That question was answered almost immediately as the two of them began to enjoy themselves in the pleasures of their reunion.

Michael Montgomery and Natalie Vincent were back together. They weren't paying too much attention to the only fact that neither seems to be thinking about. The fact that they couldn't turn back now and what would be the cost if they don't.

CHAPTER 6

The usual Thursday night poker game was in full swing at Mona's condo. The usual suspects as Mona always likes to call them were there. This is what they've been doing ever since they all met in college. Sebastian, Michael and JC sat around the poker table with her and everyone was in serious poker game concentration. Mona had the guys on the ropes again, like she stacked the deck or something. Michael's game was off not because of anything except that his mind was totally on today's events with Natalie.

"A full house again Mona, man I am out", Sebastian said as he got up from the table. "Damn, I swear Mona's stacking the freaking cards."

"Or I could just be that good big boy."

"You guys forget the cards will you look at Mic," JC said pointing to Michael next to him.

"You all remember that look from college? Chicago we must have a love connection," Sebastian chimed in. "Every since he told me about his run in with Natalie, which is way over due considering that she's Mona's best friend, I knew it was just a matter of time. Mic I know you tried it out again, huh?"

"Sebastian, shut up. You are still so juvenile. What is he talking about? When did you and Natalie connect Michael?"

"Mona I have no idea. Yes I have run into Natalie and we did have lunch."

"Sex, don't forget to mention the sex."

"Ignore him Michael, your business is your business. How was the lunch date?"

"Mona, let's just say I'm glad I got through it."

Michael thought that it would be best to keep the lid on the entire story of his afternoon. After all Natalie and he are married. It was no sense in burdening themselves with the scrutiny of all his friends. Let them just always think of him as being the one that is always in control and would never lose himself to the control of his desires.

They know that his marriage with Sonja has its ups and downs but not to this capacity. It would just open up too many roads to destruction. Until he was sure where this was going it would remain his secret.

As Michael looked around the table he wondered was there things about his friends that he didn't know. Do friends really tell it all to each other? Or are there gaps with clean versions to fill in the dirty spots. Does Sebastian have a few illegitimate babies out here in the world that he doesn't want to acknowledge, because he messes around too much? What's the mystery behind Mona's new boyfriend that clearly she's hung up about; no obsessed about?

But at least they've met Mona's new man. JC keeps his lady under FBI sequesters. What's with that? From what it seems like is that she doesn't want to meet them. JC hasn't said that directly but Michael has heard some of his conversations when he's on the cell phone talking to her. In about another ten minutes like clock work, JC will make a call to her tonight.

"Changing the subject Mona how has work been? You sure are hush, hush about things lately. Usually you have a lot to say about work."

"Well Mic, its only because the company has been developing 3 new drugs that they hope will revolutionize the diabetes industry. We have been so secretive about the details and products that I guess I didn't feel comfortable talking about it. We are in the final steps so the lid has been kept sealed tight, competition is always snooping around. Do you know that we caught my lab technician Craig having sex with some girl right there in his work area recently? I could understand the newbies but not Craig. He's worked there forever. Those newbies are always doing risky college behavior like that. That's one hell of a breach of security during this time. That's why I keep my keys, my combination to my office drawer with me at all times, for safe keeping. So you see it's been trying."

"Wow the cooperate rat race. Have you been getting anymore packages through the mail," Michael said glancing at Sebastian.

He still hasn't figured out why Sebastian has sworn him to secrecy about his, delivery. They were among friends. It could be that Sebastian didn't want Mona to blame him for her packages. Because if the sender is pissed off at Sebastian and is female, she may think that Mona is the other chick on the side, blocking her. Michael expressed to Sebastian that this could really be serious and that putting it out in the open could help them discover who it was. Sebastian told Michael to drop it, hoping it would just go away. He said he didn't need any problems with Mona, Abigail was enough.

"No. Thanks for looking out for me. I probably pissed off an old college enemy and they were blowing off some steam again, like they did back in the day. I'm sure I won't have anymore problems."

Michael thought that would be the cue for Sebastian to tell JC and Mona about his packages but Sebastian remain quiet and Michael decided to move on.

"JC when are we going to meet this mystery lady of yours, it's time?"

"Soon Mic, soon, as a matter of fact I'm gonna call her and set it up, because I really want you guys to meet her."

As JC got up from the table he stumbled a bit, but caught himself. As he braced himself on the table he didn't have to bother looking at everyone because he knew they were looking at him. Each person around the table was thinking the same thing; even though no one but Michael was suppose to know about his old drug problems.

JC on the other hand didn't know what to think. All he knows is that he has been feeling like he use to when he did do drugs, but he knew he wasn't doing them now, so what was up?

"JC, man, are you okay?" Michael said excitedly.

"Yeah, Mic I got it. I guess I just lost my balance, that's all."

That was enough for everyone to hear. Michael, Sebastian and Mona felt some relief from their fears even though they knew something had to be going on. Clearly watching JC now made it clear that JC was doing something and Michael felt it was his place to approach him. While JC made the call on his cell phone, Mona's home phone rings.

"Hello," Mona said into the receiver. "Jackson, hi,"

"Hey you, I wanted to call you quick, because I know you have your friends over. I was wondering if you would like to take our thing of ours to another level."

What does Jackson mean to another level? Is he finally leaving Leanne?

"Well what do I have to do?"

"Meet me later tonight at The Pill, I want to take you some place special, I know you will enjoy."

"Okay lover, it's a date, bye."

As Mona hung up the phone she swooned like a southern belle. This is how special Jackson made her feel. She couldn't resist her heart and her heart told her she was in love. Sebastian eyed Mona with curiosity and wondered why he never moved her like that.

"I'm only asking you to take a little time out to meet my friends, what is wrong with that? It's not like you don't have the time."

Michael heard JC talk into his cell phone. JC was trying to be discreet but it wasn't really working. He was caught off guard because Desiree said that she would meet his friends when he was ready to introduce her. Well he's ready and she's all but saying no to him. What was up?

Michael watched intently, listening to the disappointment in JC's voice as his woman obviously rejected his friends.

"Okay, okay I understand and that is what we'll do. Don't worry about that, they're not like that. I miss you too, baby."

Michael felt the same relief as JC probably did. It's not like he didn't know what it was like to have a woman in his life that pulled at him about his friends. Sonja did not like his friends, but Sonja doesn't like much of anything. She probably, only likes Michael just so.

"Well its set, Saturday night at the Pill. It'll be crowded so that will lessen the conversations; Desiree seems to be so afraid of. I guess she's shy."

Or up to something Michael thought.

****

After the guys left, Mona quickly arrived at the Pill full of excitement and zest. She was on her way to see her lover and the thrill of taking this relationship to another level energized her. As she walked in through the club the music drove through her body like small fingers stimulating her. Jackson had told Mona that he would be in the back of the club near the second bar; and there he was.

He made eye contact with her as she approached his table. Mona began to pant the closer she got to him.

"Hi Jackson," she said loud enough for him to hear over the loud music.

"Hey, baby," he responded as he got up to greet her with a kiss and as they sat down together.

"So I see that the Pill is still the thing on Thursday nights."

"I'm just surprised I've never seen you here before, Mona."

"Jackson, I'm really anxious to hear what you plan on doing to take our love thing to another level. Did you tell Leanne about us?"

"No, it's not that Mona, baby. I'm going to do that, real soon. What I meant by taking our relationship to another level is sexually."

Mona did not bother to hide the disappointed that was surely written on her face. She couldn't believe that she got worked up this much to hear Jackson talk about taking sex to another level. What was it this time, role playing?

Sometimes she felt that this was all he wanted from her, the intense sex they have. Jackson read her facial expressions.

"Maybe we should get a drink before we get into this any further."

Jackson motioned to the waitress that seemed to be waiting there with drinks in hand. She laid the drinks down on the table and winked at Jackson when she walked away and he winked back.

"I took the liberty of ordering you a drink earlier and had it waiting in the wings."

"Thanks baby," Mona took a sip. She was pleasantly surprised that Jackson remembered she likes the drink the Cherry Rose. It was a splash of cherry flavor, 7 up and Stolichnaya vodka.

Jackson held his arm tightly around Mona as he spoke to her.

"I've always had this fantasy that the woman that I love and I would be open sexually in our relationship." Mona opened her mouth to protest. She felt she knew where he was going. She was not going to agree to see other people. She's already sharing him with his wife.

"Mona wait it's a surprise, I know what you're thinking, but it's not like that, it'll take us to another level and I promise I will tell Leanne."

Being with Jackson is becoming more or less the constant overnighter. But Jackson's pleading was all Mona needed to hear as she finished her drink.

"Let's go baby," she said seductively in his ear.

As Jackson and Mona got up from the table Jackson nodded to the sexy waitress. Mona's head was swimming and she felt herself grinding seductively to the pulse of the music, wanting to touch everyone.

She was feeling euphoric and wanted everyone in the club to feel what she was feeling. Hell, she wanted everyone in the club to feel her. As Jackson whisked her away through the crowd Mona glided on the air and the clouds.

By the time they reached the room, Mona was trying to tear clothing away from Jackson's body. Inside, the room was spinning and inside of her she was spinning from the warmth. Jackson motioned Mona onto the bed that was perched in the middle of the room. This was no suite.

As he walked over to her he pulled her from the bed and embraced her. He slid his hands over her body and around to the back as she cooed dramatically.

Mona helped Jackson remove her dress and let it fall to the floor. He kissed her deeply. Behind Mona she heard movement in the room. Jackson held her too tightly for her to move around and together the fell back into the bed.

"Oh Jackson," Mona moaned. The two of them lit the bed on fire and began at each other like hungry animals.

Suddenly Mona felt the extra body in the room move again. She was well in a sexual daze as the figure moved over to the dresser and danced seductively in the mirror. Mona could only make out that it was a female.

She heard the simple music that was being played as the figure gyrated to her own reflection. So this was the surprise that Jackson wanted her to take part in, another woman; never. The figure was doing something while dancing and Mona's attention soon was diverted by Jackson again, as he embraced her.

'Karen' felt the anger build as she watch him performed his lust on Mona. It was like what she has seen so many times before. She didn't like it then and she certainly didn't like to see it happening in front of her.

The two of them were like disgusting pigs. She kept an eye on them while she slowly slid her hands into Mona's purse and lifted her keys, her wallet and a mini pouch from inside it.

Once she knew that Jackson had consumed Mona in his lust and the ecstasy pill was now in full swing, she slowly crept from the room; leaving the two to their devices.

'Karen' hurriedly raced to the adjoining room where inside there was a key making machine. There was one to program an electronic proximity card and metal key. There also was a copier and lamination machine as she spread the contents of Mona's wallet out on the bed. She began her work.

By now Mona was focusing on Jackson. Together they had no idea of what danger actually has entered their lustful lives.

CHAPTER 7

The next day Mona sat across the lunch table of the local eatery Moonbie's with Natalie. Moonbie's is the newest eatery nearest the hospital and was on the tongues of all the staff lunch crunchers as the place to be.

So Natalie had suggested to Mona that they try it out on this day. They were just about finished. It was late in the afternoon and even though Mona was exhausted and groggy from the late night antics she had with Jackson, she honored her commitment to the lunch date they had set days ago.

Actually the real reason was that Natalie said she had something important to talk to her about. Mona knew that it was going to be good whatever it is she was going to tell her. However, Mona did not need to expand her imagination too far. It didn't take a psychic to know that it was all about Michael.

There was no reason to bring up what went on last night. Mona really didn't know too much herself. It was all too blurry. But the one thing that was very clearly etched in her memory was the female form that was with Jackson and her last night.

How did she let herself partake in that filth? What in the world possessed her? It was like being out of her body and not being able to remember how she was drugged and force to do.

Mona was no stranger to wild and freaky nights but this was not on her to due list. This was too far to the left of her personality.

What heinous acts? No way could she have done that with a clear mind and she only had one drink. Jackson must have slipped her an Ecstasy pill or something.

The bastard set her up. He didn't even have the balls to face her either, this morning. He left before she woke up and took that trash with him. He has much to explain when she hears from him, much more than that flimsy text he sent to her that read:

"*Thanks for living out my fantasy, I love you.*"

Love has nothing to do with the disgusting feeling she feels as each hour of the day does nothing to expand the scenes from their late night romp. It made her sweat profusely. She would be too embarrassed if she thought that anyone would be able to see what went on. Even though she doesn't know herself, it's almost life shattering.

Well one thing for sure, she certain is beginning to slow down her antics. She actually feels disgusted about last night. Jackson's ass is in big trouble for this for sure, she thought.

"…so we slept together." Natalie said breathing a sigh of relief as she finished her story.

It took Mona a moment to emerge from her own madness to actually digest what little she heard.

"You two did what?"

"Michael and I made love." Natalie said with conviction.

"Well good for you girl. I'm not the least bit shocked because it's was written all over Michael's aura last night. Good for you. Can I tell Sonja?"

Mona paused a little and stared seriously at Natalie, and then she let out a loud laugh.

"I'm just kidding. But you two now need to tell those two loser where the hell to get off."

"Mona, it's not that cut and dry. Michael and I have families."

"So what, you say the girls don't even see Christopher on a regular, so what would be the difference if you leave? And poor Michael and his little girl are living in hell with the evil bitch."

"Mona it's just not that easy. I..."

"Yea I know you have a career. You know Natalie, Chicago Memorial is not the only hospital around. You can have your own practice apart from the hospital. You don't have to fear him, he's nothing."

"I don't fear Christopher; I fear what will happen to my girls. I love Michael, I never stopped, but I don't think we were meant to be together."

"So what has happened between you two was what, curiosity?"

"No, forgiveness, I was asking for his forgiveness. I was naive back then, Mona. I let other people control my mind and talk me out of my man. I let Sonja take Michael from me and the grim thing is that she planned that all along."

"She's a heartless backstabbing witch. If Mic wasn't married to her, I'd take her on a few rounds and kick box her ass to death."

"Mona you are crazy. I'm glad I can talk to you. We'd better get going; I have a few things to wrap up before I leave today."

****

Dr. Edwards sat at her desk in amazement, listening to 'Karen' talk with such joy. She would love to think that the medication was the cause. She had a feeling that Karen was not taking the pills. Here she is filled with excitement and self-assurance, leveled off like she is doing just that.

"...and I feel like I can do anything. I went out and did something very exciting and only for myself. I proved that my life does not need to fall prey to anyone. I'm now in control of other people. Don't you see I'm on top of the world?"

Dr. Edwards stood up from her chair near the soft sofa where 'Karen' was sitting. She began to pace almost giving the appearance that she was the one who was indeed in need of counseling. 'Karen' watched her intently.

She wondered in her mind whether she should just confess to the dear Janice about *her* escapades last night. It was just perfect. She has always had Jackson in her pocket from day one. She sent him to do her bidding. He was a success.

Once it was confirmed that he was Mona's love interest it was a simple thing of watching and taking notes. What he wanted from Mona though was much more than love.

She approached Jackson that night at that swap party after he had his little sexual encounter with Mona. She told him she could help him with his plans and she also appealed to his greedy appetite for women, the selfish bastard.

On that night they were merged together. He was a no good pig who actually disserved to be stabbed to death, but he was needed. There were so many other things to do and so little time. But last night was a milestone. She doesn't even know what was taken from her was literally her life last night and she disserve it.

How dare Mona pretend to just be friends with Sebastian? Sebastian was and still is a true bastard? The two of them have been laughing at her for too long, she thought. For too long, for years laughing in their dirty lust for each, other.

By sleeping with that slut it is no wonder he would do what he has done to her leaving her a barren wasteland, full of emotional pain.

Then she thought about him, the friend, the good guy, with the broken heart. She hadn't really been following what Michael has been doing lately.

What a waste for him to be married to Sonja. She has always been selfish and no amount of advice could ever change her controlling ways. Next time she'll bash her head in personally rather than instigate some random accident.

"'Karen' I see you've changed your hair style." Dr. Edwards said as she walked over to her window.

Looking out of it, she continued to talk to her.

She knew that visual observance was very important to her field of work; but she just couldn't stare at 'Karen' one more second. There was something going on here and she could not crack through it; something that she needed to know about.

She has tried this session for the last pass hour to get out of 'Karen' what changed her attitude but all she was getting was the run around. It was very important that she reported her activities to her but 'Karen' was very unpredictable.

But at least she was now attempting to be happy about their plans. Still she wanted to know what attributed to the positive change. At the last session 'Karen' was still full of rage and revenge, but today the flip. Maybe she is taking the pills, but Dr. Edwards' gut instincts say she isn't.

"I needed a different look to complete my mission last night."

"Mission, 'Karen' what did you do?"

"Look Dr. Edwards, I know that I've been coming here a while for your help, but I don't feel I should have to tell you every sorted detail of my activities. I mean some things are personal," she laughed.

"I understand that, really I do, however you brought these things up and frankly I'm intrigued. Beside we agreed that this is what you would do."

'Karen' paused and relaxed in her chair. She was flattered. The good doctor wanted to hear about all the sorted details, from A to Z huh? She wasn't in control, a first.

"Let's just say that I helped provide a fantasy to a very needy gentleman."

"A gentleman, so you're saying that you're involved with someone, special?"

"No I said I provided a fantasy."

"Well it must have been fantastic, because you're glowing from the result of it."

It must have been like a trigger on a gun, only taking seconds for the bullets to go from dormant to live rounds.

'Karen' leaped out of her chair and fell to floor, pounding into it with both fists with all her might.

"Fantastic? It was disgusting what I had to do. I felt like a cheap whore. They have ruined my life and I've been reduced to lying in the dark letting men do what they want to me. They…"

The doctor almost choked on her breath, with her own excitement of finally cracking the shell. This was what she wanted to hear, the truth, her truth.

She took that chance that 'Karen' would be receptive to her comfort and knelt down beside her, grabbing both her fists. She had beside her a small music box which she opened and played.

"'Karen' please tell me, who are 'they'."

The music seemed to calm 'Karen', it was lullaby music, almost hypnotic.

No. Don't let it fool you.

'Karen' thought about what she was about to say to ensure that she said what she was enticed to say.

"They're the ones that drove me to this. The music man and his whore the, CEO. The two of them are one of a kind, destruction you remember you said…"

"The music man is he the one we've been talking about all these months, the one you want to get even with?"

No, not you, it's her.

"Why would I do that? They're not very important you see I have had the time of my life and I am growing. I'm getting better, I had a life. Will you stay with me until I'm well?"

"But you said that you are angry with them, they're the ones that did this to you, remember?"

"I do."

"Then yes I will be right here for you."

Dr. Edwards let out a deep breath. As quickly as the rage came it passed, just as Dr. Edwards had planned. She was the calm at the center the eye of the storm, the focal point. So this is another long session with a short result. Dr. Edwards embraced 'Karen' like she was a child.

'Karen' sat quiet not really in the same world as Dr. Edwards. She didn't hear anything as well as Dr. Edwards' response to her question.

"I'll always take care of you. I created your strength."

She started to prepare herself for the days and nights ahead; much to do, much to do.

****

In another part of the Chicago Memorial in Natalie's office she is there talking to Mona. She had finished her work early so Mona just decided to hangout the rest of the day with her.

"So you and Sonja had words huh? I bet that was interesting."

"Natalie, Sonja didn't want any of this action. I was ready to let her have it but of course your man Michael, peacemaker, intervened. I was surprised because Abigail was there too and tried to break it up. She was kind of eerie suggesting that I call her Ambrosia, what is all that about? It was something about her eyes I really think Sebastian has married a ravening lunatic."

"No Michael did. I still can't believe he let Sonja get this far with her selfish crap."

"I'm just glad that Michael and you are back together. Whether you two end up together is…"

"Humph, excuse me."

Natalie looked up towards her door a saw Christopher standing there. The door had been open because Kelly left early and Natalie didn't want to feel shut in. The two of them, Mona and Natalie sat in shock not knowing how much of their conversation Christopher had heard.

"Natalie, I was expecting you for lunch today," Christopher said as he walked further into the office, glaring, glancing at Mona.

He despised Natalie's choice in friends. She always seemed to choose useless associations.

If it wasn't for him she would never have received her own practice. She just wastes her time with idle gossip and her hopes of keeping in touch with the little people. She never seems to understand that she should be above reproach by the less interesting. As always Christopher refused to listen to or respond to anything negative that he might have wanted to speak on. It's about not wasting time on the small stuff.

"Ah Christopher, did we have an appointment?" Natalie responded nervously.

She knew full well she will never know until he allows her to know whether he heard anything or not. Mona just sat quietly observing her friend's change of attitude as she became a Stepford Wife right before her own eyes.

"Yes we had an appointment earlier," he said glancing at Mona again, before continuing. "Tomorrow, 5 o'clock don't be late. The Riggs are joining us. You know the place."

"Yes I, I do. Oh Chris you remember Mona Daniels, the VPO of Cultrax Pharmaceutical?"

Christopher walked out of Natalie's office without saying another word. Mona began to speak and Natalie put up a hand to caution her. They waited in silence a few seconds until they heard the front office door slam.

"Ooh Natalie he is a jerk. I never dreamed. Do you think he heard us about Michael?"

"Well Mona, I guess I'll find out later tonight. But I promise you I will not be attending that 5 o' clock ego boosting session tomorrow. I don't even like Marina Riggs."

****

The elevator door to the hospital opened quicker than Mona expected. She had her back to the doors and spun around quickly to board the car. She had intended on walking out with Natalie, but Michael called. By no means did she want to block that so she left.

As she boarded the elevator, she eyed the woman that was already on board and dismissed her choice of clothing immediately. She stood closer to the entrance as the elevator doors closed. She pushed the number one button and stood impatiently at the door.

Then it hit her, a wave of recollection. She felt she knew the woman that was on the elevator and could not place her face. It didn't help that she had that God awful wig on, as if no one could tell. So Mona turned around and spoke.

"Hi. That's a beautiful outfit you're wearing."

It really was dog awful Mona wanted to say but it gave her a chance to thoroughly scope the woman out. She could hardly see her behind the large tinted Gucci glasses and hair draping all over the place. She had too much hair, but not enough to hide the face completely.

"Thank you," the woman said dryly to Mona.

What's up her tunnel Mona thought in her mind?

"It's the color. It's perfect for this time of year." Mona said glaring directly into the woman's eyes albeit through her tinted glasses.

The woman instantly snapped. She slapped Mona with her back hand and mashed her in the face; shoving her head against the wall.

"Bitch, if I wanted your opinion, I would have asked for it." Mona fell against the wall and collapsed. She instantly started to plea for her life.

"Miss, I'm sorry. Why are you doing this?"

"Because you are a whore and you should die like all whores do."

"It's you. It's you that's sending those dolls and the notes. Why, why are you doing that?"

"Shut up whore. I am going to take this letter opener I borrowed from a friend of mine and really carve you up. I'm going to carve your insides out like mine was."

The woman pulled the emergency stop button on the elevator and the alarm whistled. Mona put her hands to her ears to deafen the sound. Mona screamed at the top of her lungs and the woman plunged the letter opener into her chest.

"Are you okay?" Mona said to the woman as she leaned against the walls of the elevator.

"I'm alright," 'Karen' said realizing she had phased out again in one of her fantasy scenarios. Mona took this opportunity to get a good look at her face, but 'Karen' turned her head.

"Do you need to see a doctor or something honey?"

"I said I was fine!" 'Karen' said more aggressively and the doors of the elevator opened to the lobby. Mona left well enough alone mainly because she could not draw a name to the obscured face.

She walked out into the lobby towards the entrance. As she walked she felt this weird feeling, stop and turned around. She saw as the elevator door closed that the woman had not got off on her floor but instead was standing in the back of the elevator.

She had taken off the glasses and stood glaring at Mona with a burst of rage in her eyes; giving her the finger. Mona flipped back at her as she turned back around and headed out the entrance.

"All that I asked the dumb broad was whether she was alright woo." She said to herself.

In her mind she added another conformation on why she didn't care too much for women, too much damn drama.

She had no time for that. Jackson has not contacted her and that made her pissed. She decided that she would call him as she walked out of the hospital.

"Hey baby," he said to her through the phone.

Jackson knew that by now the events and questions of what actually happened in that hotel room was really bothering Mona. He shouldn't have dropped that pill in her drink because it could have raised some questions with Mona. He didn't need her being too suspicious.

In order for his plan to work she has to totally trust him and not implicate him once the deed is done. He will be like the doting boyfriend. He will until the heat gets too strong and he has to back away from her; for his own sake. It was a perfect plan.

"Don't hey baby me. What was that last night? I don't do drugs and that is a no-no in my profession. Do you know I could get suspended if I'm tested? Hello I'm a VPO at a pharmaceutical company. Don't ever, do that to me again. Just because I'm in love with you doesn't mean that you can put my life at risk."

"I'm so sorry baby. I didn't know that you felt this strongly about it. We were having fun. Tell me it wasn't the best night of your life?"

"I wish I could tell you, but I can't remember anything pass standing up at the table. Did you have someone in our room videotaping us or something?"

"No are you kidding. I'm not that adventurous. I did have the TV on at one point."

"What was that female in the room for?"

"Room service baby, that's all."

Mona was sure he was lying, but why? Why would Jackson not admit something like that? He never lied to her before. Maybe he was telling the truth. She was having some heavy reactions to that drug that night. Maybe hallucinations were one of them. But he asked her to take the relationship to the next level. What did they do?

At any rate she hadn't planned to be that mad at him. She just wanted him to take her life in consideration the next time he wants to act like a 20 something and feed her drugs. JC's addiction taught her well to steer away from drugs.

"Just watch it baby. I love my career."

Jackson agreed with Mona and made his false promises. The die is casted, so it will be whatever happens.

****

Natalie stirred around silently in her office. It was late. It was great to see Mona and then top off the evening with talking to Michael. She wasn't in a hurry to go home she didn't want to listen to Christopher's rants and demands.

She had heard enough earlier. How dare he, be rude to one of her friends and have the audacity to expect perfection from her. That's just telling her that he did not have much regard for her life unless it revolved around his.

He called a few minutes ago. He gave some lame apologetic speech about having too much on his mind, that he did not hear her. Natalie knew that he wasn't telling the truth. He's being as selfish as he's always been.

She sat back at her desk and brought the cup of coffee she purchased at the Starbuck's staff lounge to her lips. Immediately she paused as she looked up towards the door and in the doorway stood Sonja. She stared at Sonja not actually believing she was really there, so she blinked once and realized she was real.

"Well Natalie, may I come in?" Sonja said trying to add some dry humor to the awkward moment.

Here they were adversaries. Once best of friends and now because of a man, it has come to this. It has been years and Natalie has much to say. She felt that now was time. If Sonja doesn't go there she will.

"Have a seat. You wanted something?"

"Yes, I want you to leave my husband alone."

Does she know? Natalie thought. How could she know? Sonja has never been known for her swiftness.

"I don't know what you mean bothering your husband. Let's see if that makes sense. No I need a little more."

"Not bothering him, wanting to see him. I want you to stop trying to be with Michael again."

"Sonja cut the crap. You know I'm not the least bit interested in your fantasies. What do you want?"

"Well frankly I'm tired of living in your shadow. Apparently my husband feels like he's still wants you or something."

"And Michael said this to you?"

"No it's just a feeling, like the feeling I'm getting right now about your feelings for him."

"I see you've developed psychic powers in addition to your manipulation powers. You won't get in my head and talk me out of anything again."

"Well even if it's not true eventually Michael is going to call you and when he does you need to tell him to get lost."

"What the hell? Sonja, I really am sick of you. You need to get the hell out of here and never comeback. How dare you, tell me what to do."

"Look Natalie I don't want to fight with you unless I have to. I just want you to back off. I still consider you my friend. It's just that I'm with the man you abandon years ago. Why be mad at me?"

"You know it's not just that cut and dry. You set your sights on Michael long before I 'abandoned' him and you know it.

But because you stole him like a dirty little alley cat, your fears are getting the best of you. You came here out of desperation hoping I would forgive you for your lies and pity you. It has nothing to with Michael, it's you. Your marriage is falling apart and you need someone to blame, well by means blame me. What you took from me is going to be taken from you, because you disserve it. You never loved Michael you just wanted him because I had him. You wanted my man, my friends and my life so now you can't handle it."

"Don't push me Natalie. I suggest you do as I say, because one thing about you Ms. Perfect is that you value your career over everything else and one call from me to your husband and you're out of Chicago Memorial, on your ass. I guess I got your career too, huh?"

"Are you threatening me Sonja? Don't get cute with me. You know you don't know when to quit. You've already hurt me enough in the past. Nothing can hurt me that you do now. The Natalie that sits in front of you, you don't know her. Don't fuck with me; get the hell out of here."

"Ooh, who knew the pretty pediatrician had such a potty mouth."

Sonja said standing up from her chair.

"I've giving you a fair chance to do the right thing, Nat. Think about it" She started to walk out the door.

"Sonja, be sure to tell Michael that I said hi and that I'll be waiting for his call."

She saw Sonja miss a step with that comment. It was fun matching wits with her. This was something that she's always wanted to do but never got the chance.

She knew now that Sonja's words were just an inquiry. She knew nothing of what has gone on with Michael and her. Actually she made it easy for her to choose to be with Michael now. She did steal him from her and now Natalie wants him back.

CHAPTER 8

The next night, Saturday, at the Pill, Désiree brought her glass of Ciroc vodka nervously to her lips and drank it down slowly. She was nervous for sure and JC thought that she would go into shock at any minute. They were sitting at the bar waiting for Michael, Mona and Sebastian, to arrive.

JC noticed that Désiree had gone all out to make herself, extra appealing for his friends. It was almost as if she had gotten herself a makeover overnight. He hardly recognized the new Désiree.

He felt for sure as if he found the woman of his dreams. That she would go this far to impress his friends; it made him want to ask her to leave to make love to her all-night. But then JC thought about how he felt health wise and that wasn't good. His body seemed as though it was taking on a mind of its own and failing him.

"How long is it going to be before your friends get her baby?" Désiree asked with a little bit of an edge to her voice.

"Any minute, when I called a half an hour ago Sebastian said that he was on his way to pick up Michael and Mona."

"Sebastian, that's the one who's cheating on his wife right?"

"Yeah."

"He's pathetic. Why get married if all you're gonna do is mess around. If I was his wife I'd kill him."

"Hey ease down that's one of my buddies. And besides he's not the only one. Michael is stepping out on his wife too."

Désiree stared at J.C. for a bit as if she had gone to another world. J.C. did not knowing what was going through her mind; he just sat quietly and let her go there. After all, this was not the first time she has done this and he was just simply getting use to it.

"J.C., are you sure that Michael is having an affair? Isn't he the nice guy you're always going on about?"

Before he answered J.C. looked deep into Désiree's beautiful dark brown eyes. He was not sure but he could tell that there was more to her than meets the eye and that made him all the more interested.

She was hurt bad before he was sure of it and she was in need of a white knight to save her. He planned on being that white knight.

"Yeah, but that's not saying he doesn't step out. Well really it's kind of complicated. His ex from college has somehow gotten back into his life and I believe I don't know that there's something happening with them again. I'm kind of happy for him if he does, his wife Sonja is a bitch."

"Wow, you're friends are complicated."

Ten more minutes passed and still no friends, J.C. started to worry.

"J.C," Désiree said hesitantly.

"I'm not feeling well. I need to leave."

"What's wrong baby?"

"I've got a headache from the drinks. This is what I get for not drinking my Courvoisier."

"I'll drive you." "No I don't want to leave my car. You stay and have a good time."

Really Désiree's head was not aching, it was her boredom. How dare his friends think they could just have her sitting around in this pitiful club waiting on them to, arrive. Well she had other things to do anyway and new plans to make for her next conquest. She's not going to be with this loser J.C. too much longer.

J.C. couldn't hide his disappointment. This was the only reason why he agreed to meet with the gang tonight; to introduce Désiree. Now he has to sit and wait for them, only to tell them that she's gone. He kissed Désiree. She got up and walked towards the entrance. Hell he should just go with her, he wasn't feeling all that great either.

J.C. moved to get up. He turned to the bar and dropped a twenty on the counter; the bartender acknowledged. Once he turned back around Sebastian, Michael and Sonja was standing in front of him.

"Hey buddy, sorry we're late," Michael said shaking his hand. "We had some last minute juggling around to do."

"He means me J.C." Sonja chimed in. "I just wanted to meet this new lady of yours and spend sometime with my husband."

It wasn't that J.C. couldn't see the logic in what Sonja said it was the tone. He looked at Sebastian and all he could do was rolled his eyes to the ceiling. Also, it was obvious that seeing Sonja meant that was the reason he was not seeing a Mona standing here. This is not going to be a good night.

****

"I just simply refused right out, to be in the woman's presence any longer than I have to, she's poison." Mona said to Natalie as they climbed into Natalie's car.

The two of them had met for dinner after Mona decided not to hang with the guys tonight.

"I was looking forward to meeting Desiree, but not at the expense of hanging with Sonja. I don't know what it is Natalie but that woman really boils my blood. I think it's her aura."

"You might have a point there, Mona."

"So," Mona said continuing. "When Michael pulled up, I was standing out in front of my building waiting for him. He seemed mortified. Once I saw who was in the front seat, I shook my head. Sonja was smiling that toothy devious smile she always seems to have before the start of something chaotic. After Michael got out of the car and told me the story, I felt that I would probably go to jail tonight if I got into that car. Then I just thought instead of taking a cab to the Pill and risk going to jail from there, it would be best to call you and see if you were free. I like to limit my contact with her. I'm already pissed that she didn't want me staying at her house, when that incident with the flower box happened. I ended up going back to my condo. I love Mic like a brother, but I fear for him."

"Well I wasn't really going to mention this, you know how I am." Mona nodded in agreement.

"Well yesterday evening after you left, Sonja came to see me."

"She did what?"

"Yes girl she just barged in. I guess to catch me off guard. I don't think she was expecting what she found."

"What you naked on top of Michael? Please say yes."

"Ha-ha, No. Mona, that's crazy. She told me that she wanted me to stop seeing Michael.

So immediately I thought the jig was up, but it wasn't, she was just feeling around."

"Sonja is trash. I take it you gave her a run for her money, huh?"

"Well let's just say that she's not as strong as her nastiness portrays she is. After she threatened me that I should stop seeing Michael and I told her not to take me there, she seemed shaken. I think she hasn't changed."

"So are you going to stop seeing Michael?" Natalie was all prepared to give the quick witted response that she has become accustomed to, but hesitated. She really didn't know what she wanted to do now that she has calmed down.

Once again the old noncommittal Natalie has arisen again. But the here and now Natalie was determined to be heard. The here and now Natalie was deeply in love with the man she lost and he has found her again.

They have established their feeling for each other and it seems that Michael is ready to take the next step; but was she. There was always a road block of some sort causing detours. It was as if the fates refused to make it easy on them.

Michael Montgomery is her soul mate and she is his. So Sonja be damned, Christopher be damned it's time the world gets an opportunity to see true love. No she will not stop seeing Michael.

As a declaration of her new found independence was, the fact that she stayed a little longer with Michael. She was supposed to have dinner with the Riggs and Christopher.

Christopher was so mad at Natalie that he actually raised his voice to her. That was something that he has never done. She was dedicated to her new cause and that was to cut the strings to all the mind manipulators. No one is going to direct the rest of her life anymore.

"No Mona, I'm not going to stop. Not until if at all until I'm ready. Michael Montgomery is mine."

"I hear you. That's so funny that she would be at the hospital because I had the strangest encounter with some woman I thought I knew. She was trying to hide her face. What was Sonja wearing?"…

****

It was around 10 o'clock at the Pill as Michael, Sebastian, and even Sonja settled back with JC drinking. They had all reassured JC that it was understandable about Désiree.

JC was just barely holding on, himself. He felt weak and queasy. Michael noticed JC's behavior and tried not to believe what his mind was trying to convince him of.

"J. you don't look so hot yourself. Maybe you should go home too. It's pretty chaotic in here with all this music and people."

"Yeah, I agree Mic. I'm fine though. I'm just worried about Desiree. But I think I will leave; sorry guys."

"Hey J, don't worry about us, Mic and I will find something to do," Sebastian said.

He meant to exclude Sonja. She only decided to come tonight in order to piss off Mona and she got just what she wanted. But that doesn't mean that the rest of them should have to suffer.

One thing about women like Sonja, is that their never satisfied. They always try to take more and more from their men and Michael better watch out. They all watched JC get up and leave the club before exchanging any words.

Finally when he was gone, Sonja seemed to explode instantly.

"Sebastian, do you think that I drink Michael?"

Sebastian was caught off guard slightly and before Michael could intervene, he responded.

"Sonja I don't think about you at all."

"Michael," she said looking at Michael. "Are you just going to sit there and say nothing to your friend?"

"Sonja, Sebastian answered your question. You didn't seem too kind when you asked it so I guess you got what you got. However, if this opening line with you two is going somewhere near an argument, than I'm getting up and leaving."

"No I simply didn't appreciate his obvious attempt to exclude me as if I'm just a tag-a-long. I have better things to do."

"I'm sure Sebastian wasn't trying to take you there. It was probably a guy thing, right See."

"Yes,"

"See Sonja..."

"No, not yes to your question, Mic yes to hers."

That was comment that Michael did not need Sebastian to make. He is always being too brash, leaving others to clean up or better yet pay for his dirty deeds.

"Michael Montgomery this is it. I've had enough of your friends. It's obvious that they do not respect me. It's like I'm trash to them. You need to put a muzzle on your friend."

Michael was trapped. He was trapped not because he was caught in the middle. He felt as if he was trapped in a cage, in this marriage. It's not hard to see that Sonja's on a mission.

Slowly but surely she is competing with Mona, Sebastian and even JC for his attention.

She is purposely becoming at odds with them to run them off; but Michael is not allowing that to happen. These friends of his are the only tie to reality that he has. Now that Natalie is back into his life, there isn't a place for Sonja. Sonja is not Michael's reality, she is his nightmare.

"Sonja maybe you should just go home." He had to say it.

He had to make this choice, right here, right now. It wasn't that Sebastian was right; he knows that Sebastian was being childish. A man doesn't say these things to his wife. Not even if they are at odds. However, Sonja has to be stopped. She started this game. She established the rules and she has not let down one minute.

'It's either her or me,' he thought. *'And it ain't going to be me.'*

Sonja stared at Michael for a minute in disbelief. What did he say to her? In all the years that she has know him he has always given her what she needs or at least what she wanted. What changed now? Natalie Vincent, she thought as anger began wielding up inside of her.

Sebastian sat quietly looking from Sonja back to Michael. He too couldn't believe what he just heard or maybe the music was too loud. Michael disregarded Sonja? Now Sebastian knew for sure that Natalie and he are sleeping together.

It all made sense. Michael was never the kind of guy that would not be loyal unless he was being pushed. Sonja is definitely pushing Michael and hard. No she doesn't just drink Michael; she consumes him a piece at a time and what she spits out is nothing but an empty shell.

'Well go ahead with you bad self Mic,' Sebastian thought amusingly.

"So your wife has to go home and you stay and hang out with your buddy? What kind off marriage is this Michael?"

"Sonja what kind of fun do you think we'll have? You started this remember. You set the stage, first with Mona and now Sebastian. I came out here to have a good time. Now there's tension, there's always tension with you."

Well I guess you've said all that you needed to say, huh," Sonja said glaring deep within Michael's eyes.

It was almost she thought to herself as if she looked deep enough she would eventually see Natalie Vincent hiding in there. She's the cause of all of this and she's going to pay for it.

Sonja was so angry within her thoughts that before she knew it she had picked up her glass and threw the contents into Michael's face. Then she got up from her chair and threw down sixty dollars she retrieved from her purse.

"Don't bother to get up gentleman, sit and enjoy your drinks; there on me." Sonja walked off in a huff as bystander stopped and looked on.

Michael sat still wiping the watery liquid from his face with whatever napkins he could find. Sebastian knew that Michael was mad as hell. He didn't say a thing to Michael. He felt that if he spoke to him, Michael would somehow take out his frustration on him.

Away from their table near the bar, one woman threw her head back in hysterical laughter. If not for the volume of the music she would have caught the guys' attention. 'Karen' knew she wouldn't be heard and so she cut loose in a burst of laughter as people looked on.

****

Later that night, Natalie and Mona drove down the street leading to Mona's condo. Once into the community Natalie looked up towards Mona's windows.

"Mona, look up at your windows."

Mona followed Natalie's instructions. She instantly saw that every light was on in her place. Behind the sheer curtains a figure was seen walking through the condo.

"Oh my God, who is that," Natalie said in pure horror as she parked the car directly across the street and turned off the motor.

"I don't know, but I better call the police."

"Do you think it's Jackson?"

"Jackson doesn't have a key to my place…Hello 911; I like to report an intruder…"

Mona talked to the 911 dispatcher, for only a brief moment once they committed to sending the police. Additional minutes went by like hours and the ladies watched the intruder slowly turn off each of the lights in Mona's home. About a moments later someone emerged from the lobby doors of the condominium.

"Mona look, that's…"

"I know Natalie, Abigail Black. That witch, what was she doing in my apartment?"

Mona jumped out of Natalie's car before Natalie could say anything. Mona sprinted across the street in seconds just as the police pulled up. Angrily she was upon Abigail immediately.

"You have two seconds to tell me what in the hell are you doing here, Abigail?"

"You should know you called me and ask me to come here; then you didn't answer you door. You mind telling where you were and what do you want?"

"I didn't call you and you need to tell me why you were in my condo. Is it you sending me all those boxes of dead roses?"

"Roses, I'm not sending you any roses. Why would I do that? And I was not in your damn condo."

"Did someone call the police?" The officer said not knowing who to talk to.

"I did. Officer I know this woman and clearly it was her that was in my condo. There's no other reason why she should have been in my community."

"Is that true Miss?"

"No, I've told her that the only reason why I'm here is because she called and asked me here. Look Mona, I don't know what kind of games Sebastian and you are playing, but I don't want to play. It's enough that you're sleeping with my husband, now I'm being set up too."

"So Miss, you're saying that you were not in this lady's apartment?"

"No I was not! Look like I said I was at the craft store where I work sometimes and I got a call from her on my cell phone asking me to come over. Sebastian must have given you my number."

"Why would I do that Abigail? It's not like we're friends or anything."

"Anyway I thought it might be important, like a confession that she's sleeping with my no good husband. Who knew it was a set up."

"Sleeping with, girl nobody wants Sebastian Black we're just friends."

Mona said trying to sound convincing. Okay, well, she did at least a couple of times; just to see how he was. But since then Abigail needed not to worry about an encore performance.

"Your husband is Mr. Sebastian the Morning Lover? Aw man, he's..." the younger police officer said but the other older officer flashed him a look and cut him off.

"Ms. Daniels did you see Mrs. Black in your apartment?"

"No but why else would she be here?"

"Good question, you ladies stay down here while we investigate. What condo number?"

"Ask Abigail she should know."

The officer shot Mona a look.

"Okay my condo number is 33F." she said reluctantly as she handed her keys to the officer.

Mona Natalie and Abigail watched intensely as the officers went upstairs cautiously. Natalie turned slightly and noticed that Abigail was staring at her.

"Abigail is something wrong?" Natalie intended her question to be harmless, but if Abigail takes it the wrong way then so be, it.

"No I'm just looking," she offered.

Abigail viewed this Natalie carefully. She wasn't like the studious, trustworthy Natalie she remembered from years ago. This woman looked as if she was a full of flair. Maybe Sonja has a point to be worried about her connection to Michael.

It's never good when the competition offers a lot more than you can give at the time. But truthfully even though it goes against everything that she should feel, Michael belonged with Natalie. She would never say that out loud.

"I was thinking that I haven't seen you since college, you look good."

"Thank you, so do you."

"You're welcome. So things look like…"

"Ah, hello, can we stay focused. She broke into my home." Mona said, disgusted that Natalie was even talking to Abigail.

"Look I said I did not. I was only responding to you urgent message."

"What message"?

"Like I said you called and asked me to come by. You wanted to talk about Sebastian."

"I've known of you for over twelve years, now. Have we ever talked and especially about Sebastian? Hell no, so don't try and lie here, you're caught."

"Whatever. So Natalie have you had a chance to catch up with Michael?"

"Abigail…"

"Actually I go by Ambrosia now."

"Okay Ambrosia. You sound as if I just popped back on the scene here in Chicago. I've always been here. I never left."

"Oh I was under the impression that you just got back in town."

"Who gave you that dumb ass notion," Mona chimed in. "Sonja Montgomery?"

The mere mention of Sonja's name attached to Michael was supposed to affect Abigail, but instead it crashed down hard on Natalie. It was just another reminder of the terrible wrong done to her life.

"I'm trying to be nice," Abigail said.

"Don't be," Mona countered and suddenly Abigail stepped up and slapped her, hard.

It was probably loud enough to wake up the whole entire neighborhood. Natalie by being too close to them was brushed aside and pushed to the ground.

The battle was on as Mona forced Abigail to the ground. They rolled on the concrete actually punching faces and pulling on each other's hair. Clothes were being ripped and poor Natalie frantically tried to break up the fight once she got up.

Soon after several minutes into the confrontation the two police officers returned and started pulling the two females apart. Again Natalie was shoved aside again, this time by the quick responding officers.

"No, no let me at her, this is a longtime coming," yelled Mona.

"Yes it is," Abigail yelled back at her.

"You ladies need to break this up or we're taking you in," warned the older cop.

After a moment with no resolution made the police made their move.

"Okay here we go downtown."

CHAPTER 9

"Man Michael this is crazy. Why do you let Sonja get to you like this? We're out, she's gone and all we have to do is make the most of, it." Sebastian said to Michael as they exited the Pill.

"I'm not in the mood for partying right now Sebastian, that's all. It has nothing to do with Sonja."

"Bullshit, if you ask me you need to step to that broad and show her whose boss."

Michael stopped Sebastian on the sidewalk.

"Bas watch your mouth, after all, that broad is the mother of my daughter. You need to show some respect."

"I hear you man. But you know, see it from my point of view. I know you're not happy. I know that you and Natalie have been playing doctor and nurse. I know that deep down under all that respect you want for the mother of your kids, that's all she is to you. You didn't even say your wife. I know that you're not digging that broad…"

"Damn it Sebastian, didn't I just tell you to cut that out. Just leave it alone. I have got this and I don't feel like hearing your dislike for my 'wife'. You don't care about nobody but you and you've been like that since I've known you. Try to focus on your own wife and why she seems to be so unhappy with you that she has to take on a new personality just to deal with you."

Sebastian just stared at Michael for a minute. Then the two of them proceeded again to Michael's car. On the way Sebastian thought about what Michael just said to him.

It was kind of true, he was a selfish bastard, but Michael didn't need to throw Abigail up in his face. Besides isn't that the way everybody expects him to be. It's not so easy to turn off a persona once you get it going in full throttle.

Mic's right he's been like this since day one and now 'Mr. Sebastian, the Morning Lover' is a hard suit to take off especially since it fits so nicely. It's like being merged with a god and the best portions of each have created this super being that can't be stopped. 'The Morning Lover' takes what he wants, he always has.

What has happen to Michael over the years? Has Sonja made him too wet behind the ears. Michael used to be the type of person that every second of the day was spent debating and challenging something.

If it bothered Mic, he was on it. Now it seems as if he's a poster or a clip of a new song or something just running hype. You only getting just enough to try to capture your attention and that's not worth a second spin. This is what Sonja has reduced him to and he doesn't even realize it.

"Oh what the fu…" Michael shouted out.

Sebastian's attention was drawn to what Michael was upset about.

"Unbelievable."

There in the parking space Michael parked his BMW only a few feet away from the Pill was his car. It had the word **'Cheater'** and a question mark scratched onto the hood in big bold letters.

****

JC knocked on the door of Désiree's apartment. When she opened it he barely recognized her. She had her hair pulled back which was unusual for her even before the latest makeover. That's when JC noticed that she seemed familiar to him, as if he's known her before now. Désiree quickly pulled her hair down and it fell to her shoulders.

"JC, you left the club? You didn't call."

"I wasn't feeling good so I decided to check on you before I went home, some night huh?"

"Yes."

Désiree didn't really want to let him into her apartment. She was tired from all the emotional baggage she accumulated tonight. How could she tell him the real reason she had to leave the club and not meet his friends?

This thing with him is getting deeper than she should have let happen. He's showing up at her place unannounced. Suppose she had someone else here or was making some plans. After all he knows how she is; he can't possibly be willing to settle down with her like this. He has to wait until she's finished.

"Can I come in?"

"Uh huh baby." Desiree wanted to sound as convincing as possible, but she was tired. "I could come back tomorrow baby and let you rest."

"Yes that would be good. I am tired. But," she had to tell him, to warn him. "You have to stop seeing me."

"What are you saying?"

"I'm not good to be with. I have these issues and I don't want to end up doing something that's going to hurt you."

"You can't hurt me."

Just his patronizing words began to cause her to have a headache.

"No it's true. I have stuff on my mind and I really feel for you. I can't keep on seeing you."

"Désiree," He said embracing her and whispering in her ear. "Tell me what it is."

She wanted to melt in his embrace. She felt the power of his love soothe her and she felt the trust that he felt for him. But there was something controlling her, stopping her from telling him the truth.

"I just don't want to be a disappointment for you and to your friends. What are you doing with me? I'm an exotic dancer. I don't count. I'm nobody. I strip for men and they touch me and I please them. I even go as far as they want just to make ends meet sometimes, so you see…"

"No I really don't? You are you."

What will make him go away? Can't he see it's for his own good? Very well, it's his heart if, she kills it then it's on him. *No tell him.*

****

"I can't believe she would do this, damn. What is wrong with her?" Michael said pacing back and forth in front of his car while waiting on the police to arrive. "I can't believe she would actually go this far."

"Well what are you going to tell the police when they get here?"

"You know what I'm going to do. I'm going to say it was vandalism. You know how much it's going to cost out of pocket if I pay for this. Look how deep she carved into the metal."

"I knew that Sonja had a hard on tonight, but this one is huge. Umm, heads up Mic here comes, Chicago's finest."

Michael walked over to the police officers to make his statement. As he was doing that Sebastian's cell phone rang.

"Hello,"

"Sebastian, I need you."

It was Abigail and she sounded upset.

"Abigail what's going on?"

"This is Ambrosia and I'm at the police station. I need you to come down and bail me out. Please, don't ask me any damn questions, just do it."

"Yeah, I'm on the way."

"Hey Sebastian, I made the report."

"Yeah well good we gotta get to the police station. Abigail needs to get bailed out of the Precinct two."

"What? What the hell happened?"

"She's not telling, so we'll find out when we get there."

****

"Are you feeling better baby?"

"Yeah a little," JC said to Désiree as they lie together in her bed, after making love.

"Why did you want to stop seeing me?"

"I know it was a silly thing for me to say, but that's how I feel sometimes and I wanted to keep it honest."

He couldn't do anything but admire her honesty and she is so beautiful. He gazed into her eyes and realized how much he loved her. He looked again and realized as he propped himself up on his elbows that he at least had this feeling before, but he wasn't sure…

"What? Why are you looking at me like that?" Désiree asked almost frightened.

"Have me met before?"

"I don't know what you mean."

"You just look like someone I know but I can't really think of who. It's just something about your eyes."

"My eyes and you're just picking up on that now. I hope she's a real classy lady, whoever she is." Désiree said as she got out of bed and disappeared through the bedroom door.

She seemed to hang on his last word and JC wondered what was in her tone. It was almost as if Désiree was a little nervous about his simple inquiry. What is she hiding? Is she involved in some illegal stuff that she don't want anyone to get close to? Why did she want to kick him off so bad?

She has been acting kind of strange lately with her secret calls. Could she be trying to tell him that she's a call girl of some sorts? JC loved Désiree and really deep down inside he didn't want to know any more than he had to.

When she returned she was carrying a tray with a bottle of liquor and a couple of glasses.

"I thought we would celebrate."

"What are we celebrating?"

"A rejuvenation of our love and after we make our toast you will be mine forever."

That was like music to JC's ears. That was what he wanted and now he was getting everything. JC clinked glasses with Désiree.

"JC wait." She said intensely.

He paused for her to continue as he watched her curiously. She just stared at. She opened her mouth to say something but couldn't. She wanted to tell him but she just shook her head.

JC nodded and gulped down the liquid while Désiree squealed with delight. He enjoyed her delight, even though her personality seemed to, changed strangely, immediately. He started to feel even worse than before as he lay back onto the bed.

****

At 2:40 a.m. Sebastian and Michael walked into the 2nd precinct and made their way towards processing. This was a crowded night for the beginning of the weekend. Mona and Abigail sat at different desk with their backs turned from the entrance.

"Sebastian isn't that Mona at the other desk? What is she doing here? What's going on?" Michael asked.

"I don't know but look whose walking in over there?"

Michael looked over to where Sebastian was pointing and he saw Natalie walking in carrying a cup of coffee. She saw him and smiled. Sebastian walked over to where Abigail was sitting and Michael went to Mona, but he really wanted to run to Natalie.

"Abigail, baby what's going on? What are you doing here?" Abigail didn't say anything right off so the officer whose desk she was sitting addressed Sebastian.

"Mr. Black your wife was involved in a brawl tonight. She was brought here for disorderly conduct and aggravated assault."

"A fight with who?"

No one answered him but the cop looked over to where Mona was sitting. That explained it all. He guessed it was bound to happen that the two of them would eventually fight over him. The cat must now be out of the bag, more trouble.

"Can I just take her home now?"

"Yes. Post bail and she's all yours. But Mrs. Black understand that you need to get a hold of your anger and try to resolve this feud that you and Ms. Daniels have between you. It's going to just end you up here again or worst and the next time we will keep you."

"Yeah," Abigail said dryly as she stared intently at Sebastian. He walked off to post the bail.

Michael walked up behind Mona.

"Mona, hey so you didn't want to party, but decided to come up here instead." Michael asked trying to lighten the mood.

"Mic fancy meeting you here. I guess the Mrs., over there didn't have any money on her, while she was burglarizing my condo and had to call the hubby."

"I'm hearing assault. What the hell happened? What are you talking about, burglarized?"

"We got into a fight outside of my condo. I saw Mrs. Psycho over there roaming through my condo when Natalie brought me home earlier."

"So you're saying that Abigail broke into your condo? What was she doing?"

"Going through my stuff I guess and probably leaving another doll. I don't know why you men don't believe what I say. It's crazy."

"Mona I just find it hard to believe that Abigail would break into your condo to just roam around. What would she be looking for? Did the police find a doll?" He looked at the officer and he shook his head. "So Abigail, most likely was not there."

"The police weren't even looking for a doll. So then you tell me why she was in my neighborhood? When she was coming out of my condo complex, just when I saw a prowler there, and I'm done?"

"Well you've got me there. Sir?"

"Ms. Daniels did not provide that theory to us until after the ride here. So basically I can tell you that in her condo I didn't see any visible discrepancies. You can go now Miss but I caution you on anymore displays of public violence."

"Ooh Michael I'm public enemy number one. This I should add to my resume. I'm out coppers."

"I'm out coppers?" Mona got out of the chair.

"Well the police are pissing me off. I'm the one who has to live where they couldn't find the intruder. So what am I suppose to do now, go home and get killed by Abigail Black, the lady killer? This is ridiculous."

"Mona calm down a minute I need to talk to Natalie. Give me a few and I will drop you off at a hotel."

Michael left Mona where she was standing and went over to Natalie. She was just waiting in the waiting area for Mona.

"So you were fighting, too?" Michael said to Natalie smiling so deeply it made Natalie giggle.

"Yes I was the ring leader. I have been secretly grooming Mona for my gang and tonight was initiation night. We did good huh? Arrested like all the other Gang Mamas"

"I'm turned on Ms. Vincent. I didn't know of this dark side of you."

"Michael this is crazy. Mona is way off chart."

"I've known this for years. So what's your version of story? Is Mona telling the truth, did Abigail really break into Mona's condo?"

"All the evidence points to her doing just that and I did see her at the entrance to Mona's building. But Abigail says she didn't break in. The police say that there was no forced entry and nothing seemed disturbed. Of course we couldn't verify that because of the fight. I really don't know what to believe. She was there."

Michael leaned into her almost whispering into Natalie's ear.

"I enjoyed being with you the other day, thank you."

"I ...can't begin to...it was good. I loved being with you too."

"We have to talk. We have to decide..."

Even after he said it he wished he hadn't. It was too permanent, too forceful. It was almost like he was giving her an ultimatum and he wasn't even sure where he wanted to take this.

"Natalie I don't mean to come off like I'm forcing you to some conclusion because that's not where I'm coming from but I..."

"Michael I know what you're saying. I really did mean it when I said it was good being with you. It was more than good but I just need a little time to digest it all."

"Are you gonna see me next week, Thursday? I really like to see you again."

Natalie paused. She stared pass Michael like a deer caught in headlights. He wondered what brought on the shock that he was now seeing in her eyes. He turned and saw Sonja marching in the police precinct like she was going to war.

Sonja locked eyes with Michael and never faltered. He stood transfix knowing it was too late to move to a safe enough distance away from Natalie. It was no need now the deed is done and this was bound to happen. It was just moving quicker than he was ready for.

Sonja approached the two of them and made sure that her aura was enough to shake the planet. Natalie stood her ground but to her discredit she did flinch a little.

"Michael, what are you doing?"

"Sonja, what are you doing here?"

"Me, first, my question first, why are you here with Natalie Bower?" Sonja's desperation in her voice betrayed her and Michael wish he could recover fast enough to exploit it.

"Natalie was here with the girls and I was trying to get a neutral party's version of the story what's going on?"

"Natalie is that whore's friend, if anyone could tell the truth it would be Abigail. I see you can't be trusted. Here you are reminiscing while you should have been calling me to tell me that my friend had been arrested. Abigail shouldn't have been the one to call. But I see why you may have been a little distracted."

"Sonja, don't make a big deal out of nothing. Natalie thanks, have a good one, okay. It was good to see you."

Natalie looked at Sonja and remembered their visit from her the other day.

"No Michael, thank you. The pleasure was all, mine. Don't be a stranger." She ended looking at Sonja.

Sonja looked at Natalie thinking that this was far from being over and that she should just slap her, but remembered that she was in a police station.

Michael walked over to Sebastian and Abigail who were getting ready to leave the station. Mona joined them.

"Michael and Sebastian thanks for coming and seeing how I was doing. You guys are great friends." Mona walked off towards Natalie.

"So you came for her, Sebastian?"

"Abigail the two of you just had a heated, knock down fight, so of course she's going to take a jab at you through me. You have to see that. Let's go."

"Ambrosia! And all I see is a woman trying to sleep with my husband, again. You can't seem to refuse the attention can you?"

"Don't feel bad Ambrosia, Michael has his whore here as well. Let's go, I brought my car."

Natalie and Mona were walking by just in time to hear Sonja. Enough is enough Natalie thought, it was time she dealt with Sonja here and now. When Natalie was about to respond, Michael's cell phone rang.

"Hello."

"Michael!" the urgent voice sounded over the phone.

"This is Désiree JC's girl. Something terrible has happened and he's in the hospital."

"What happened? Where is he?"

"He's in Chicago Memorial. He was having problems breathing. Please come quick!"

Désiree hung up the phone.

"Sebastian, Mona we have to get to the hospital JC is there and it's serious."

Natalie wanted to embrace Michael, something that Sonja should be doing, but she simply stood there. Sonja just shook her head. He was terrified, scared so whatever the caller told him it was just as he said, serious. She was going to follow him to the hospital to be there for him and if Sonja causes any trouble she was going to ready for her.

CHAPTER 10

JC lay in the emergency room hospital bed wondering how he got where he was. The doctor told him that he had drugs in his system and he knew he didn't. But it was there from the damn blood test, drugs, Crystal Meth.

The doctors determined that the drugs weaken his heart and caused him to collapse. JC had admitted his drug use during college, but he has been clean for years, six. It was strange how the drugs got in his system. He couldn't worry about that now, he needed to recover.

He was still groggy from the emergency room. Now he was in his own room, alone. He was semi conscience during all the rescue procedures, he endured. How did this happen? He thought. Last night started off with making sweet love to Désiree. All of a sudden he kept getting sicker and sicker until he couldn't breathe. What was happening to him? He was the picture of health months ago and now this.

Where is everybody? What was taking them so long? Desiree said she called them a while ago. He knew it was early in the morning and the guys were probably hung over from the night earlier. They were probably just getting home, barely beating the daylight. He felt like he was dying. If this was going to be the last hour he wanted to be with his friends.

The doctor said he couldn't really determine anything until he had further blood results and that was hours ago. So no one is going help him? Where is Désiree? She's been gone a little while as well. The curtain to his room opened and the doctor that had been working with him came in. He sat down on a low stool that was next to the bed.

"Jordan I want you to be honest with me," he said sounding like he was about to ask JC to reveal the secrets of life.

What could be going on? He thought. Whatever it is, JC was certain that he had no knowledge of it and didn't like it.

"I want to know how long you have been dependent on Methamphetamine. There's no sense in denying it because it's in your blood system and while you were asleep we checked your arms. You have needle marks everywhere."

JC couldn't believe his ears, it was like this was years ago. Maybe he was waking up in the rehab center that he stayed at what he thought was six years ago. Maybe his life these past years was a drug induced dream and now he's waking up to reality.

This dream must have been God's way of letting him know that the time was near. He was monetarily successful in that dream. The only thing he wasn't successful in is when he attempted love.

He allowed himself to fall for Désiree in spite of the warning signs that were clear from the start. Somewhere along the way the Crystal Meth came back into the picture and brought him from his wonderful dream.

He did use to blackout back in the day but that hasn't happened in years. So now he was blacking out again and in that time he does the Meth. Were they doing the Meth together and he didn't remember? But JC knew that even though he would welcome a second chance at his college years, this was the here and now.

"Doctor, I can't explain what is going on. I don't do drugs, not anymore. I had a Meth problem, years ago, but I've been clean. I've been clean for six years."

"Well Jordan, it's in your bloodstream. I can't just negate the fact that it's there. It was so abusive that you caused yourself some heart problems. You need to stop or you may have a heart attack. You know I'm going to have to notify the police, those are procedures. But I want you to relax. You're going to be in here for a sometime. We are going to move you to another private room on another floor, so we can deal with your addiction. Do you have family here?"

"No, but my girlfriend is here. I don't know where she is now and my friends, Michael Montgomery, Sebastian Black and Mona Daniels are supposed to be on the way."

The doctor didn't say anything else he just nodded and left the room.

JC drifted into sleep and didn't notice until he awoken again that Désiree had come back to the room and was sitting next him. She was looking at him in this strange way that unnerved him, just staring at him blankly.

"Désiree..."

"JC baby, how are you feeling?"

"It's touch and go but, I'm not worried, I got you now."

She nodded, and smiled slightly, but JC didn't believe her sincerity.

****

Michael, Mona, Sebastian and Natalie walked into the lobby of Chicago Memorial in panic. All of them had different thoughts on their mind but all were concerned about JC's safety. They were all about to board the elevator when Dr. Edwards walked out of it.

"Natalie, there you are, I really need to talk to you. I'm so glad that we ran into each other, hi Mona."

"Janice hi, everything's alright?" Natalie asked then realizing that she was holding everyone up. "Janice, hold on a minute. Michael, go on and I'll come up as soon as possible."

She eyed Michael with what Mona thought was peculiarly. To Mona it seemed as though Janice was sizing Michael up as she stared at him intensely from head to foot. A thing that, Natalie surely wouldn't like.

"Hi Michael," Dr. Edwards said.

Michael nodded and followed everyone else into the elevator. He was watching Natalie with curiosity. He didn't know the woman that spoke to him. He keeps forgetting that Natalie has a life apart from him and his friends as the door to the elevator close.

Natalie watched the elevator door close wishing she hadn't stopped to talk to Janice. But Janice sounded like she needed Natalie more than Michael at this point. However it didn't stop her from being concern for him.

"Janice what's going on? Why are you here on Saturday, this early?"

"I had an unexpected appointment with one of my patient today. Natalie she is tougher to crack than the Pentagon and I think she's dangerous."

"Janice you know you can't disclose anything that is revealed in those sessions unless you want to lose you license or unless you have her committed. Has she threatened your life?"

"No, not directly but I know she intends to hurt others. The 'music man and his CEO whore' were her exact words. I know I haven't kept anonymity amongst my clients but I know that I can't do it now. What should I do?"

Surely she was joking, Natalie thought. What do psychiatrists do when patient get out of control? Who do they get help from

"I don't know. When you said you had an unexpected appointment what did you mean?"

"I got a call from my emergency service that my patient, 'Karen' was hysterical and that I needed to have a session with her. Once I met with her here you could tell that she was up all night long and had been drinking. She said that she did something that she's sorry about that is going to hurt a lot of people. All she says is that she wanted to do is fit in and to be liked by people. She says that she might not be able to handle it all."

"She sounds like someone I know."

"Yes the female version of Christopher ha, ha."

Natalie didn't feel like sharing that laugh. It was a joke, but this was not the time. Natalie knew it was not true about Christopher, but it was insensitive. Out of all the people on the list to be reminded of she hasn't taken the time to think about Christopher. Why hasn't he called her? There really wasn't a reason, since the girls were with her mother for the weekend. Was he even at home?

Lately Christopher has been giving her the impression that he was moving on without her. So why has it been hard for her to move on with Michael?

He was everything she needed in her life and there was no reason to juggling it in her mind over and over again. But of course Michael and she cannot just pick up where they left off. They can't just sleep together and live happily ever after. They need to date again and get reacquainted.

Why didn't Christopher call her to see if she was alright? This is the first time she has ever stayed out till the next morning and no calls. What's up? That selfish bastard! Why does he always have to be in control?

"So am I going to have her committed or what, Natalie?"

"Uh what, yes I guess you...no Janice I think that's your responsibility. I don't have a degree to assist you with this. Besides don't you always tell me that these people are always just acting out in those sessions?"

"Well yes but..."

"I have to go now there's a friend I need to see."

"That's right I forgot to ask who those people Mona and you were with."

"I'll tell you some other time. But I didn't know you knew Michael Montgomery."

"College, why were you with him?"

"See you Janice."

Janice watched as Natalie wriggled out of the conversation and quickly boarded the elevator. She really wanted to know more about what was going on there, but her own pressing matters made her let up.

'Karen' is a ticking, time bomb not some drama queen, not following instructions and rebelling. She's got some serious stuff that she is not telling her on her mind. Stuff that will cause the process to, go against the plan.

****

Michael finished talking to the doctor who was reluctant at first to even give him any information until JC told him that Michael is his closest relative, a brother. He had to try hard to erase his personal feelings and not let his disappointment in JC interfere. The doctor left him in shock revealing that JC has a current drug problem and it has messed up his system. JC was doing so well.

When Michael and Mona walked into JC's room he was there wide awake, lying in bed.

"Michael, Mona I'm glad you guys are here. This is crazy and I know you know all the details but it's not true. I don't remember doing drugs and I don't know how it's in my blood."

For a moment Mona wanted to scream. How in the hell could JC let something as meaningless as a drugs take over his life again. He's on the top of the world with this new girlfriend and his career; but then she thought of Jefferson.

He hadn't called her back when she called him at the police station. She was at his beck and call, that's like a drug.

She shook the thoughts from her mind.

"JC baby, you don't need to pull this off to get our attention. We've told you that before. How are you feeling?"

"I've had better days, how's everything?"

"Good." Is all that Mona could say, she was holding back her tears, which is what she never wanted the boys to see. Michael wanted to tell JC of the events that happened after the club last night, but it was not about him, it was about JC now.

"Where is Désiree?"

"I don't know she must have left. I don't know why she would do that."

"So do you know how long you're going to be in here buddy?"

"Not a clue. Hey, did Sebastian come?"

"Yeah hold on."

Sebastian came into the room after Michael retrieved him. Michael stood out in the corridor as the hospital staff bustled about. At the end of the corridor a little ways from JC's room, a woman in a nurse's outfit stood motionless glaring at him.

He looked down the hall and noticed her. They connected for a bit. He felt a familiarity and then the woman quickly walked off. Déjà vu Michael thought, how many times has that happened?

He was tempted to follow her to find out who she is, but thought against it. She is just this woman in the corridor staring at him and he was staring back at her. What's the mystery in that? Though it has happened many times like this before, some woman just staring at a distance then disappearing.

This intrigue that is going on is getting out of hand and his curiosity was getting the better of him. Against his better judgment he was going to take to the hunt anyway when his cell phone rang.

"Hello."

"Well did I piss you off that much that you didn't want to come home to me?"

"And good morning to you too, Sonja," he said a bit annoyed.

"JC is still in the hospital and we're here now, you know that. Besides we need to talk about what you did to my car, but not now."

"What are you talking about your car? I don't know what you're talking about. Anyway I'm at the hospital too with Abigail. I'm coming up and guess who else is with me? Time's up, it's Natalie. We're on our way in the elevator, don't you move."

In that moment a text from Michael's co-worker, Shanna popped on the screen. 'Call me ASAP' is what it read.

"Yeah," Michael hung up the phone.

He wasn't ready for any foolishness with Sonja but he had no time to think about her shenanigans. The car was enough and she's not taking him there today, he was too tired.

He started dialing Shanna's number on his phone.

"Shanna hey what's up, I just got you message?"

Michael listened intently to Shanna. When he hung up the cell phone he was grinning from ear to ear. Finally there was something wonderful going on and he wanted everything to be alright with his friends so he could share it.

The news was earthshaking. The network interested in his cable talk show has agreed to sign the show into syndication, *Deena* is going national. This was his baby and it was really exciting having this opportunity. It was almost the equivalent of a life long journey and now he was there, at the door and it was wide open.

****

JC looked around the room at his visitors, Sebastian, Abigail, Michael, Natalie, Mona and even Sonja, all his friends and theirs. They had spent most of the morning with him. It was now noon, but no Désiree.

She called him earlier to let him know that she had to be at the strip club and that she would come by later. What was later? What was she afraid of? Why was she not trying to be around him while his friends were here?

Désiree puzzled JC and she also started to make him question her loyalty to him. Here he was laying in a hospital bed in his condition and she goes off to work. Maybe it's time to cut her loose.

Once again, it seems that he had to, sit back and watch something else good happening in somebody else's life. On top of that Sebastian seems a bit standoffish, he seemed a bit nervous. JC will never betray him. The always agree that the secret was between them no one else.

"JC its time we cut out, I need some sleep." Sebastian said.

"Yeah we'll try to come by tomorrow." Mona said.

"It's cool, guys I'll catch up with you then."

He watched as everyone left the room. He thought of Désiree it will be a long night without her as he drifted off to sleep.

****

Later that evening the door to his room opened and she was standing there in a nurse's outfit. JC looked at her with puzzlement, what was she doing back here? It was clearly pass visiting hours because he was told that by the nurse from earlier, just a little after the others had left. She looked different but it was her. What was she doing?

He parted his lips to ask her, but she placed her index finger to her lips, using a shushing sound to quiet him. She approached the bed. She bent down to him and rubbed her chin along his forehead, down the side of his cheek, then tasted him with her tongue. JC could barely hear her as she whispered above his head.

"I had to see you again. I have a surprise for you and I just couldn't wait to give it to you. You see, you're supposed to be unconscious."

JC didn't speak, he was sure that he was dreaming, but felt the warmth of her breath on his skin. It was almost intoxicating and she smelled of alcohol.

"Medical science can be so unpredictable. There's the differences of our bodies, differences of sex and also enter in the tolerance factor. You know for example, how much pressure the body can take from physical, mental and most effective, drug abuse. You remember the drug abuse right. But if you really search your memory you will get a flashback of the other abuses as well. No matter. You begin to slowly give the person poison every time you see them and you do it effectively because you may not get to see them that often, maybe just once a week, you know at play. They have their own lives as well. You have to be friendly and you have to be encouraging. Most of all you have to allow them to trust in their self ego, which in this case, you do not have, one. You gave your ego over to Sebastian years ago. What a waste of intelligence. I have watched you for longer than I can remember and you have just sat on the sidelines living in the shadows of that loser. Don't worry about it, Sebastian is next and then everybody else will follow in our crowd. Why leave anyone out?"

JC tried to move towards the emergency call button, but for some reason he couldn't. She was here earlier, maybe she snuck him something that has caused him paralyzes. Why is she doing this? He thought he knew her better than this. What did he do to her? What did Sebastian do to her?

"What I have here is a small vial of potassium. When I inject you with all of this, you will go into cardiac arrest and well if you're lucky you might fall into a coma. But if I get my way you'll just die, instantly. No matter, either means you won't be in my way. You see you're getting too close. I'm sorry that this is where it ends for you, but I just can't take the chance on you remembering. Don't worry, the hospital staff is wonderful here and they will try to save your life. But don't count on it being a success."

There was nothing that JC could do but live the nightmare. He couldn't cry out for help and no one came to the room to check on him. He was at her mercy. He couldn't believe all the times he was in her presence and he did not see this sickness, this evil.

Surely there was a mental breakdown and he believed what she was saying about wanting him dead. She was going to kill him. He had to die with the knowledge that she was going to do this to everyone else that he loved and they won't even know what hit them. What did he do to her?

His thoughts were broken from the pinch that he felt on his left arm. She didn't even bother to hide the assault. Surely the doctors will know what happen but how with all of these needle marks in his arm?

Maybe they will see her on the video from the hallway. She will not get away with this he prayed. His mind flashed as he felt strange sensations traveling through his body. There was a hint of pain in his chest and he gasp.

"Well I guess I'll be on my way. I have a home to attend to."

No, this isn't right. Help him survive.

JC watched her stand upright her mind in obvious cluttered. She walked uneasily towards the door as the pain started to increase within his chest. Suddenly she stopped, clutched her fist, turned back around, returned and bent down to him again.

"Oh I forgot. Just in case I am wrong about you and you are just that stupid to know what going on, let me enlighten you."

She whispered in his ear faster than his mind could accumulate the shock of what she was saying. Once she was finished, he had to look at her again to, make sure he believed what she was saying. Then she told him the reason why this was happening to him and he remembered that night. He remembered that he was there when…

JC fell into unconsciousness and 'Karen' was satisfied beyond the feel of pleasure. As she passed by the shiny glass picture frame on the way to the door again, she stopped to check out her reflection. She listened to her mind, searching for the weak voice that tried to prevent her from her mission. Once she felt she had listened enough she opened the door and left out. JC was all but memory to her now. It had to be done, number one.

CHAPTER 11

An hour after leaving the hospital, Natalie dropped Mona off at a hotel instead of Michael and came home. She totally agreed with Mona's decision to stay at a hotel. Whoever, was in her apartment last night may come back.

She noticed that Christopher was no where to be found and that her home for the past six years was suddenly very cold. She made her way through the house into the kitchen where she saw a note attached to the fridge. Picking it off the refrigerator she instantly knew it was from Christopher, not the housekeeper.

'You were too busy to come home or call, huh? Well it's a good thing that I am going to be Chief of Staff at the hospital. The staff knows that and alerted me that they saw you come there. We will talk when I get home. I will be late, be up.'

Natalie felt the first tinge of anger come over her. If Christopher was as concern and angry about her not calling, then why didn't he call. She knew that this was just another way that he wanted to exert his control over her. She was being rebellious and he didn't like it.

They were into the final match now and she brought in a pinch hitter or ringer, something. She was not going to be home tonight for him to find her. She'll call her mother and have the girls stay with her for the week. Then she will finally get her life back in order. After that she'll call Mona and let her know she needed to stop by the hotel once she's had enough sleep.

****

That evening Natalie made her way through the nightly streets of Chicago. It was interesting because normally in the late evening hours she would be home with the girls. She would patiently be waiting for Christopher to grace her with his presence. Now she was headed towards Mona's condo.

Mona told her that she wasn't at the hotel anymore that she had come home. Once she had a chance to sleep she realized it wasn't any use in running away from Abigail Black. Natalie's mind was traveling in many different directions.

Suddenly without warning her car was struck in the back by another with its lights off. Natalie almost lost control as her vehicle swerved left to right. Once she got herself together she managed to pull over to the side of the street, but the gray Mercedes pulled off.

Natalie started in pursuit but thought better of it. It was enough that she got the tag number which indicated that it was a rental car. She didn't need to kill herself going after a rental car when she could just report it. She simply proceeded to Mona's, shaken but unharmed.

****

After Natalie arrived at Mona's she reported the hit and run to the police. She was sure to call from her cell phone. She didn't want to bring anymore attention to Mona than she's already gathered over the last few weeks.

It was enough that strange things were occurring. Now it seem like someone was going out for blood. She had to get the troubling thoughts out of her mind and relax. She decided that she was going to be more alert from now on.

Natalie chatted a little more with Mona about the string of events that has happened recently.

"It's unreal. Someone has a real problem with use."

"I know Natalie; I can't begin to know who it could be."

Natalie spotted Mona's college yearbook.

"You've been going back in time Mona?" Natalie said pointing to her year book on the coffee table.

"Oh, yes I guess that thing with the roses made me want to look back and see who could still hate me that much. It didn't last long. I saw a few people that I wished I had kept in contact with and some that I'm glad that I marked off."

Natalie laughed at her comment. She sat down her coffee cup on the table. She began flipping through Mona's college year book, not really focusing on the contents until she came upon Janice's picture.

"Janice Prentiss." She said.

She had forgotten that Janice had told her many years ago that she had gone to CU. She sure has changed, Natalie thought.

The Janice that she saw in person could barely be matched to this Janice in the yearbook. How a career, confidence and years, can make you over. She truly wished, she could be made over and make the right decisions. She was scared, worried. She was constantly concerned about the past events.

Just for the hell of it could Sonja go as far as to try to run her off the road? If so than what's next if she decides to go after Michael? She doesn't really know her anymore, do we truly know anyone these days. Should she buy a gun?

It was silly to think something like this. Why would she allow herself to be moved by Sonja Price? She would hope that Sonja would be woman enough to step aside and let the man that doesn't want to be with her, move on.

Michael is an excellent father she was sure of that and she intended to make sure that he remains that way. Michael

Montgomery. What were they doing? What did he see in her she thought? Why would he want to take the chance that she could break his heart again?

"Mona I just don't understand why Michael carries this torch for me. All I keep doing is hurting him."

"You made one mistake eight years ago. Had the two of you stopped and talked about all this before you married those jerks it would have been handled sooner. But it's not too late. You two can find happiness again like you are now."

"You're an optimist. If he just would forget about me he probably could learn to love Sonja again."

"Are you kidding? You have to understand Natalie that you're really the first and only true love Michael has ever had. Those other girls that he was dating in college before you were nothing. Even Kimberly, she was this snotty rich girl that put Mic through mental hell, because she was mental as hell. Now that was hurting him. Mic didn't know it, but JC had a thing for her too, which was so funny."

"What happen to her?"

"After Mic and her broke up, it was like three months later and she was gone. She must have left campus to attend another college. Who would have cared anyway that Ms. High Society snob was leaving campus, she was not liked really."

"I don't remember her, but that's not saying too much. I was a loner and the campus was huge."

"Beside there were more exciting things going on. It wasn't like she was pregnant or anything? I mean with all those other dumb girls that got pregnant when they opened their legs without protection and had to leave. And the others were stupid enough to get a back alley abortion instead of going to real doctor. You know the whole embarrassment and not telling the parents thing."

"She wasn't pregnant?"

"No, not Miss Uppity that would, have killed her. Then again if it was Mic's who knows because she was really obsessed with him. I said she was crazy. Well I'm just saying that during that time there were several girls getting pregnant by their boyfriends and dropping out. One girl did leave campus after she ended up pregnant from a sexual assault or did she leave? I'm not sure. She was supposedly drunk or something and some guys attack her at some frat party. I don't remember the story too well but it was something like that…here she is, that's Kimberly, Kimberly D Stanford, that's Mic's ex-girlfriend."

"She looks familiar."

"Yeah, well she was into everything at UC so who didn't probably know her; plus her family is filthy rich. I don't know why her picture is here she didn't graduate from UC. Anyway that's why Mic's so hung up on you all he's ever dated were losers. Don't let me get started on your girl, Sonja."

"Please don't, I'm still reeling from her visit to me."

"It's just typical pushy delta sorority bullshit. She just can't get that crap out of her."

"But you know something Mona; I do vaguely remember something about that assault story myself. It was one of the DS. I remember they wanted us to keep it hush-hush for the reputation of the college and the sorority. Mona, Abigail Black can't have any children."

"She was a delta with you wasn't she." Mona asked.

"I think so. I really wasn't focusing too much with them; I just wanted to be in that sorority, you know to enhance my career."

"But what's your point?"

"Well she has certainly been acting funny lately, at least according to Michael. Maybe something bad did happen to her and it's just affecting her now."

"Well if you're talking about the attack, Abigail graduated, here's her picture. Besides she's been with Sebastian forever."

"Well then a back alley abortion."

"Sebastian would have told Mic."

"Are you sure?"

"No. But anyway she didn't seem too traumatized when we were in college."

"I don't remember her being there."

"She was there, we didn't get along. I know you were so into Mic that the two of you were in your own world but she was there. Sebastian always kept us apart. She was probably the one who sent me those dead roses and the note. It could be her now. I think she really believes I slept with Sebastian."

"Well did you?"

"Why are we even talking about this nonsense its ancient history?"

Natalie noticed that she didn't really answer the question. She wanted to tell her friend that she was not here to judge her. What they said to each other was in the strictest confidence. How could she judge Mona when she was sleeping with her married lover?

She decided that she was not going to pursue the question any further. Instead she would rather concentrate on the current issues relating to these odd occurrences. It wasn't nonsense to Natalie, it's more than a coincidence, there was a pattern forming here with a common denominator, but what was it?

So far it involved dolls and dead flowers. Abigail Black collects dolls. Sonja's craft store specializes in them. She couldn't dare ask Sonja if there has been a large portion of her inventory missing or bought in secret. There would be no way they could sit down and discuss anything that serious. Not anything at all in their current state.

Mona's notes always called her a whore, which could allude to her questionable involvement with Sebastian. Michael says that Sebastian tells him that Abigail has been hanging out late and coming home drunk. This was something that she has never done, before. Natalie doesn't have to be Janice to realize there's a trauma there.

"Mona, I think you'd better watch yourself from Abigail."

"Abigail Black is no threat to me, Natalie. I know what your thinking and I have considered it but Abigail doesn't have the nerve. Even though, she had rummaged through my condo."

"It fits though Mona. You have always been there as an obstacle and threat to take Sebastian from her."

"If that what's she's worried about she should give herself a rest. There's no curiosity there anymore; we are just friends."

"Well, maybe she doesn't know that."

"Maybe, but don't worry honey she's not dangerous. Somebody just likes pissing me off."

"Well what about me? I got a package too. What are they trying to tell me?"

Mona just stared at Natalie. This was something new, that she didn't know this. As Natalie, tells her the details of her strange delivery. The more she hears the story, the deeper the horror of her reality chills her bones.

"Why didn't you tell me?"

"I just got one while we were at the hospital earlier today, in front of my office door."

Natalie was not going to mention anything because she didn't really have time enough to digest the craziness of it all. There were pictures of ceramic dolls with their head broken off and the note reading 'Don't stand in my way bitch. You don't want this to happen to you'!

Maybe she should have told Mona about it while they were at the hospital, but everything that was happening with JC prevented her. She understands that Abigail was pissed and a little leery of Mona, but what was Natalie herself doing that would piss her off? Unless just being Mona's friend, disturbs her or maybe because she's Sonja's friend.

"Sonja Montgomery." Mona said in realization.

"Don't be insane."

"I'm serious she's insane enough to do something as insane as this. You were so willing to believe that it could be Abigail when all the while it's her friend. Now that you're in the equation it's obvious."

"I'm not listening to anymore Mona. Sonja is not sending me anything."

"Well it's just like you want me to believe that puny, mousey Abigail Black is Madame X."

"Okay I see your point, then who?"

"Madame X or Mister X. Somebody's trying to play games with us Natalie and it's not that serious. That's why I came home. Of course I brought a new lock. You never can be too sure and soon I'll get a gun. Now on a lighter note did you and Michael make plans to get together soon?"

"It's in the bag almost like playing Poker."

The two of them burst into laughter.

"I got to get going Mona. I think I have avoided the inevitable long enough. I have something very important I need to do."

****

"The whore," Sonja said to herself. "How, dare she, mock me."

The Montgomery home was silent to her rampage. There was nothing and no one to respond. Sonja hadn't seen Michael since he woke up a few hours ago and took Tiffany to see her grandmother. It was clear to Michael he said, that Sonja was mad as hell and he didn't want his daughter around that.

Sonja continued her rampage throughout the house and she started to smash things. All she could do is think of the contempt she had for, Natalie Bower. Natalie is a sore in her freaking side and she needs to be dealt with.

She was hearing voices in her head now. She knew they were her own thoughts that were bursting out. It was all at once calculating and playing out scenarios that, she was happy no one could hear. If so they would think she was crazy, but she was angry.

How could Michael do this to her and in front of everyone she knew? That slut and radio asshole, they were a hell of a bunch they were. The only one with any respect is poor JC and he's suffering.

"So Natalie wants to play games with me huh? Well I don't think she know who she's messing with! I invented this game, that's how I won Michael and I plan on keeping him."

Sonja was out of control now and she was not letting up. When she sat down on a stool on the end of the kitchen island, she let the tears pour from her eyes. She was not going to lose Michael Montgomery, not to Natalie Vincent Bower. No matter what she had to, do.

She climbed into the shower to calmed down, although that didn't help her calm at all. Once she put on her clothes she knew what she had to do and she wanted to do. This was her revenge and no one was going to keep her from it, she thought as she stormed out of her house.

****

Sonja arrived later at her craft store and she was still fuming. It was the only place she felt at peace. It was where she would always be calm amongst her creations, but she wasn't. She immediately wandered around musing at her work. She°a hand in crafting some of the items she sold in the store. This was her passion.

She always had that talent but it was not utilized like she wanted when she was younger. She blames those in her life for not seeing her creatively and helping her along; not just punishing her for minor things. That is the reason why she appears to be so bitter. No one has given her a chance. She's always had to take what she wanted.

On the outside Natalie approached the door to Sonja's craft store. She didn't want to confront Sonja at home and leaving this letter was the only logical way she was going to get a goodnight sleep. Having this Michael stuff on her mind was not going to allow that.

As she approached the door to her surprise it was unlocked and partially opened. As she walked in with caution she saw the closed sign facing her. Sonja met her half way in.

"What do you want Natalie?" Sonja said vehemently as Natalie walked further into the store to the cash register.

"Well I thought if my old friend could come to see me at my place of business, I should by all means do the same for her."

That wasn't true but the parameters changed.

"How are you? You look tired?" Natalie teased.

"Do you think I really care what you think?"

"Well not really but you seemed so distraught when we last talked I thought I'd come and see how you were. Could you tell that, Michael enjoyed seeing me the other night at the police station?"

"I should kill you. How dare you come in here, in my place and taunt me with my own husband. What happened to you, you use to be..."

"A weakling too inferior to your, brilliance? Nice? Well things change. I'm still nice, but…no matter that's not important. I wanted to know dear friend," Natalie said as • walked up to her and stepped in almost touching noses with Sonja. "I want to know what you did, to make sure you ended up with, Michael?"

Sonja couldn't believe what she was hearing. Natalie couldn't possibly be this bold and this daring to ask that question.

"I have no idea what you're talking about. You left him. He's with me now, that's all there is." She said waving her off.

"No something else was going on. You stole him. I didn't see it before."

"I answered your question, now leave."

"You know something Sonja. You don't know what you are doing. You don't even know what's going on around you. Your whole world is crashing down so far and so fast, it's like a building on fire." Natalie said with anger in her tone.

She was about to explode so she turned and walked out of the door.

Sonja seemed as if she was holding her breath the whole time and she finally let out a sigh of relief staring down to the floor. She doesn't scare me, she thought to herself. I'm the villain in this story not her.

Instantly Sonja looked up as she saw a five gallon bucket crash through her store window.

"What are you doing, are you crazy? I just replaced that window." She said to the figure as the bucket's content began to spill onto the floor.

It looked like red blood.

"I'm calling the police," she said as she attempted to get to the exit.

By now the liquid was all over the entrance floor, blocking her. That's when she smelled the gas fumes and the figure said tilting their head to the side, "Like a building on fire," and ignited it with a blow torch as Sonja watch in horror.

"Natalie!" She screamed.

CHAPTER 12

She swirled in joyful circles around her bedroom. Her thoughts were purely full of satisfaction. 'Karen' had accomplished her first real step. She had infiltrated the fold and started her revenge. She's been right under their noses for all these years, just waiting and they've been fools. Poor JC had to be the first though.

She told Janice that this would bring her enjoyment and she was sure it did. This was the way it had to be. It had to be done. She was not going to allow anyone to block her goals and she had to do what the voice was telling her. She was destined to be with him once again and it was time that his wife was eliminated. She will die like all whores do. She paused as she thought she heard a noise. She opened the door and walked downstairs, he was home.

****

"You think that you're so smart Mr. Black," Abigail said hovering over Sebastian. She startled him from his sleep on the couch. "You think that you can sleep with that mouthy whore and not think I would find out about or even suspect you. Yes dude, I know about you two."

Really she didn't know but he didn't know that and she needed to know. She needed to know whether or not she should love this man and she did so very deeply but he needed to be punished.

"I did not sleep with Mona. You know she's just my friend."

He was lying of course he had to be. That was what he does best. He was the king of deception and he wasn't going to lose out on the opportunity to drop one now.

"You're just jealous and I don't know why. You're a vibrant woman yourself."

Abigail was sure he was lying but she relished in the fantasy that she knew her husband could always make her believe and enjoy. He was disgusting but she loved him deeply.

He held his hand out to her and once again she took it. He led her and she followed him up to their bedroom. She allowed him to begin his process on her, again.

It was the same demeaning process that she has allowed him to perform on her year after year, since college. But she never really accomplished anything for herself. She hated what he did to her in all of the pleasure of it. This was an assault on her innermost feelings and all of her defenses rose up to warn her of his deception.

As he laid her now naked body onto their bed he did to her things that people in love do. And she wasn't sure anymore that she loved him. Maybe it was the thought of finally being able to invoke passion in him. Sebastian was good. He was a lair and she knew that but he didn't act like he was lying right there as they moved rapidly in their hunger for each other.

Sebastian really was good, she mused again as she fought hard to hold on to all of the disgust she felt for him. She knew deep down in her heart that he slept with Mona Daniels and countless other women. However, tonight he was all hers and she drew security and strength from that.

Sebastian knew that he was not called 'the Morning Lover' for nothing. He loved women and he loved sex which made the combination extraordinaire for his willing partners. So making love to Abigail was not something hard to do. She always had that beautiful body; she kept that up for him. She was prettier and classier than most of the sluts he bedded down.

He loved her; sure, he couldn't see himself with any other female. Only if she would just fight back he would probably cut down on his other activities. He liked that. He liked it when they fought back. That made the sex more exciting and meant that they really wanted him with a passion.

The more he thought about what he desired the most the more intense he made love to Abigail. Her 'Ambrosia' persona took over and met him with power.

This was his thing, the only thing that has every made him feel like he was on top of the world, conquering women. Now he had to be 'Mr. Sebastian, the Morning Lover' for all of Chicago, twenty four-seven. He loved the music, the talk, the attention, the men even envied him. He was full of greatness.

He wanted to share in Abigail's dream in wanting a child. Will he ever be able to admit to her or even to himself that guilt that he feels, the shame he feels. Maybe that's why he won't allow her to get that close to him whenever he would allow himself to even think it, let alone say it.

Abigail was never petty. Not even in the heat of an argument did she ever blame him. She just blamed herself for not being the woman to give him a child.

But it was his fault. He was the one who convinced her. He picked her up and finally he drove her to the clinic. This is where he allowed the doctor to abort their unborn child and Sebastian promised that he'd be there for her. They were still in college, so young.

Now through his guilt he allowed his twisted anger to come in. He blamed her for letting this happen as if it was her idea. Mainly, because the reward for their act against God was that Abigail will never be able to have children.

Yes, he knew she blamed him, but she will never say anything as he looked into her eyes. For a second he saw emptiness, darkness, just for a second and she reverted back to him as they lay in their embrace.

****

"Hello."

"Mr. Montgomery? Michael? This is Dr. Whalls, the physician that was tending to, Jordan Carpenter."

"Yes."

"I wanted to call you personally. Sir, I'm sorry to inform you that Jordan has died."

Michael's mind fell off from the conversation. He heard the doctor but he didn't believe it.

"Jordan had left instructions that you were to be called first whenever any emergencies arise. He was very clear."

Michael had to get himself together. He has his daughter in the car to be concerned about.

He had just left Sonja at the hospital after they managed to calm her down. This thing with the fire at the store is crazy. Sonja insisted that Natalie set the fire after the two of them got into a heated argument.

Michael didn't believe it but was curious to know why Natalie was at the craft store tonight. He wanted to call her to find out more and he was going to do that before the doctor had called. His world was upside down now and crashing fast.

Taylor doesn't need to see her father losing it and think that her mother is in trouble. There was plenty of time for him to react later, after he dropped her off at his mother's. His mother will be heartbroken when he tells her about JC. He had to take his mind off this.

"Yes, that's right. Um, I'll be right there."

This going back and forwards with Sonja didn't seem to be bothering Taylor the least bit. It was good that the two of them had enough common sense not to argue in front of her and keeping comments about each other to themselves.

"Daddy how long will Mommy be in the hospital?"

"Just a few days more honey. You miss her huh?"

"Yes. I like it when we are all together."

"Yes so do, I."

He had no choice but to go along with what his daughter was saying. At one time he did enjoy being together with her mother but now he wasn't too sure. What is going to happen between Sonja and him was nowhere on the horizon, but a lot was becoming clear with Natalie.

He never really thought clearly about what this might do to Taylor until he heard her tonight. This complicates this move he is trying to do with Natalie and there is no doubt about it.

He was doing a good job of keeping his mind off JC's death. He didn't like thinking about his Sonja troubles much. That was like death, he thought as he pushed his car peddle little harder with his foot.

****

"Are you sure, a heart attack?" Michael questioned in shock to Dr. Whalls as he sat in his office at the hospital. "How is that possible, JC is only thirty, healthy?"

"Well as I was saying before about the recent Meth use, it weakened his heart. But he shouldn't have had a heart attack that's the strange part. He went into cardiac arrest earlier, then into the coma and then...you know."

"Strange? What do you mean strange?"

"With Jordan's Meth use he should not have these high levels of potassium in his system but it is there and that level brought on the heart attack. You see Meth lowers potassium"

"Doctor, do you think that potassium was given to him by mistake?"

"You know I'm not going to say that because there is nothing near potassium that was prescribed to Jordan. It's got to be the Meth that hurt his kidneys and then his body just produced too much and with his weakened heart it just killed him. Of course I'll know more once the autopsy comes back. They'll be a thorough investigation I assure you."

Michael wasn't sure he felt comfortable about that explanation. He's the first to tell anyone that he has no knowledge in medicine, but it seemed like the doctor was dead certain this was the cause of JC's death.

How was he going to tell everyone? They needed to know. JC didn't have any family that Michael knew of because he never spoke of any. They were all that he had.

****

Four days passed as Michael in his latest routine, stopped by the hospital on his way back from taking Tiffany to his mother. It was strange not being honest with her. Especially when she asked what happened to her mother that she had to be in the hospital so long. She disserved better than she was getting from Sonja and he. It was a mess and it's about to get crazier.

He does love her mother but he loves, no he has always loved Natalie more. He knows that he wants to be with Natalie but it'll take time.

He felt that she didn't have to know that nearly four days ago her mother was almost killed in the store fire, set be who? They had argued once more about the encountered and each time he abruptly left. He was already overwhelmed with taking care of JC's personal effects; he didn't need this from Sonja.

She insisted that it had to be Natalie, even though the person wore dark clothes and a hood. She admitted it to the police that Natalie wasn't wearing it seconds before. Still she insisted it was her.

The police asked her and she took great pleasure describing in detail, her encounter with Natalie, prior to the fire. Of course the security footage was destroyed with everything else in the store. All her dreams, dashed away in a fire, a fire set by her nemesis.

Now Sonja lay uncomfortably in her hospital bed, thinking.

Once she gets out of here, this is far from being over. Natalie will die for this. In fact, Sonja reached for the phone.

"Yes, you can. Will you connect me to Dr. Christopher Bower's voicemail please? Thank you...Dr. Bower, my name is Sonja Montgomery and I have some very interesting information regarding your wife that you need to hear. If you're interested I can be reached in room..."

Sonja smiled as she thought of the sweet revenge she will have once the wheel start to flow in motion. Natalie Bower will not know what hit her.

****

Christopher listened to Sonja with interest but no emotion. It was a wild accusation but it made since. Natalie has been acting strange like she was pulling from him or something, but to torch a building for the love of another man, he can't believe that.

Then there were unexplained absences that he thought were due to her friend Mona, so he didn't bother to ask. Their marriage has been unraveling and this couldn't come at a worst time.

A scandal like this would upset the board's choice to make him Chief of Staff. All of his planning would have been for nothing. He decided that he would find out what it is that this lady wants and provide it for her. Shall he say discretion?

He didn't have time to watch Natalie day and night and he didn't want to confront her because it really was not that important. Marriages have their dirty little scandals, the need for outside connections. All that was important was that he becomes COS.

Sonja was sure that Christopher Bower was angry, however he didn't show it. He didn't seem the least bit interested. Well it's only because he is so elevated in his position that he has to always appear nonchalant.

What would it mean if the head of the department staff is so easily buckled under pressure? She was sure that when he gets home Natalie will immediately be smacked around a bit; for causing what could be a big scandal at Chicago Memorial if this got out.

****

At Chicago Memorial, Sonja laid restlessly in her bed. Michael had returned to the room with Tiffany, quickly as he had left, because she missed her mother. He then left again making some flimsy excuse about having to call the station about that damn *Deena Show*.

What a crock he only wanted to have time to be with Natalie, she thought. He had probably gone to her office plotting her defense with her. Sonja could barely stay focus on the conversation she was having with Tiffany for worrying what he was doing.

About an hour later before the actual end of visiting hours, Michael and Tiffany left to go home. Sonja thought about her life and the conditions of it and how much she hated Natalie Vincent Bower. Thoughts of her flooded Sonja's, mind. It was so much that she thought that she was hallucinating. Especially because in that instance she saw the door to her room opened up. She thought Natalie stood in the doorway in a nurse's uniform.

"Why are *you* here?" She asked the woman angrily, but the woman did not answer.

As the woman walked further into her room she saw that it wasn't Natalie, just some random nurse.

"Oh I'm sorry. I thought you were someone else."

"Now, now dear," the nurse said walking towards her bedside. "That still is no way to talk to someone; no matter who it is. You really need to learn how to be more gracious." She scolded Sonja, while preparing a needle with fluid inside. "This will ease all of the pain and some that I know that you are having right now..."

She injected the medicine in Sonja's arm.

She appreciated the concern from the nurse. She didn't appreciate her little flippant mouth. She thought this one was a little bit strange and of course she wasn't her regular nurse for this shift. She began to feel the effects of the medicine coursing through her body, but she couldn't move.

"What, what is this? I feel...I can't...move."

"Oh you know how our bodies react strangely to different meds. I'll be sure to find the right one that agrees with you the next time. You see I thought you would need this since you've been so tense that you think that your husband is sleeping with your nemesis."

She bent down close to Sonja. Sonja eyes opened wide, shocked with horror. How did this nurse know what was happening in her life.

"Next time bitch when you decide to steal a man, make sure he doesn't already belong to someone else. Because your life may be at stake…"

The nurse straightened her body up and checked herself in the bathroom mirror before she departed.

Sonja laid there motionless hoping whatever she had in her system would not kill her. This nurse, she sounded as if she could be Natalie, but Sonja was not sure. She was really in and out of consciousness and it was clear she didn't really know who the nurse was. She sounded like…the store.

* * * *

Later that evening at Cultrax Pharmaceuticals, Craig McNair, Mona's lab technician sat at his desk with 'Karen' cradled in his arms. He thought how lucky he was to be able to pick this one up right at the carryout down the street from the building. Who would believe it? It was so easy.

'Karen's' thoughts were purely on her mission. She had to woo this buffoon so that she could get close to Mona's office. What would be the best way but befriending the closest and the most available, her lab technician?

"I have always enjoyed the mind. I mean what it takes to really process all this stuff that goes into processing medicine. Is the team really your staff or do you have a boss?"

"Well of course I have a boss but she doesn't know what's happening. I'm the one that informs her and guides her through all of her meetings. She's just the face of this project."

"What project is that?"

"I can't tell you…" he said as 'Karen' kissed him seductively. "Are you trying to get me fired? I couldn't possibly tell you what we're working on you could be with one of our competitors."

Immediately 'Karen' jumped off his lap. She was able to make her move now.

"I can't believe that you would think I'm working with some other company. When I saw you in that coffee shop that day, I thought you would be interesting to go out with. I knew you worked at a lab. Most brilliant guys do. But now that I know how you really feel, I think I will leave now."

"No 'Karen', you can't, I'm sorry. I didn't mean to make you feel like I don't trust you. Stay so I can take you on a tour."

"Well I don't know it's not every day that I allow a man to insult me and take the insult lying down, but I really love…uh like you so, okay."

Craig couldn't believe his luck. This sexy woman is really into him. She seems as though she has a fetish for eggheads. Well that, he is not, but that doesn't stop him from trying to get next to her. She'll problem do anything he wants.

They left from his office and walked out into the main hallway. Hand in hand they toured the semi vacant building. It was nearly clear of staff and whatever staff was there was focusing on their own projects that they didn't notice the contempt she had for Craig in her eyes.

An hour later they returned to Craig's office and she instantly started kissing him the moment he closed the door. Craig was excited because this chick was hot for him and must really love brainy men.

She ran her hands all over his back and encircled her arms around his neck. This was the oldest trade in the book but it still had very strong merits these days. What made this geek think that he was that desirable to bag a hot woman in less than a week, 'Karen' thought?

With her left hand she reached around and turned the diamond ring that she had on her right finger so that top of the ring was now on the underside of her finger.

Once there she flipped the fake top of the diamond ring off and there was a thin short pin-like needle protruding in the missing space. She instantly stuck it into the back of Craig's neck and he gasp as he felt the pinch. She was getting too good at this and she was on a roll.

Once Craig began to slide down to the floor behind his desk, 'Karen' felt it was safe to exit his office and use his keycard to access Mona's office.

What are you doing? They don't care about you, their using you. Stop.

Once again 'Karen' ignored the voices the intruded in her mind and continued on her mission. This is where the real work began. She pulled from her purse the key and keycard that she reproduced the other night belonging to Mona. Actually she just switched the keycard. This gave her full access to what she needed.

CHAPTER 13

On the way home Michael was conversing with Shanna on his cell phone.

"No I think it would be great. We'll just get the old and new crew together at the cable station and really turn it out. I could use a celebration. After all this isn't just a milestone for me, it's for the whole crew. This is the big time, we should celebrate I…"

Michael was cut off by the car in he saw in his rearview mirror. It was that grey Mercedes again. It was following him. He couldn't see the tag or maybe he thought he was reading it backwards wrong, 'e-g-n-e-v-e-r', revenge.

The car tried to maintain a safe distance from Michael and even though he couldn't really tell who it is. He could tell it was female, though. Female, but who could she be? He ruled out Natalie a long time ago, simple because they've been seeing each other.

Years of this behavior, it was not the same things but stalking just the same. Someone was always lurking, watching Michael go about his day to day life but never identifying themselves.

"Michael?"

"Ah Shanna, could you get the list together for me please."

"Sure thing, this party will be the best." Michael hung up with Shanna and his cell phone rang again seemingly wildly.

"Hello."

"Michael!" Sonja yelled into the phone. "She tried to kill me again. She came after you left and poisoned me with something in a needle. Natalie is trying to kill me to get you."

"Sonja, get a hold of yourself what are you talking about. Who came to your room?"

Why would Natalie do that? It is always something about Natalie?

"I'm on my way."

****

Shortly later Michael ended up at Chicago Memorial and was comforting a hysterical Sonja. The doctors had assured Michael that there were no foreign substances in her system. She was the picture of health they only had her in the hospital because of the prior injuries from the fire.

The police had come and gone again from taken a second report alleging Natalie to the crime. They also were not willing to take the report any further. Especially after the doctor's confirm that hallucinations can occur from taking the heavy dosages of pain killers. Sonja had requested it because she swore she was in excruciating pain.

"I want to go home Michael. I'm like a sitting duck here. Natalie is out to get me and if it isn't her, than its Mona. I was not imagining these things. It happened the nurse came in here and she knew things that only we knew. I want to go home."

Michael didn't see any other alternatives, Sonja would be hysterical at the hospital and there was no sense in keeping her here if the doctors will release her.

****

Around noon, Michael sat in the sound booth with Shanna going over this weeks' taping of the *Deena Show's* airing.

It had been three weeks since JC was buried and things kind of gotten back to normal but things will never be the same. JC should be here for this. It was strange not to be able to feel the full joy of what was happening to him. Maybe as time goes on Michael will feel fortunate again.

"Michael the final sequence is complete. This one is ready for viewing."

"Good I'm glad I'm exhausted. I think I'll leave early today."

"Okay if I need anything I'll give you a shout."

"Thanks Shanna, you are the best."

The whole show had moved to its new home in this short time. It was a matter of weeks and was across town from the old cable station. The old place is what he has called his second home for eight years.

Michael drove from the TV studio. It wasn't until he pulled into the cemetery where JC is buried that he even realized he was coming here. He missed his friend more than he thought. To Michael, JC was the kind of guy that tried to see the bright side of everything no matter what. His forgiveness was uncanny.

Once he was upon the location where JC laid to rest, he saw a woman at his gravesite knelt down talking to the ground. She was enveloped in her despair for JC that she didn't notice or hear Michael as he walked up behind enough to hear her conversation.

"I didn't know JC. I didn't know that you love me until you told me too late. I feel like I hurt you unnecessarily. It didn't have to be. Michael didn't need to know…"

Désiree paused as she felt the aura of Michael's presence. She doesn't turns around.

"I'm sorry Miss I didn't mean to intrude. I thought I come to see if you were alright, because you sounded upset. You knew JC? Do I know you?

"I'm…..Désiree." She said with a pause as she turned around with dark sunglasses on.

Michael could barely see her tear stained face through the glasses. He didn't know how much JC cared for this woman. They never got a chance to meet her, but he knew she was something special.

Although she made the call to them, once they got to the hospital she was not there when they arrived. She never came to the funeral either.

"Wow…it's good to meet you. I didn't know this thing with you and JC was that serious."

"I didn't either," she said staring at his grave. "I didn't find out actually until that day."

It was unbelievable that this woman that seemed to elude him and his friends can stand here and tell him that she loved JC. Michael just didn't believe it.

"Well how are you? Are you going to be alright?"

She just smiled at him. It was good to know that he was as loyal as JC believed he was. She knew it to be true, too. So she nodded.

"You mentioned me when you were talking to JC. What didn't I have to know? I didn't mean to eavesdrop but I heard it."

"I might as well tell you. I didn't want you to know that JC was in love with an exotic dancer."

Michael breathed deeply with a sigh. This was all of the mystery, what she did for a living. Who was he to judge, his lover is married with two kids?

"Well to put your mind at ease, if JC love you than I'm sure that doesn't mean a bit a difference. I'm glad that you were together. He seemed happy."

Désiree let out this blood curdling scream and ran off. Michael was so caught off guard that he didn't have any time to react. He just watched her run off to her car, a red Mercedes and screeched tires as she hastily pulled off. He stood motionless at the cemetery not knowing what had just happened.

****

"Hey Natalie, are you busy?" Mona said over her Bluetooth as she was driving in her car.

"Hi Mona, I'm leaving work, what's up?"

"Word on the street has it that the Blacks are going away for the weekend. Our buddy is getting some stupid award for playing music and cracking jokes. You work roughly four hours a day; get paid crazy money and now they give you an award."

"Michael didn't mention this to me. That's wonderful for Sebastian. Maybe Abigail and he can rekindle their relationship while their away."

"Girl please, Sebastian Black likes his relationship with Abigail just the way it is. Don't look for a change this soon."

"Mona you are terrible."

"That I am. But I didn't really call for idle gossip I called to invite you on a treasure hunt."

"What kind of treasure hunt?"

"The kind that you do when you have keys to the Blacks' house, are you in?"

"How did you get keys to Sebastian's house?"

"Well last year they went away for about a month so that Sebastian could do a stint at a struggling sister radio station. I guess to boost listeners. It was in another city so Michael was asked to house sit. A couple of days into the sitting gig, Mic couldn't make it one day. He asked yours truly to fill in, to turn something off or on I forget. So of course I had to stop by my favorite locksmith and get a set of keys made, just in case, thus my request to you to have a little fun."

"Why did you have their keys copied?"

"I'm Mona Daniels, have we met?"

"Remind me never to have Michael house sit. I can't go into Sebastian's house uninvited."

"Will you relaxed it'll be okay. You are going because I invited you."

"But."

"But nothing, I will not take no for an answer. You were the one who said I had to watch out for Abigail Black. Well this is how I'm watching out. I'll either find out that she is just as I thought, crazy, or she really is a lovesick bunny in love."

"Mona I just can't. It's breaking and entering."

"I have a key. Be there in twenty minutes."

Mona hung up the line with a tap on her Bluetooth. She was amused that she held certain powers and controls certain aspects of others' lives. It would be no harm to go to Sebastian's place and snoop around at bit. It's not like she hadn't been there before.

****

After retrieving Natalie, the two of them were standing in the middle of the Black's family room looking around in the dim light.

"As much money as Sebastian makes you would think that he would have an alarm. Let's go upstairs. Whatever you do, don't turn on too many lights."

"This is not encouraging to me. We are going to jail, again."

"We are not." Mona and Natalie scaled the staircase like too teenagers spending the night in a creepy old house. First stop on the tour was the Black's bedroom. The two of them looked around the rooms.

"Mona, what are we supposed to be looking for?" Natalie whispered.

"Something out of the ordinary and why are you whispering, I mean we're here by ourselves?"

"Oh."

She followed Mona out of the master bedroom to check the secondary rooms. They got to the last room on the end hall and opened it. Flicking on the lights Mona let out a shriek.

"Natalie do you see all this?"

"I do. I don't believe it."

Around the room Abigail had turned it into a mini version of Sonja's craft store. The many ceramic dolls line the room like a school house classroom; dolls of many sizes. In the corner were a few boxes of long stem rose's type.

"It is her. It's been her all these years. I never thought it could be."

"I know Mona. This means that she tried to run me of the road."

"This means a lot of things. I am going to kill that crazy witch."

The two of them began taking pictures with their Smart phones. Natalie began backing up to get a wider span and as she was doing that she knocks into the small dresser that was position behind the opened door.

Instantly, items begin to fall off of it including a small music box that hits the floor and opens. Music begins to flood the room as the ballerina spins on her side dancing to the baby lullaby.

"Tell me that I do not hear what I hear Natalie."

"I can't tell you a lie. We better get things back to normal and go tell Michael."

****

"...and you did what how could you do that to Sebastian?" Michael said angrily as Mona stood before him.

She was trying to get him to see pass her bad deeds and focus on what they found out instead. They were at the TV studio where Michael had to return to do what looks like an all-nighter.

Every so often Michael would look at Natalie but she averted her eyes from his to avoid the scrutiny.

"I guess you didn't hear what we just told you that we found? I think that should supersede any thoughts of disappointment from you Mic. The woman is a deranged psycho and I am her first target."

"That's crazy. I've known Abigail for twelve years I can't believe it. You do know that since the fire at the store both Sonja and Abigail have been storing, what items they could savage from the store room, at our two houses. That is probably what you saw, inventory from the store."

"Including a music box? You know when I replayed the recording for you on my cell phone, that it's the same music. We've been hearing that all these years. I am going to call the police so they can lock her up as soon as they get back from their weekend."

"You are not. Mainly because you and *you*, Natalie I can't believe that you were in on this, are going to be locked up too for trespassing, breaking and entering."

"Michael I..." Natalie tried to say something but Mona cut her off.

"Ha the jokes on you, I have a key."

"Sebastian gave you a key to his house?"

"Well not exactly. I just have a key."

"How can somebody just have a key? Mona as much as I love you, this is wrong on so many levels. Where is your loyalty to your friends? It doesn't matter how you feel about Abigail, this will hurt Sebastian that you did this. He doesn't want to admit it but there is something between Abigail and him that, is not going to go away. Please don't continue to do this Mona, you're stretching."

"I understand Michael. I'll drop it. But I'm going to keep my eye on Ms. Ambrosia like a hawk now."

"I'll be taking that key."

Natalie giggled at Michael silently as he retrieved the key from Mona. The mere thought that anyone who could contain Mona Daniels was hilarious, but he did.

The entire trip over to TV station, she was treated to Mona's ramps and raves. She went on and on about how she finally will destroy Abigail Black for the hurtful things she's done in the past. It was all the mockeries, the accusations, all of it.

Michael says a few words and she sensible again. She loves that about him and it just added one more reason to be in love with him.

"Every time you get into trouble I get to see more of you. You should do that more often." He said.

"I'll be sure to rob a bank on Monday." She counted with a grin.

"Will I see you on Thursday?" He whispered to her.

"I wouldn't miss it for the world."

****

It was midnight at Chicago Memorial inside Dr. Edwards' office. There was moment there but it was not Dr. Edwards, it was 'Karen'. She was hastily rummaging through files that were in the office. Most of the drawers it seemed as if she had keys to and the others she used the gold plated letter opener to gain access.

Drawer after drawer she riffled through them with her flashlight looking for something in particular. She did it with too much ease as if she knew her way around. Through her frustration she cursed at ever defeat. Then she came to what was a small glove box drawer in the desk. She had never seen that before it was a new attachment.

She pried on it until it fell open and the document filled drawer displayed its contents to her. With the flashlight she studied the papers briefly and decided that this is what she needed to be free. She was going straight to him so he could help her to solve this issue. She can't be allowed, forced to continue on this way, she didn't want to.

This is what you are to do. It's not over. You're not done. Destroy the evidence for her.

'Karen' started to round up her fist with the documents inside to destroy them.

No don't do it, you'll be free, run, run, with them run away, take them to him.

Then she shined the flashlight to the desk and saw another picture of the husband. She instantly went to it and cradled it in her arms when she picked it up from the desk.

It didn't have to be. It should not have happened. She started to cry and the tears didn't let up. As she cried she realized that now was the time to take back her control and she bolted from the office like the voice told her to.

CHAPTER 14

Mona walked around her condo the next night wishing that Jackson hadn't called and cancelled their date. She really wanted to see him and be with him to take the edge off. Ever since she found out that Abigail was the stalker, well supposedly the stalker, she has been tense. She didn't know that her involvement with Sebastian would turn out this way. It was just that one time to clear away the entire mystic of the two of them from over the years. Abigail couldn't possibly be that weak that she would seek revenge on her like this.

Maybe she should leave Chicago and start anew. It is time for some normalcy in her life and maybe in another place would be the place for her. Mona continued to muse on her life choices, walking to the sliding glass door of her balcony.

She looked out into the nightlife of the city below. She looked down on the street level below. She looked at the coffee shop on the corner street. That place she swore she would never frequent again. They mistakenly gave her a cup of dry coffee grounds instead of the percolated cup of coffee that she ordered.

Suddenly, she realized there in front of the closed shop stood a female with long hair and sunglasses on. She was standing perfectly still, looking up towards Mona and that caught her attention.

Abigail, she thought as she stared at the motionless figure across the street. The woman just simply stared at her from the street level until Mona couldn't take anymore. She ran to her front door, opened it and down on the elevator to confront who she felt was Abigail in disguise.

Once she was on the street, she ran to the area where she knew the lady was standing but she was no longer there. Hell, she thought, why would Abigail wait for me to confront her? She knew she wasn't even supposed to be in town. What did she do with Sebastian?

She went back up to her condo and found that she had left the door wide open. She didn't think anything of it, just that she must have left it that way while trying to get down the street so quickly. She closed the door and sat down on the sofa to try to calm her nerves.

As she closed her eyes and the silence became background noise to her, she heard a faint ticking sound coming from behind the sofa she was sitting on. Mona got up to investigate the sound. She went behind the sofa and she saw an old style alarm clock like the ones seen in the old cartoon movies and a note posted nearby it.

She quickly read the note.

'I know what you did and one bad turn deserves another as they say. You aren't the only one with a key. Next time you will die bitch like all whores do. Oh you will die.'

When the alarm clock wound down to twelve the clock exploded, causing Mona to fall backwards from the sheer shock of it all. She wasn't hurt because it was such a small compacted implosion, almost like a small lab explosion when mixing the wrong chemicals. She immediately ran to the phone.

****

Later Michael and Natalie were standing outside Mona's condo in the hallway. The police was there and had roped it off. This time, this incident drew more than just the two police officers that Mona and Natalie had met before. The bomb squad was there came as well.

It unnerved her, the fact that someone had a key to her home. They purposely toyed with her to get her to come out of her condo. All, so they could set that small bomb between the time she went downstairs and came back up.

That thought further unnerved Mona to her core and so she decided that she was going to again check into a hotel. This time it was for an extended stay. By the time she calms down she will have made arrangements to move. Even though the bombs caused no real damages, what was coming next a bigger explosion? Could she be in it this time?

Natalie cradled her friend in her arms. She knew that Mona wanted to cry but she was being. She didn't want them to know that she was this vulnerable, but Michael knew.

****

Across town, at that moment, at a restaurant called the Grifton Bistro, Jackson sat at the dinner table with 'Karen'. They seemed very cozy almost intimate.

"You were great. Everything was there like we thought and it was like cheating on a test. I take it that you took care to make sure that your face was never view by the camera correct?"

"I said I did, didn't I? The guy was so full of his dirty little lust that he didn't see what hit him. By the time they find him he'll be a dead, cold case. I didn't want to do it but it had to be done. No loose ends. Thanks for getting me that stuff to make that small bomb, too. This will keep them guessing for longer than we need to pull this off."

"I enjoyed it and well you had to get rid of the evidence didn't you? What more than a bomb to erase any trace of being somewhere you're not supposed to be."

"Next time let me try fire. I never tried fire before."

****

The next day at the hospital after Natalie had spent her some time with Michael she sat in her office preparing for the next patient.

"Natalie, I would like to talk to you," Christopher said as he barged through her office door.

"Christopher, I expect to have a patient in about twenty minutes okay?" Natalie seemed short with him he thought. What has happened to her in the last few months that she is so rebellious? It was like she was becoming this other entity that he couldn't understand.

"I think it is now time to talk more about this accusation that Sonja Montgomery said to me. She said that you are being too friendly with her husband and that you purposely set her craft store on fire. I'm not asking about the craft store because I know you better than that. But what do you say about the husband?"

"There's nothing to say. I thought I would spare you the gory details of this nonsense; but I see I have no choice. This is really incredible that you would take the word of someone as devious as Sonja Price, someone that you don't know. She pretended to be my friend in college so she could, how, should I say, steal my boyfriend at the time. As much as I know it sounds very juvenile today back then the betrayal of a close ah someone I thought was a close friend hurts deeper than you can imagine. If you had friends you would know what I mean. But everyone is beneath you, so it's hard I know to grasp that concept. Yes I have seen her husband around, here and there usually with her and she is just worried that karma is what they say it is. Now is there anything else you would like to talk to me about?"

Christopher looked at Natalie and just shook his head. What she said made sense, but she didn't have to be so aggressive with what she said. He has plenty of friends but he doesn't have time to cultivate such things.

He has goals and his trying to get her to see what the goals are, but she insisted on getting wrapped in this world of gossip. He knew he didn't have to worry about her being unfaithful. Why would Natalie want to give up a man of his status for a fling?

"No I think that will do. I will assume that there will be no more need for this conversation in the future."

"Not unless you bring it up."

"Just see to it. I'm very busy. A lot is riding on discretion."

"Twenty minutes, time."

Christopher left in a huff.

How dare he try to exact, some kind of control over this situation. She loves Michael and now there is no turning back.

Sonja will get hers. She has been a very busy bee lately. Not only did she dispatch Christopher to interrogate Natalie like a ruthless dictator but she also made sure that Michael would not be able to invite her to the studio party at the cable station.

That one caught Natalie off guard and bothered her. When Michael planned the details he bounced them off of her to see if she agreed with some of the details. It was going to a night to remember and he wanted her to be there with him.

Then Sonja involved herself totally. Michael and she knew that he would not have any peace if he didn't allow her to participate in everything. The irony being that Sonja never respected Michael's interest in his craft.

Sure she tried to fake it Michael would say. It was too obvious that Sonja didn't care or allowed herself to care about what was the core of Michael; his heart and soul.

Natalie did however. Especially back when they were deeply in love, sharing their hopes and dreams together. She knew what made him tick and he did her, just like now.

So this Saturday is the party and she will be alone when she wished she could be with the man she loves. Sonja Price be damned, you will not win.

It seems that Sonja was more distressed about losing Michael than she cared to admit. Who would have imagined that she would talk to Christopher and accuse Natalie of, how did she put it, being too 'friendly with her husband' and setting fire to her craft store, why would she do that?

The idea that Christopher fell so easily for that information hook line and sinker, then approaching Natalie with it angered her deeply. But denying the information to him, did not deny the longing in her heart to be with Michael.

It only served to authenticate the fact of her love for him. Christopher appeared to take Natalie's word for it. Mainly she thought because he did not want to face the possibility that she could be interested in another man. It would destroy his already fragile inflated ego.

Regardless this will surely come up when the time comes that she eventually tells him the truth.

CHAPTER 15

Saturday evening, Michael and the rest of the staff was having a good time as his friends mixed into the crowd. Mona brought Jackson who had been missing in action for a while. She felt it was just one of those 'Fu Paws' of relationships. It has to come about that they would need some time apart and also the fact that he's married even further complicates things. Sonja was there and Michael tried to be the perfect husband sharing a night of fun out with his wife.

So far things were going the way they should. If it wasn't for the fact that he wished he could be here with Natalie; it would be perfect. This was the furthest thing from perfect. It was not fair but this was reality. Sebastian and Abigail too were having a good time until Mona decided to ask Sebastian to dance and he had the audacity to do it.

They were on the make shift dance floor on the stage enjoying themselves like friends do. But Abigail stared at, no glared at her husband and her nemesis wishing that she could cut their throats. Mona does taunt me, Abigail thought. She insisted on playing these games but tonight will be the last time she would have to deal with her. It was time to do something about this and do something Abigail will.

The party had whine down. Michael, Sonja, Abigail, Sebastian, Mona and Jackson were together talking and listening to some music in the sound booth. Abigail didn't feel like staying after watching Sebastian cozy up to Mona all night. She felt herself filling with anxiety.

Sure they pretended very well that nothing is going on but she can see it. She should just kill them both. As she moved further into the sound booth, she reached into her purse. It could be so easy she thought as she pulled out the bottle of Xanax and pop two in her mouth.

She put her hand back in her purse and fished around in it as she waited for the Xanax to take hold.

****

Natalie sat in Janice's office sipping coffee. She had run into her friend the psychiatrist when she was leaving her office. She convinced her to spend a few minutes with her. Then she started sharing stories about her patients and Natalie about hers, which went on for hours.

Natalie however needed the break and the different company. Too much of Michael and all of these events were heavily on her mind. She needed desperately to clear her head and get away from all this trouble that Sonja has caused her anyway.

Janice didn't know anything about Michael's and Natalie's affair and she wanted to keep it that way. She really wanted to attend the party for Michael's production team that was happening right now, but she knew she couldn't because of Sonja.

Janice just talked on about her patients and most of their business as Natalie eyed her with amusement. This was the kind of stuff that Janice was always being frowned on, revealing private counseling information in casual conversation. But she decided to let her vent anyway.

She gave herself a pat on the back for keeping all her troubles to herself. Then she realized that she had wandered too far away from the conversation that Janice was having with her.

"...Natalie?"

"Oh Janice I'm sorry I was thinking," She said as she looked around for something to use as a cover story. Then she looked to the desk. "I wanted to ask you about your statue, the one that Everett gave you. What happened to it?"

Dr. Edwards looked to the spot where the statue once sat and recalled in her mind the day 'Karen' destroyed it and Janice's closest link to her dead husband.

'Karen' was heartless to do it and it took Dr. Edwards a while to get pass it in order to move on in their sessions together.

She felt that way mainly because after all that has happened, she really did love him so very much. She didn't expect things to go that far. 'Karen' will indeed have to be corrected for this.

"'Karen' pushed it off the desk during one of her mad outburst and it smashed into pieces. I wanted to kill her that day. I had just recently told her how much I cared for that piece. I angered her and she meant to hurt me."

"Really, I tell you Janice I do feel for you. Your profession is really stressful."

"I know, when people see me they think that I just have this casual career with a few people that come to talk about how bad their day is, but some of my patients can be dangerous, even murderous."

"You better be careful."

"Take for instant 'Karen'. A classic case of a mind manipulated by hate and revenge, so much that she could be controlled and turned into a deadly ticking destructive bomb if one wanted to do so."

"Wow can someone be so consumed with hate that it's all they think of?"

Dr. Edwards nodded.

"It seems like there's a lot of hate and destruction going on lately in so much abundance."

"And it is up to us college educated professional to see them safely through it."

"Oh that reminds me I saw your picture in a UC yearbook. I forgot you had gone there. I barely recognized you. I have to say you look one hundred degrees different older. You look good."

She looked at Natalie with strange recollection.

"That picture, I had forgot about that? Thank you for reminding me."

"Why, don't you have a year book?"

"I didn't get one, I wasn't too fond of college," she said sternly as if she was trying to drive the point home.

"I get it, Janice." Natalie agreed with her only because she wasn't really listening. This time her focus was on Dr. Edwards.

She looked at Janice this time wondering what she had missed, not in the conversation but in her time as Janice's friend. There was still so much mystery after she returned to CM after her husband's mysterious death.

"Janice what happened to your husband, was he ill?"

"No he wasn't. It was sudden and an accident. He fell down a flight of stairs and smashed his head. The autopsy..." She breathed in deeply to hold back tears. "...proved, that, his skull was crushed from the fall. It was an accident."

"Oh Janice I am so sorry. I didn't know."

"It's quite alright. I've gotten over the shock of it all. It's just one of those things."

Natalie noticed that it was a nonchalant way of responding to her inquiry. No point in causing Janice the pain of talking about the ordeal any further. She didn't want to pry, so she decided to move on from the question just in case she was trying to mask her true feeling.

"I hope you don't mind me asking but have you had plastic surgery or something?"

She looked at Natalie with apprehensiveness. She was becoming quite the detective lately. She really didn't like sharing her personal information but she was a friend.

"Yes I did, recently after Everett died. Do you like it?"

"You look like a million bucks, Janice. I don't think I would have the nerve to do it at least not at this age."

It was as she suspected but that is so common these days that it really isn't worth talking about. Women are getting things like this done earlier in age. She just couldn't get over how much Janice just looked like someone she didn't know. Well she did look familiar but nobody that came to mind. It was like she could put her face on someone else's body if she could remember who?

She didn't really want to bother with small talk about Janice's procedure anymore but after all she decided to sit here with her. She had other things on her mind like these attacks.

The attacks were going a bit far. Mona's latest incident means that someone is really close, closer than the two of them would like to admit. Who would have known about this unless it was Abigail herself? She had to be the only one who knew they were in her house.

There was so much on her mind worrying her. Puzzles were forming all around her slowly piecing together to be what? For certain Michael was the only one that never got what the other received. No hostility was pointed in his direction at all.

Years ago all of the sudden there are these random attacks on Michael's friends. The only things that happened to him were the mysterious woman and the BMW he says parks near his home and at work regularly. It was possibly, the same BMW that nearly ran her off the road.

It only began after she and Michael began their affair. Right after that the packages came to her office. It never got really serious with everyone until now, but everyone is claiming years of odd occurrences. This is definitely one person with one goal but what happened to bring this all on?

Sebastian, Mona plus JC's death they're all surrounding Michael but not affecting him directly. Abigail was always in Natalie's mind as the culprit only because Mona and Sebastian seemed to be the main targets especially with the explosion at Mona's condo.

What did those two do? Did they simply have an affair and it finally drove Abigail to do these insane things? But then Sonja's craft store was set on fire, she's Abigail's friend. JC didn't do anything, did he?

Maybe it still is Abigail and she was trying to frame Natalie. That definitely would be a good way of eliminating your best friend's enemy while you are on a rampage. Maybe it's all of them. Maybe they all did something to Abigail and she is not about to forgive it.

"So Natalie," Dr. Edwards said looking at her desk clock. "You think that your friends are being taunted by some...what was the term you used?"

"A very tortured, woman. I use to think that it was my friend's wife, then his best friend's wife and now I feel it goes further into his past like maybe they all conspired together to cover up something. But my friend Michael seems to be involved. But I just don't see Michael doing something wrong."

"Michael? Well what's so special about Michael? Is he some incredible love or super boyfriend or something?"

"No. Why would you say that? I was nowhere close to that ballpark. These are friends of mine from college."

"Sure, sure, you know me I'm always looking for a scandal."

"Well, maybe I should say that about him, he's truly one of a kind."

"I know he is..."

Natalie stared at Janice as she seemed to travel away from the topic for a bit. That same gazed that Sonja use to have back in college when Natalie would speak about Michael to her. A gaze she ignored and then Sonja stole him from her.

Now does she have to worry about Janice going after Michael?

Janice noticed her reaction and returned casually to the conversation.

"I mean something has definitely got your attention and it's been like that for months. Is he more to you? What do you think he and his friends have done?"

"The only thing I know is that one of my friends' wives can't have children and I never got the story about that. That wouldn't be anything to mention except now she has taking on this new persona, changing her personality and calling herself by a different name. That's when my red flags flared up. I think she's upset that she can't have children and her husband is supposedly having an affair with another woman, I think she feels that they mock her in some way."

Dr. Edwards smiled a bit before she spoke, when she started her facial expression shifted and became serious.

"A new personality, really, that is such a weird coincident. The woman that I am treating, 'Karen' she fits that story."

"She can't have children?"

"Yes, she did before but had to get rid of it. It happened about ten years ago when she was in college and she's never really made a full recovery because she felt forced to do it. Some very devastating things happened after that, following her through the years. It was impossible with all that pain anyway. I've been trying to get her to move on with me but she won't let me in. Instead she revels in the hate that she feels for the man responsible and now she wants to claim his friends too. She has been following them all around for years doing destructive things, deadly things to them. She especially wants to punish the two that she calls 'Mr. Radio and his CEO whore'. I don't know how they fit into it. She talks in riddles."

Natalie started to speculate on what Janice was saying and then compared it to what was happening around her. Maybe Abigail was pregnant by Sebastian and had an abortion those years ago, but didn't' want to do it. He must have forced her.

Mr. Radio and his CEO, whore, whore, Mona. Mona received packages stating that she will 'Die whore like all whores do'. This is too much to be a coincidence, this is too close. Mona is this person idea of a whore and…Sebastian has got to be Mr. Radio. That's what he does, he is a radio personality.

"Janice what did 'Karen' say about Mr. Radio and his CEO whore?"

"Something about following them around and even one time getting, close enough to touch the two of them. I'm convinced that he was the man that betrayed her. She also talked about losing his love and that the woman, she has to be this CEO, she says has mocked her; when she called him to tell him something that she needed him to know. On her last visit with me, she spoke, really determined to fulfill this mission of revenge that she's hell bent on. She is really talking about murdering people. It was like talking to a pre-serial killer. I started to have her committed because she was beginning not to obey my direction anymore. But she darted out of here so fast and I haven't been able to reach her this past week."

"Do you think she meant what she said?"

"About the revenge, yes she is serious. So much that she sent chills through my body. I mean who can get through to a woman who is determined not forgive the man who violated her."

If Natalie was to believe that Mr. Radio is Sebastian then this disturbed woman has to be Abigail and they were going together, in college and their together now, what can be Abigail's issues? No baby? She continued to listen to Janice intently.

"She said she tried to play music to help him see what she needed him to know. I never understood what she meant by all that. She is really a tough subject to crack with the encrypted conversations through her sessions it's really hard to follow her."

"Music, baby lullaby music?" Natalie said slowly, choking the screams, threatening to come from her throat.

"Yes lullaby music." Dr. Edwards said casually. "I couldn't understand that. She mentioned she was going to have them altogether one day soon to end it all in some sort of massacre. How did you know it was lullaby music?"

Natalie didn't answer her. Instead she dropped her cup of coffee to the floor, as it slipped from her fingers. In her mind she screamed, Michael.

She recalled hearing that music at Sebastian's and Abigail's home. That night when Mona and she went snooping there, she dismissed Mona's claim then and wish she hadn't.

"Natalie what happened? Are you okay?"

"Uh nothing, I have to go Janice."

Natalie quickly got out of her chair and bolted out of Janice's office, as if she was being chased in a Slasher movie. As the door to her office opened and shut, Janice gazed down at the broken coffee cup, on the floor, peculiarly.

"Not a problem," she said as she smiled, leaning back in her chair. "You don't want to miss the party, I know. That's going to leave a stain…"

Natalie hurried hastily through the hospital halls and down the emergency stairway. She exited through the doors to her car parked in the garage and she thought to herself. That was it. That was the end piece to the puzzle.

She now knows that Janice has been counseling the very person that has been after everyone in Michael's world for years and she had to warn him.

It was the celebration at the cable station, the one that Sonja was so determined that she didn't attend. This was the very gathering 'Karen' said to Janice that she will have her vengeance, a massacre.

She dialed hastily as she drove through the parking garage. It's Abigail Black.

****

It was Abigail all along, Natalie thought. She was by now in her car racing to the cable station where Michael was having the party at to warn him. She couldn't believe that this Karen' has been having sessions with Janice, is Abigail. Natalie really thought that Mona was just being too hard on her.

Now she felt the sting that Abigail tried to hurt her by running her off the road. What did she do? She was the one sending the packages and from Sonja's craft store. Sonja is probably helping her. Sonja hates Mona just as much as she hates Natalie.

It made sense because no one person could have been at Mona's condo that night they saw the intruder there. Abigail was probably going to get the car while Sonja was roaming around. But why did she set Sonja's store on fire unless she thought that Natalie was still there arguing with Sonja or that should be implicated. But it backfired.

It all fits, she thought. Natalie pumped the gas pedal harder as her car lunged forward to accept the new speed. She decided she had better call the police and tell them what is going on. She'll make them aware that she thinks that the person is armed and that she is female as she sped to the cable station. Michael, beware of Abigail.

****

Abigail moved towards Mona. She was going to confront her because she felt that she had the strength now to take it all the way. It had to be done. She was no longer going to accept the goings on that Sebastian and she have to be doing. It was dirty that they did this to her.

The door to the sound booth opened and Désiree step through. Abigail turned to see the new comer, as did Michael.

"'Désiree it's good to see you," Michael said surprisingly. "How have you been?"

Jackson instantly turned to see Désiree standing there and paused with shock. He didn't say anything, he just back away from the crowd close to the rear of the sound booth. This is not what they had discussed, why is she not sticking to the plan? Why is she calling herself 'Désiree? Why is she here?

Mona noticed Jackson's reaction and just observed him. Did he know this Désiree? She was after all some stripper trash and well, that seemed up Jackson's alley. What really was in the back of her mind was that one question. Was this the mystery woman Jackson so reluctantly didn't want to; confess up to being in the hotel that night?

If she was, then they have a problem, because she was JC's woman and she had to know that Mona was JC's friend. If that was the case then she was about to kick some fake ass and this was just the beginning of what maybe going on.

Michael told them all about meeting her at the cemetery and her weird behavior. This would explain it if Jackson knows her too.

"Jackson do you know her?"

"Uh no Mona not really."

"Wrong answer, 'uh, not really' is not an answer. Either you tell me or I'll ask her and set it off. She's my friend's girlfriend and he's dead because of drugs he swore he hadn't done. Something's up."

Jackson just stood there transfixed. She could blow everything that they have planned. What is going on with her?

"Michael I need to talk to all of you." 'Désiree said stepping slightly further into the medium size sound booth.

Michael felt her panicky behavior like she was desperate about something. It was strange that he would see her now this night after only meeting her that one time and the way she ran off from the cemetery. How did she even know to come here tonight?

She was strange he thought as he turned off the music. Désiree stood not moving now and everyone gave her their full attention.

"Okay 'Désiree. Everyone this is 'Désiree, JC's girlfriend. The one I told you all that I met at the cemetery. She has something she wants to tell us."

"Good, now," Desiree said as she pulled out a 9mm handgun from her purse. It took only a moment for everyone to realize what they were looking at.

"Desiree, what the hell are you doing? It's not funny."

"No Michael it's not. It hasn't been funny for me for a long time." She said with confidence while waving the gun around. Then she seemed to struggle to say what she said next.

"Not since we dated."

Désiree paused and breathed in a little to give herself time to move forward.

Tell them, tell them now. The voiced screamed in her head.

Everyone stood perfectly still in the sound check booth as Désiree stood crazily, shaking her head, in front of the only exit pointing her gun in their direction.

No one could figure out what it was that she just said. Mostly everyone in the room knew Michael and she was never in his life. She was someone no one knew.

On most minds it seems that JC has once again picked the wrong woman and this one is the worst and craziest of all. Did she snap? What was she going to do kill them because JC died?

Sonja instantly looked harder at her thinking that she was somehow Natalie behind all that elaborate slut getup she was wearing. Désiree noticed her looking and pointed the gun at her.

"Stop staring at me you ungrateful, sneaky witch. I should shoot you first. You've been taking Michael through hell and to think he chose you over me."

"It's Natalie, I told you." Sonja said cockily not knowing how serious this was.

"Désiree," Michael said ignoring Sonja's outburst. He stepped towards her trying to take the opportunity to defuse the situation. He wanted to draw her attention away from Sonja's foolishness. "What is going on? Is what happened to JC upsetting you?"

"Michael, I don't want to do this. JC has nothing to do with this. This is about you."

Michael didn't have a clue as to what was going on but the more he looked at Désiree the more she was familiar to him. He just couldn't place her face.

She had so much hair and makeup on that she could really be anybody underneath those thick reading glasses. It was obviously a disguise. Natalie? Michael felt his cell phone vibrate on his hip. He was curious to know who it was but didn't want to upset Désiree by trying to answer. At least not right now.

"Desiree." He said to her, trying to keep her calm. "We've never dated I don't know what you mean."

She stared at him and felt a tinged of anger build inside of her.

He doesn't even know who I am, she thought.

Of course not the voice replied *you're not yourself right now. It's not you, he never really knew you. Tell him what she wants you to do, tell him the truth, tell him...*

Kill him, kill them, do what you're told, she thought.

No.

The rage wanted her to kill him for his betrayal. However the inner voice from her safe place reminded her that she looked differently from the last time, so long ago when they met briefly.

Do what you're told, she thought again.

"Michael you know you've always had a good heart. I'm sorry that I never saw that pass my own needs. But that's why I'm back and I've changed myself for you so you won't see what he's done."

She pointed at Sebastian and then brought the gun up to match the aim of her other hand.

"He's the cause of all of this Mr. so-called Sebastian the Morning Lover."

"I don't know you. I've never been anywhere around you, Désiree. All I know is that you were JC's girl. What is all of this?"

"What is all of this? What is all of this? I don't know you. Oh you are soooooooooooo innocent." She mocked Sebastian teasingly. It was all, his fault. "You don't like not knowing do you big stud? You don't like not being in control cause you like to be in control, don't you?"

Abigail stared at her and then back to Sebastian. Once again the penis he uses to guide his life has gotten him in some trouble and she about to pay for it, again.

"You like to use women and dispose of them like they don't exist like nasty chewing gum. Once you've suck the flavor from it you spit it out. Does your wife even know that you slept with that CEO whore over there standing by my incredibly, dumb damn husband?"

Mona was confused and shock by the fact that Désiree knew that she slept with Sebastian. She watched her smile and revel in the delight of causing Sebastian this pain. How could she be Jackson's wife?

Abigail lowered her head. She had just about all that she could take in this thing with Sebastian. What is going on, she kept asking herself?

Sonja smiled with vindication. She had guessed that Mona slept with Sebastian and was right. It also, probably means that Michael is sleeping with Natalie. He will pay.

Desiree knowingly nodded as she told herself in her mind that there was so much more pain to come. When she leaves she will have enacted a revenge on all that caused her pain and stood in her way. She will have the man that she loves with her.

She told Janice that, as this 'Karen' that she calls her, that it will be impossible to contain her once the revenge starts. You can't control that sort of redirected pain. Not when someone is controlling you with it.

No don't fall into the pit. We had this planned. You were going to tell the truth...

SILENCE! The voice in her said. Let us begin our plan.

CHAPTER 16

"I told you she was nothing but a slutty little whore, Abigail," Sonja chimed in as they were all standing perfectly still while Désiree held the gun on them. "All this trouble that this whore friend of yours has caused Michael what do you have to say?'

"He doesn't have anything to say bitch because he's not my keeper." Mona interrupted, lashing back at Sonja.

"Tsk, Tsk Mona, you have always been under thumb with that stupid woman huh? Sonja, I don't believe that Michael was that stupid to marry you. If he only knew what you did, *only knew what you did, what you did, what you did...*" she repeated in a sing song.

Michael didn't say anything. He was still trying to piece all this together. Who is Désiree? She says she married to Mona's boyfriend, Jackson, but she was dating JC. Then there's her anger towards Sebastian, no understanding that one. It's almost like she knows everyone in the room.

"It's time you get to the point Désiree. How do you know everyone?"

"No Michael not Désiree," She pulled off her wig and took off her glasses. She tried to stop herself. "It's me...it's not Kimberly, it's your Kimberly."

Michael stared at Kimberly closely. What was she saying? This was not Kimberly Stanford, she was not this crazed looking; but yet it did seem like her. What happened? Mona, Sonja, Abigail, Sebastian and even Jackson stared in shock and no one made a sound.

"Yes I can see that knowing that made you all wonder what's really going on. Well why don't you ask Sebastian, he really does know, right baby?"

Sebastian shook his head, innocently.

"Kimberly, K," Michael said compassionately. "I know you. I know you can't be evil."

"Michael, poor goody, goody Michael, you don't know nothing of what's going on around you. What these people you call your friends do. Not so much Mona and JC though they disserved everything I have done to them. But the Kimberly Stanford that you dated all those years ago is gone, dead. As dead as those dead black roses everyone has been receiving over the years. Yes this is what I've been reduced to and I owe it all to Sebastian."

Everyone turned to look at Sebastian but he had that clueless look on his face.

"Of course he would act like he's *so* surprised. He's just so innocent you just want to eat honey off of him."

Abigail gave Sebastian a knowing look as she approved of what Kimberly said. Sebastian always appeared clear of guilt, but was far from that.

"Yes he's the man, especially in those college days. Frankly Ambrosia I don't know how you put up with him all these years. Girl do you want a gun too? Anyway Michael remembered the day of the break up? Well you broke off the relationship."

Michael didn't say anything, he just nodded.

"Well I have a story to tell you about later that night. And you remember the story about that night too Sebastian, don't you? When poor broken hearted Kimberly came to your apartment, the one you shared with Michael, later that night. It was real late and no one knew a poor girl who was so upset and been drinking was there. You figured you would take advantage of the situation and wanted to have sex. Tricking a drunken girl after letting her in the apartment saying Michael would be right back you made your move. Of course you were told no. But you know no woman is supposed to say no to the morning lover or did you know that? So he rapes her. Not once, not twice, but over and over until he was done. You know those handcuffs he kept in your place? Those things were around her wrist for three hours so much that her wrist bled from the strain she put on them. She was handcuffed because he didn't like the way he was scratched up when her hands were free. Yes that's right the incredible, irresistible Sebastian Black couldn't take no for an answer. Poor JC he was there that night watching the whole thing, too Meth out to know what was going on. He was killed him for being weak. You don't need weak friends in your life Michael. Oh yes and guess what I found out during my research over the years? Mr. Sebastian is the reason why JC had this heavy drug problem. He was his supplier, because Mr. Sebastian didn't have the cash he led you all to believe he had. You want to know what else. There were at least 20 women that received his brutal attention. How lucky can you be?"

Yes that's the truth. That happened. Tell them the truth.

No one in the room could take their eyes off of Sebastian. He looked at everyone, pleading with his eyes for forgiveness. He could see their disgust and their hope that she was lying. But he knew it was the truth. He did exactly what she said. It was like being before a jury that you knew was going to vote guilty, unanimously.

Michael saw his best friend, a friend now for longer than he could remember as a stranger. He remembered back to the night in question. He remembered coming back to the apartment that he shared with the guys off campus, and hearing what he thought were two people making love. It was just Sebastian and his latest conquest.

He turned around and left spending the rest of the night over at Mona's, she lived off campus as well. He thought nothing of it. When he came home the next day he noticed the scratches Sebastian's had on his neck and face. He asks him about them and he told him that his latest conquest was a wild one, damn bastard.

The pit of Michael's stomach ached like hell as he realized he could have stopped Sebastian. Stopped him from violating yet another woman because he believed all of what she was saying. Stopping Sebastian then would have stopped this darkness that is in Kimberly now. Now they were all here under the wrath of someone who has clearly gone over the edge. Kimberly is dangerous. How was he going to reach her?

Mona remembered her own version of the story as well. She asked Sebastian what girl scratched him up when she heard him bragging to JC; later that week at her apartment. He was so cynical in his response about it that it made her skin crawl. Over the years she never encountered that about him again so she put it out of her mind.

Abigail couldn't believe what she was hearing as well, he did it. It was always in the back in her mind.

"Oh this was just the beginning of a wonderful life. After the attacked I made it back to my cousin's dorm room. She's so wonderful with her analyst babble. She and her boyfriend at the time tried to convince me to call the police but I refused, I couldn't risk a scandal. I especially didn't want you to find out about this Michael and think that I slept with Sebastian to get back at you. So I went on with the pain and without you, hoping you would come back to me. Then about a three month later I found out that I was pregnant. So of course I had to get rid of Sebastian's demon seed. My cousin's boyfriend was a pre-med student and so to avoid attention I let him perform this back alley abortion on me in his off-campus apartment using borrowed equipment from the med school. It worked but I still left school. I was trying to get on with my life. A year later I started dating the son of one of the owners of a pharmaceutical company, filthy rich. We were so in love him and me. He immediately wanted to start a family. When I went to my doctor..."

She paused and the gun in her hand shook violently.

What are you doing? You were doing alright at first. Tell them who it is.

Mona tried to ease pass Michael in an attempt to grab for the weapon. Kimberly recovered and growled at Mona.

"You should be the first I shoot whore bitch. If I were you I would go back and stand by Jackson my ungrateful husband. Yes Mona I know girl you are so shock. Well that's your problem for being a filthy slut whore that you don't profile the men you fall in love with. You see in the society where I come from that is what the rich do. We profile our prospects. You have to seek out their portfolio so you know what you're getting on paper. So you see that my husband knowing that I was from a prominent family didn't know anything else, so it was easy to make him fall in love with me. As I was saying after a trip to my doctor I found that because of my cousin's inept husband ah boyfriend I was left unable to bare children and of course since I couldn't produce an heir, I was asked for a divorce, plain and simple. Once word got around I was cast out not only in my husband's world but in my own world. I was barren. No man wanted to be with me other than for the obvious reasons because I was very beautiful, you see. So the words begin to spread about the woman who fell from grace and her need to do anything to belong. I was quite the one in bed. Since Sebastian showed me that men like it rough. I decided to be rough and very nasty. Soon I didn't want to be with any other man, just you Michael. So when I got cast out I decided that I should give thanks to all that were involved in my downfall. Of course Sebastian you disserved the mighty prize and you're going to get it. But you Mona, you didn't come on board until you taunted me about my baby, those last years a CU. Do you remember that? DO YOU REMEMBER THAT?"

Mona didn't know if she should respond or not. The fact is she did remember that night years ago at the guys place when they were playing their regular poker game and she answered their phone.

There was this creepy music on the other end, the first time she heard something like that. Then there was the female voice talking low so low that she couldn't distinguish what she wanted.

So Mona did what she normally does when she feels someone is trying to prank her, she fights back.

"I'm sorry I didn't know. You weren't speaking up. I thought it was one of those sorority girls making trouble for me. I..."

"Shut up, it's always about you isn't it, savvy Mona, savvy Mona. You see if I had known I would have kept my baby. I wouldn't have giving away my only choice to have a child. Michael I didn't really want you to be involved. I just didn't like your wife. I've been a prisoner in this hell since you did this Sebastian and now you have to pay."

"Kimberly, I thought that was something you wanted. I didn't think I was hurting you," Sebastian pleaded, not really believing he heard himself, but she was holding the gun.

"ARE YOU INSANE? Do you really think that I wanted to be handcuffed and violated all night by my ex-boyfriend's buddy? Get a damn clue. You did exactly what you've been doing all your life, taking from the defenseless but I'm not weak anymore, oh no."

Do it now! Her thoughts screamed.

Kimberly got so enraged that she pointed the gun towards Sebastian in the direction of his lower body and pulled the trigger. The bullet went immediately in his upper right thigh and Sebastian fell to the floor wrenching in pain. Abigail ran to him to stop the bleeding.

"Ha, I was aiming for his penis. I promise I'll aim better the next time."

"You have to stop this Kimberly. It's not too late to stop," Michael said.

"Michael I want to...I don't want to stop. I can't stop. This is what I've been dreaming of. This is his fault and I will not be cheated of the revenge."

****

Natalie arrived at the cable station back entrance. She hoped she wasn't too late to stop Abigail. When she entered the door that was already open she saw the security guard lying on the floor. She went towards him and saw that he was dead. Blood was rushing from his skull from a gunshot wound.

She instantly started looking around fearing she would run into Abigail hastily trying to leave the station. She removed the gun from the security guard's gun belt and walked off towards the backstage. She never had any experiences with a gun but she did have the notion to just point and shoot. Hopefully it will be that easy if she had to use it.

It was dark inside the area she was at. She was scared but she was so worried about Michael that she didn't care. How could she make him believe that his best friend's wife is crazy and bent on revenge?

Natalie had only really been here once with Mona and didn't seriously take down any directions. They could be anywhere. Then as she walked further in down the hall she heard muffled yelling. She slowly but hastily moved toward the sound. Once she saw the light in the sound booth she determined the voices were coming from there.

"You will go to jail. What revenge is that? You don't know how this is going to hurt people. I have a little girl."

"I know Michael, really I do, but I can't leave any witnesses. She told me I couldn't leave any witnesses if it came to this. But you and me..."

"Who told you to do this Kim?"

"Who? No I meant that this is what's been on my mind all this time, all these years, the voices. Stop it Michael, stop confusing me. I know what I have to do."

Natalie stepped up to the outer door of the sound booth. She peered in the window and saw Abigail pointing the gun at everyone who was hurdled to the rear of the booth, Michael in front of them.

She then saw Sebastian bleeding like crazy on the floor and she wondered where the police was. There kneeling beside him was Abigail.

Immediately Natalie knew she was wrong about her all this time. This woman was someone else. She could see little of her face, not enough to recognize her.

She breathed in deeply as she held the gun tightly in her hand. It was now or never that she had only that one chance to catch the woman off guard by opening the door and getting off a shot.

She has never shot anyone before and never even shot a gun. The thought of it made her sick, but Michael and everyone in that room lives depended on what she did in the next few second. Even Sonja did not disserve this.

"So you see Michael it is necessary and we will finally be together. I just…"

Kimberly noticed that Michael's attention went from her to something behind her and then back to her.

Is there someone there and should she take the chance to look. It could be a trick?

You have to look. You must look.

Quickly Kimberly looked behind her and sees Natalie in the window of the booth door, immediately pointing the gun in that direction. Instantly rounds of bullet fire sounded off as everyone duck and dived to the floor. Kimberly shot at the door of the booth screaming like a banshee.

Before she could turn back around to shoot at the others, Michael who hadn't dive for cover tackled her with his full weight and yelled.

"Natalie!"

Mona, Jackson and Sonja got up and ran to help Michael contain Kimberly. She was howling with expletives and twisting her body trying to break free, until Mona hit her hard one good time and she lay limp.

Quickly Michael ran to the outside of the booth and Natalie lay unconscious as the police rushed in with paramedics descending on them. Michael cradled Natalie in his arms.

"Natalie, oh God, please no. You can't leave me please no, don't leave me. I need you. I love you."

Sonja was standing by Abigail by now when she heard him. She was pierced in her heart with what Michael declared. This life threatening situation and he chooses who he really loves and who he is concerned about.

It hurt her deeply more than she wanted to outwardly show. She sobbed silently amiss the chaos as Abigail comforted her. Mona surprised herself as she felt something for Sonja, so much that she shed a tear.

Michael thought of nobody but Natalie as the paramedics worked on her trying to bring her to consciousness.

CHAPTER 17

The next day, Michael stood by the large window of Natalie's hospital room peering out. Actually it looked as if he was standing guard on the highest point in the world, to prevent her from any further harmed.

He should have been able to see through Kimberly's disguise. How could she have been so close, to him and he not recognized her? It's not like she had that much of extensive plastic surgery, just a few minor changes. But of course it's been over ten years and faces fade. Especially the faces you never expect to see again.

It had been years since he saw Kimberly and truthfully after he met Natalie he had forgotten about her. She really did become this ghost of his past.

It was crazy the things that were hidden from him, that he didn't know. His best friend was not someone that he really knew. He was a monster. How could he have given drugs to JC? Then again how could he hold Sebastian to any high regard? Not when he's in his mistress' hospital room, hoping her husband doesn't come charging in, demanding who he is?

It was Mona's idea, a good one at that. It allowed him this time with Natalie. He would wait here all day for her to wake up. He knew he couldn't. Kimberly almost ended his life and he feared that the same thing could have happen to any of them last night.

Mostly he was thinking about Natalie. She risked her life last night running into a situation sight unseen to save his. She was his. This was his choice. How could he choose anyone else? Not Kimberly, not Sonja, no one.

He thought of Sonja and the look she gave him as he cradle Natalie in his arms. He saw it. It was brief but he saw it. How could she think he would do anything else? She knows that the two of them are having problems and she hasn't been the least bit understanding.

It wasn't as if Natalie had been in their presence, physically all these years. At this point there was nothing Michael could do. The façade has faded and the jig was up. It was refreshing that Sonja now knows where she stands. It will make everything much easier. But it won't be easier on Tiffany.

She was the real victim here, but what was he supposed to do, stay in a loveless marriage fighting constantly with her mother until he's forced to leave anyway? Better off to make the change now and help her deal with the madness of it all. He hopes that Sonja doesn't take him through too much bullshit that he backs away completely. Well no that would never, happen. He would challenge Sonja for Tiffany, she is his heart.

Natalie began to stir. Michael lunged from the window to be by her side as she turned toward him and opened her eyes.

"I don't believe it." She said groggily.

"Believe what?"

"I don't believe that you were an angel all along."

"You're not in heaven," he laughed. "Or the other place. It's Chicago Memorial Hospital your home away from home. You loss a lot of blood at the scene last night and passed out from that. The bullet went through your right shoulder and came out the back, cleanly. How do you feel?"

"Tired."

"Baby, I don't know what I would have done if anything had happen to you. I love you baby."

She looked at Michael for a moment before she spoke. He probably will never know how much she really loves him. She was never really good at expressing her feelings, but taking a bullet for the man you love should count as something toward the deal. He was hers and she was his.

"Well you won't get rid of me like that. To think hiring a hit woman to bump me off and she turns out to be a lousy shot. But, I'm dedicated and I love you too damn much to let you go that easily."

Even as she said it she couldn't believe that the words were coming out of her mouth. It must be the pain killers because she spoke the words too easily. No fight with her mind about the morals. It was all about the love she has for Michael Montgomery.

"I hear that."

"So what happen to the shooter?"

"She ended up shooting herself with one of the officers' gun. He got too close to her while she was being taken out. She faked being unconscious and pulled his weapon. She tried to kill herself with it but it was superficial. She kept screaming 'I must die, I must die'. They carted her off to the physic ward where I hope she stays for a long time."

"I know about the dead security officer. Was anybody else hurt? Is Mona alright?"

"Well beside you, Sebastian was the only one who got hit by a bullet in his leg. Kimberly shot him before you got to the station. She was really determined to kill us all, but thanks to you she didn't. Bass will be alright physically, but I don't know…"

Michael had no more to say on the subject of Sebastian. He cut himself off. His one little selfish act could have ended more lives. He's already ruined Kimberly's life to where she felt she had to kill JC. He felt guilty that Kimberly had to endure that because she felt she had to come and apologize to him that night. JC certainly disserved more than what happened to him.

He didn't want Natalie to know any of that. These things were pissing Michael off about Sebastian and this is why he chooses not to think about his dirty deeds. He'll deal with it some other time. At any rate his life with Abigail is going to be pure hell from now on.

"Sebastian is here as well getting prep for surgery. The bullet is being removed."

Suddenly Mona bursts through the hospital room's door in a huff.

"Michael, quick, Christopher's on his way here to see Natalie. You've got to go."

"Damn. Natalie baby, I won't be far," he said as he bent over to kiss her. "Feel better okay."

"I did that when I opened my eyes. I'll see you later."

"Mic, it's now or never."

Michael really didn't want to leave. Deep down, not too far down inside, he wanted to confront Christopher. So a chance meeting like this was right up his alley. He wanted to inform him that he was here take back his woman. That his services to her were no longer needed and if he needed to he would fight for Natalie.

This was all circulating around in his head, but he thought about how much commotion it would cause Natalie while she was recovering. He decided he would wait it out. He has waited this long, he could do that again for a little while more, but only for a little while more.

Michael walked out of the room proudly, while Mona stayed inside. As he approached the corner of the hall to turn towards the elevator he passed Christopher. He wasn't too sure it was him because he only saw a picture on Natalie's desk. Something she says was just up for appearances sake. The two men glanced at each other but it was more of a glare on Michael's part. It was a normal afterthought exchange.

Christopher's mind went to total instant recall as the man passed him. He has seen him before here at the hospital. He has seen him with that woman that Natalie calls her friend, Mona. What is he doing here on this floor? Whatever the reason it had better not involve his wife and the reason why she was shot at some lowly cable station last night. What has Mona Daniels gotten her into? The tip from Natalie sorority sister Sonja Montgomery may just have had some validity to it. Maybe this Mona Daniels needs to be removed from Natalie's life.

When he entered the room he was not the least bit surprised or elated to find Mona in Natalie's room. He couldn't hide his disappointment and felt that he didn't need to hide it. His days with Natalie seem to be over. His image was something that he didn't want tarnished and by God he was not going to disappoint that.

"Natalie good you're awake what happen to you? How are you? Why were you at that cable station last night?" He asked her hesitantly while he looked sternly at Mona.

Mona caught the signal that Christopher wanted some privacy with his wife. Of course he should have that; it is his wife, even though Mona knows the real truth.

After Mona departed Christopher dove into Natalie as if she wasn't lying helpless in a hospital bed recovering from a gunshot wound.

"I don't want that woman near you again. She's nothing but trouble. Why were you shot?"

"Chris, I'm not really feeling up to the question and answer period right now. I just happened to be at the station when that woman opened fire. I'm told the story is in the papers."

"I am about to be the Chief of Staff at a prestigious hospital. All that my wife can tell me is that she just happened to be some place and a woman opened fire. This Mona did she take you there?"

"I was here with Janice and found out that the shooter was going to the party, so I went to warn Mona. When I got there it all happened in a blur."

"Natalie, that doesn't even make sense. I don't think you know what is at stake here. I will not have my children endangered while you go about galloping through the city like a teenager running after a married man."

She couldn't believe what he said or was it that she couldn't believe that he could admit this to himself out loud.

"I'm tired Christopher," is all that she managed to say to him.

"I will not have my children subject to this, just remember that."

In that they had in common. That was all she could think of these days. How was she going to factor Michael into the lives of her children? How could they be together because Christopher will not go in peace? He will try to make her pay for what he feels is her destroying his perfect world.

So he believed Sonja after all. There much she had to think about. She didn't know if she had the strength to fight Christopher and be that love for Michael.

Yes she agrees with her husband on that one thing. She will not have her girls endangered for any reasons. Even if it means that she may not be able to have the love of her life in it. This will need much thought.

****

Three days later Mona sat bright and early morning behind her desk at Cultrax. She was still getting used to Craig not being there with his energetic smile. A heart attack, how? He was so young. He will be missed greatly.

It has been a crazy few months and she has learned a lot. One thing is never to trust men again. How could Jackson have been married to that crazy woman and not know that she was a murderous bitch? She killed JC without so much of a thought and he said that he didn't know anything.

Once the police raided Jackson's home, the evidence was there. Kimberly had everything kept in one room as if it was a museum. She had all of the clothes that she wore at each attempt on everyone's life. The boxes of craft items and fake dead roses were there. Baby dolls with no heads. It was scary to think of. She even had their pictures sprawled all around his home.

But no way did he not know what was happening in his own home. That's why he fled the state. There was no trace of him yet that Mona knew. According to the Illinois state police Jackson Crane just disappeared.

He was on the run. It looked as though he was prepared anyway to go somewhere. The police are thinking Mexico. It was a mystery. Maybe he planned to leave. Maybe he didn't know a thing about it. But the bottom line is that he's gone and without an explanation.

"Ms. Daniels," the female voice on Mona's speakerphone said. "There is a group of high level executives heading this way. I thought you may want to know."

"Thank you Vickie."

Mona got up from her desk. She decided that she was going to greet the gentlemen to find out what would bring them to this level of the complex. Usually if they wanted information about products they would send a messenger or schedule a meeting. What was happening to make these greedy execs, rush her office area?

It must be something about Jackson. She told him that her career was everything, why would he, aid that crazy woman? Now she has to stand in front of respected share owners and explain how she was involved with a felon, her married lover. But how would they know that?

Mona walked out of her office. She stepped out into the open area of her office section, where all of the offices intersect. One of the execs pointed her out to the police. She was greeted by them.

"Mona Daniels, you are under arrest for selling company trade secrets, the theft of documents and samples of the most recent pharmaceutical products that your department is developing. Come with us." The police officer said.

She almost fainted. Is this real? She would never do like this to Cultrax, to herself. She was the most ethical person she knew. She built, no rebuilt Cultrax on her back, there's got to be a mistake.

The police put Mona is handcuffs right in the middle of the Cultrax building once they were there. The execs wanted the rest of the employees to see what would happen to them if they decided to sell company secrets.

Employees were all in their individual offices. Looking out of the glass windows that separated the buildings on the inside, creating a street effect. In fact that area was nicknamed Main Street, because it connected the entire four building sections around it.

At first Mona had her head held high because she knew she was innocent. Once it sank in that this company would never risk being sued she knew it was serious and she lowered her head.

She knew they would not go this far if they weren't certain. What is going on, she thought as she was placed in a federal police car that was waiting outside in the courtyard entrance, with the motor running?

****

Later that day Michael listened intently to Mona, at her condo, as she explained in details what happened to her earlier. Of course she called Michael as soon as she was able to make a phone call. She had told him only that she had been arrested and needed her lawyer. She wanted to get the ball moving on her defense and have support at the same time.

Michael called her lawyer and then Sebastian. He wasn't really talking to Sebastian right now but he decided that he would let him know what was happening. He waited on calling Natalie because he just wanted her to get her rest. She had already been through enough.

"Well this is what they're saying, that I gave Minolta Laboratories my copies of the new diabetes medicine that we are about to release to the market. It was found that Minolta was developing the pill from some of my samples and notes. Of course it was going to take time for them to fully develop the pills. They have to be sure it is what we say it is, but they have the jumpstart they needed. But it is definitely what Cultrax has. It's my baby. Why would I do that? With this project I was going to be setup for life. Their saying that I received a fifty thousand dollar payment to a bank account that isn't, even, mine but was apparently opened up by me, recently. There were airline tickets brought supposedly by me to Puerto Rico that were open tickets, so that I could leave at a moment's notice they said. It was all very well planned. I had even supposedly brought a villa there. Whoever set me up made this plan almost picture perfect. Even my lawyer says that it is going to be hard to punch holes in this story. And my career, my credibility, everything is gone. Guys I may even go to jail."

She started to cry.

Michael got up and went to her to comfort her. This was not a way that he had ever wanted to see Mona. She was always strong-willed, smart and ahead of the game. He knew she felt helpless.

"Mona there has got to be an explanation for this. There has got to be a loop. No setup is full proof. We're missing something. All we have to do is pull on the right string hard enough and the answer will fall like rocks down a mountain. All we need is the string." Michael assured her.

"I don't know Mic. I don't know where I could begin. It looks like I just walked out of my office one day and handed over all my information to Minolta. They paid me a deposit and I look like I was fleeing the country."

"Mona, that's it. That is it. Jackson Crane. He fled the country, well Mexico, but he's still in hiding. He may have something to do with it."

Jackson again, well that could be possible but how could he have done this.

"No Michael that's just too farfetched but I appreciate you trying to help me."

Michael just wouldn't let it go.

"Mona, how much about Jackson do you know? He just came out of nowhere and you never really said where you met him."

Mona was never going to tell Michael because then she would have to tell it all. That was the night that Sebastian and she were together sexually for the first time.

She didn't want Michael to know that. He was already having a hard time with what had happened to Kimberly because of Sebastian. She didn't want to add fuel to the fire. She never wanted Michael to look at her the way he now looks at Sebastian.

"Not much I guess."

****

When Michael got home later Sonja was in not so rare form. She was angry because Michael went to comfort his sweet Mona on top of all the other things that were going terribly wrong. This was the first time in four days that they were really able to discuss what happened at the cable station that night.

Sonja was staying with Abigail all this time and decided just today to come home. Their daughter was now permanently over her grandmother's for the rest of the summer until this nasty business was solved.

"Well I see this line to get your attention is never ending. You go to anyone but me in times of crisis, don't you? JC dies you're right there. Sebastian gets shot, off you go. Mona gets arrested, again can't wait to be there. And your precious Natalie is shot, you declare your love for her. I knew you were seeing her, you lied to me."

"I never lied to you because you never asked me. You just made innuendos and I never responded. How do you expect me to tell you something like that when I wasn't sure myself?"

"It's easy, you say, Sonja I'm seeing, sleeping with Natalie because I'm in love with her. I hate you."

"I guess you always did huh? What did you ever like about me other than the fact that you took me from Natalie."

She glared at him speechless. He said her dirty little secret, the one she thought he never knew. How did he know?

"Why would say that? Who told you that?"

"I really never knew until now, but it was something that Kimberly said about not believing what you did. She saw a lot of what others did not. She saw our good and our bad. So I believe while she was watching me, she saw what you did. I don't even care what but it is probably why we never really clicked well. I'm just as guilty myself. I moved on too fast after Natalie when I knew that I was not over her. For that I am really sorry…"

"Michael I still love you. I want this to work for you and me."

"I…"

He couldn't say it and be honest. He didn't know what he wanted to do. It's not like Natalie is beating a path to his door. They were having their fling but nothing was concrete.

He spoke out of turn that night at the station only because he thought he was going to lose her. He wasn't yet ready to declare it to the world and definitely not to Sonja. But the cat is out of the bag now and there was no pretending, not anymore.

"I'm not focusing right now…"

"You are giving me mixed signals Michael. I'm not going to be here forever. I will get a plane ticket. Taylor and I will be out of here, back to Michigan with my family."

Tickets, Michael thought, the tickets that Mona supposedly purchased. We can start there. The time and date had to be stamp on them even the location as to when and where it was purchased. All of the receipts and everything Mona's lawyer had to have copies of. If they trace it, maybe they can find out who really set all this up.

"I got to go Sonja, something just came up."

"What, I didn't hear any calls. Are you telepathic now, Michael?"

"I don't want to get into now with you because it'll be taken out of context. I just gotta go."

He left just like that. Like, they weren't even married. Like, they were just roommates. Sonja just breathed in deeply and that was it. So it begins she thought. All of her plans were coming to an end.

****

Jackson Crane groggily got out of the bed. The constant knocking on his motel room door made sure he would get no rest. It must be the front desk manager, he thought.

He looked over to the nightstand and saw his wallet and car keys lying there so he knew he hadn't left the items at the desk. He had paid the bill in advance to cover the short time he would be there.

Then he paused just as his hand was about to open the door. The police, he hadn't thought about them. After all this was the meeting point that he had set-up with Leanne well Kimberly.

She must have told the police that this placed was where they agree to meet and she would again frame Mona. She was supposed to kill them all that night and he would help her move Mona's body from the murder scene, to dispose of later.

This was so that she could continue on as Mona until they were out of the country, secretly returning via Canada to the United States.

It was an ambitious plan but Kimberly told them that it would work. She didn't count on herself losing control of the situation.

So the police were finally at the door and his perfect plan is going to hell. With all his planning and putting up with that psycho to, only be betrayed by her.

This was something that he could have done on his own, but he allowed his lust for Mona to control his thoughts. He wanted to have fun and felt that he could show Kimberly how to really be loose.

He knew she was unstable but he pushed at her anyway. Who knew she had these issues with sex and this trauma. If he knew he would have definitely taking another route.

It was a beautiful ride. He had the money and more on the way. His contact paid him a pretty penny for Cultrax's information and still don't know how it was all accomplish. Best they didn't.

The banging was intense now and Jackson knew before long the police would get tired of waiting and kick in the door. So he breathed in deeply, grabbed the door knob and opened it.

"Kimberly," he said in surprise. "What are you doing here? I thought you were taking in by the police, that you were shot. It was all in the news."

She stood at the doorway smiling so broadly that you would have thought that she had won the lottery. He was a disgusting, perverted, idiot, she thought but that means that her work was almost done.

"You can't believe everything you hear."

She was different he thought. What has happened in those few days that changed this weak and confuse woman into the seemingly strong willed goddess. Could this be new personality suddenly taking over her for good now? If so she needs this one.

Just by the aura along Jackson felt her power and his lust stirred for her like in the beginning when they first met. She was exactly the same as she was then. It wasn't until later that she turned pathetic and weak.

"We need to get out of here and to another motel. I'm sure the police know about all this."

"How, did you tell them anything?"

"Everything, I couldn't stop from falling into their traps. I had to give them the plan or I wouldn't have made bail."

This was crazy. The papers said she was wounded when she attempted to kill herself with a weapon she grabbed from one of the police officers. Now she is standing here none the wear and ready to flee.

"Jackson, you look like hell. You need to relax. Let's have a drink. I brought some brandy that should help you to calm down. Sit down; I'll fix you a drink."

She went over to the musky nightstand, sat on the other bed and began pouring the drink. He was leery of her so he kept his eye on her, just in case she tried to slip something in his drink. She was different and she seemed untrustworthy.

As he continued to watch her with scrutiny, she became aware of him.

"You are going to worry yourself into a heart attack if you keep this up. Here you go."

She handed him the glass of brandy and he took it with confidence. He had been watching her the whole time so he knew the drink was safe. He had to be cautious.

He had seen her pour it directly from the bottle into the glass, one of the glasses that were already in his room. He drank down the liquid quickly as if it was just a shot.

"Now don't you feel better?" She said to him resealing the bottle without pouring a drink for herself.

Jackson nodded and then instantly felt himself begin to feel sleepy.

"Something doesn't feel right. What's happening?"

She got up from the bed she was sitting on and sat beside him on the other bed. In her left hand she held a needle filled with a liquid substance.

"I'm happening."

****

Natalie thought about Michael as she lay in the hospital bed contemplating her marriage. Everybody except Christopher now knew that Michael was in love with her. She can safely guess that they knew she loves him as well.

What a nightmare they endured and when she thought she was going to lose Michael again it made her reckless. It could have been her that died that night along with the security officer.

Christopher questioned her for four days straight about why she rushed there to the cable station that night. He was told by one of the staff that she was seen hurrying out of the hospital in a panic, no doubt heading to the station.

That story was at least corroborated but did it do any good? She could only use Mona as an excuse. She was going to save her friend she said. She just couldn't let her die with knowing that she was in danger.

He questioned her about Michael. He told her he knew that he had come to see her while she was in the hospital. He knew he was there last night. He just left it like that.

This was the first time in their entire marriage that she felt he was the least bit threatened by someone else occupying his wife's time. It was a milestone that Natalie thought may try to trap her in this marriage forever. He couldn't be that concerned could he?

Just then the door to her room opens and in walks Janice. She was dressed like she was going on a date, but Natalie knew she hadn't begun to date; even though her husband was dead all these years.

"Natalie, how are you?"

"I'm fine Janice, how are you?"

"I'm sorry I've been gone a few days, I had an emergency myself. I heard about that nasty business with 'Karen' ah Kimberly. I did not know she was talking about your friends.

Mona, my God she was a target as well, that VPO whore. Talk about six degrees of separation. It was a lucky thing that I decided to discuss that with you or she would have killed more than just a few people. The papers were very vivid and I had to instruct my assistant to release all the data I had on her."

"I couldn't believe my fortune that you and I discussed all of that. It was almost like the information fell in my lap."

Dr. Edwards looked at her friend and smiled.

"Well that was my free gift to you. After all you are my friend and I'm glad you're safe. But I warn you, you better be careful from now on because I can't give you any more free passes."

The two of them giggle together like school girls.

"It must have been scary."

"Yes for my part in it was terrifying. I was about to shoot her. I've never thought of doing something like that before. I was so…"

"Are you serious?" Dr. Edwards said in disbelief cutting her off. "You were going to shoot her. Oh you must tell me the gory details."

Natalie was sure that Janice did not mean to sound so sinisterly interested in what happen that night at the station. To any outsider it surely sounded something straight out of a psychological thriller. But it was all too real for Natalie each time she told it.

****

"So that's what we thought when we investigated the airline tickets Sebastian," Michael said to Sebastian while he laid stationary in his hospital bed at Chicago Memorial.

Two grueling weeks had passed by and Michael wanted to share the information he had on Mona's case with Sebastian. It took Michael this long to face his buddy.

"It was that Thursday night when Mona met Jackson at the Pill. First a bank account was created in Mona's name. Fifty thousand dollars was posted into the account. There was a purchase of airline tickets and a villa in Puerto Rico."

"So Mona is cleared right?"

"She's with her lawyer now. They still want to know how Minolta got a hold of Mona's company information."

"This is so weird that this is happening to her. Are there anymore leads?"

"Well Mona says that she is certain that Jackson slipped her an Ecstasy pill and that there was some woman in her room. Maybe…Se turn up the TV, there's some breaking news."

Michael said pointing to the TV hovering above Sebastian's bed.

'…and the California State Highway Patrol, is certain that the man found dead at the Seaside Motel, near the San Diego Freeway, is Jackson Crane. Jackson Crane is the alleged husband of deranged murderer Kimberly Stanford. Crane fled Chicago right after Stanford attempted to murder 95.8 radio personality Sebastian Black better known as 'the Morning Lover', his wife and several other people three weeks ago at a party at local cable station KXITV. Black was seriously injured in the incident and is recuperating at Chicago Memorial Hospital. Police say that Stanford had been stalking her intended victims and was not clear how long. It is not certain that Crane had anything to do with the attempt but he was there the night of the incident. Crane was found in the motel room dead from an apparent heart attack. Police say a large amount of money was in the room as well as various drug paraphernalia. Chicago 7 will follow this story.'

"Damn Mic now all my business is out there all over Chicago and everywhere. I'll have to leave here before the groupies come."

"Se Jackson Crane is dead. He died of a heart attack."

"So?"

"Did Jackson look like he could have a heart attack to you? The man was in great shape. You could tell he hit the gym on a regular."

"Once again so?"

"JC had a heart attack and you know so did Mona's coworker. And you remember when Sonja said she was attacked by that nurse? Her potassium level had risen but not enough to give her a heart attack. Sebastian it makes sense kind of. These murders were all Kimberly and the attempt as well. Now the only one that doesn't make sense is Jackson's death. Not unless there is someone else."

"Michael let it go. That loser probably was using some of those drugs the police found in his motel room with him. He probably was on steroids or something. Now I do believe that he may know more about how Mona got setup, but Kimberly was acting out there alone."

"No that's not what she said. Remember she said she's making me do this."

"Good luck with that Mic, the ramblings of a craze killer. Besides I was only in intense pain, near passing out how could I possibly miss all of that?" He said mockingly.

"Well I got to say this that you brought it on yourself. What were you thinking?"

"Mic please don't, do this here. I will talk to you about this when I get out of here. I already have too much on my mind with Abigail not speaking to me. It's a good thing that I have a room here because she told me that I was not welcome at the house, she wants a divorce."

"Okay buddy, I'll back off."

"How's Natalie?"

"She's okay, just recovering slowly. I think I'm going to ask her to leave her husband. I promised her while she was recuperating I wouldn't press her about it, but just as soon as she's healed I will do it."

"Just prepare yourself just in case she says no."

CHAPTER 18

Sonja had been living over at the Blacks with Abigail, she had officially separated from Michael but most recently rescinded the decision. They were still not totally together but Sonja wanted to come home so she could resume rebuilding her store. Sebastian was staying over Michael's house once he got of the hospital.

It didn't take Abigail but three weeks from there to file for divorce, unattested. She told him that if he didn't want her to go public with their story, he would sign the papers and he did. He moved out of Michael's when Sonja came home and into a condo in Mona's neighborhood.

Mona was cleared of all she was accused of doing. Cultrax made a public apology and Mona was given all the perks she wanted. It was Jackson and Kimberly who had stolen Mona's identity and created all the false evidence that led to her downfall.

The evidence was found on Jackson when he died at the motel. He was an employee at Minolta Laboratories and was trying score big there. They found out that a number other Minolta employees was involved in the big payout. Jackson really was on the run.

His meeting Kimberly was totally consequential that night at the Yahoo swing party. There were letters written to him in detail how they would proceed in their corporate crime. However there was no indication that Jackson knew what Kimberly was up to.

It didn't make since to Michael because Jackson and Kimberly were married. They lived together so there was no need to send letters of instruction. They could just discuss it when they were together. It was as if someone was trying to make sure that all the evidence pointed to those two.

Michael couldn't put his finger on it but it seemed that with Jackson's death, the attacks and all the weird stuff just stopped. The mystery remains. Kimberly wanted revenge and Jackson wanted money. But there was someone else, he was sure that wanted something as well, who?

There was no lead on how Jackson met his end. But his death became questionable. Once again it looked as though someone wanted the world to believe that he was a drug user.

The police, however, decided that it was foul play. This was due to Michael, bringing attention to the facts. He exposed that the few people that Kimberly, medically had access to, had high levels of potassium in their body. That was the link, but to what?

****

It took Natalie about exactly two and half months to fully heal once she was out of the hospital. She wasn't feeling herself even after she had laid off the medication about a month ago. She was taking it slow and enjoyed the time away from the routine life she had fallen into. However, when she was with Michael there was nothing routine about that.

Even during her last few nights at the hospital, Michael would sneak in to see her with the help of Mona. She was in an arm sling, then a cast and then not. He sat patiently watching her heal slowly but surely each day. Michael on those days would sneak out and none would be the wiser or at least they hoped.

Now Natalie was free to resume in full swing their love affair. Michael had promised, during the entire time that Natalie was recuperating, to never bring up the question of leaving their spouses.

It was noon, Thursday and Michael met Natalie at their usual spot, the Montage hotel. Like always they would have a drink, sometimes it would be wine or champagne or other times it would be juice.

Today it would be Château Pichon-Longueville, Lalande 1986 a special occasion to build on. It was well over three hundred dollars for a bottle. With all his good fortune and Natalie's love why not romance her with one of the best little red wines?

When they met this time in the room the air was different. It was as if the cosmos had tipped itself off of its axis. He noticed that Natalie seemed distant and he couldn't understand it.

He pushed the thoughts aside as Natalie walked towards him and kissed him deeply and their lovemaking was on. Michael held her closer to him as his tongue encircled the fading scar left by Kimberly's bullet.

He wanted her to know that he remembered the sacrifice she made to end up with this. No woman had ever given him anything more. Natalie moaned in pleasure as if to let him know that she confirmed what he was thinking. They made love.

****

An hour later they lay beneath the silky like comforts, their passion cooled and eyes never leaving one another's gaze.

"Natalie, leave Christopher and marry, me."

He wasn't being fair, she thought. He had lulled her into a sense of comfort, euphoria, with his sex, his presence. He dropped this big request on her, knowing very well she would love to say yes.

Leaving Christopher is something that she has been entertaining over these last few months since she rekindled things with Michael.

Easier said than done; she liked things the way they were because it was safe. She didn't have to worry about disappointing Michael and he couldn't know that she had flaws. If she went with him he could suddenly realize that she wasn't worth the wait and she could end up with more problems.

She had to think of more than just herself, did Michael know this? They weren't this college co-ed love mates with a full life ahead of them and no responsibilities. At any rate the question was here. She had to be honest and it was time to face him with her true feelings. Once again she didn't trust enough in their love to see it through.

There was again an excuse to deny real love; deny Michael. What the hell was wrong with her?

"Michael it's complicated. You just don't know how much. You're not looking at the big picture; you don't see."

He got up from the bed and walked over to the window to look out, not really at anything really.

"I see you and you see me and I know that you love me. I know that you have never stopped loving me and that is all that I'm thinking about right now. So I'm asking you, do you want to be together or what?"

Natalie got up and went into the bathroom. She closed the door without responding.

He heard the shower start to run as he left the window and sat on the bed. It was like a desperate feeling that Michael felt. Maybe if he could reach down in his heart and rip it out he could spare himself the pain of what he was feeling.

He loved Natalie with all his heart, he knew that, more than any man should ever love one woman. How is it that he can't be with her? Who is making these damn rules and why couldn't he win.

He sat back on the bed and decided that he would take a break from all this drama. But how could he escape it. It hurts just as much not to feel anything as it did when he felt something. If it were that easy, it would, have been done without hesitation. It was with him everyday like some bad drug habit that just keeps coming back.

Natalie was his habit that he could never break. A drug that showed so much potential in the beginning and when it got too much it was snatched away without so much of a smack across the face. Maybe he should go talk to Natalie's psyche friend Janice Edwards; maybe she could help him make some sense of this nightmare he couldn't wake from.

He knew that he had to make the only decision that would give his mind some ease. Could he make it? The number one question that will never have an answer, Michael knew the answer to. He may have to put Natalie out of his mind and stop living a lie.

Natalie emerged from the bathroom refreshed after taking the shower. The first thing she did was look at Michael with all her heart. She really did love him.

"I'm not getting what I want," he whispered to her.

"What did you say Michael?"

He didn't know if he could repeat it. It was crazy. Here, he is with the woman of his dreams, his soul mate and he couldn't talk. It was too much and he had to stop playing games. It was time to pay the piper for all that he has gotten; his chance to be with his love again. Maybe that was all it was meant to be, a chance.

At any rate it was time to make the decision. It would be great if he was one of those men that found being with two women the stud thing to do, but that wasn't how he was. He loves this one woman and if that makes him weak, then hell that is what he is.

Natalie Vincent had his heart locked. But if he can't have her, than he has to get out of this, because he can't freaking think, just having part of it.

"I'm not getting what I want, Natalie."

"You're not giving me a chance to breathe and take this all in."

"Natalie, it's been months. You and I both agree that we were in marriages that we never should have been in. You tell me that you love me, but you won't commit to me. I mean really, what is the problem?"

There was dead silence in the room as he thought in his mind that he went too far with his plea. She was now thinking that she was not being fair to Michael again; just stringing him along.

"I agree, you're right, but this man is the father of my..."

"...children, yeah, I know and did so much for your career, blah, blah, blah. Damn Natalie you can't have it all. Something is going to be rough. If you're going to be with me, it's going to be rough in the beginning. But I've had eight years to think about this and I've never stopped wanting to be with you forever. But you know," Michael said as he stood up and walk towards the window again. "I'm tired of trying to convince you to stay with me, that choice is at least mine. I don't want to be with Sonja anymore and you're all I have. God, why can't you see this, don't you love me, Natalie?"

"Michael, just give me time..."

"Time's up baby. It's all I can do to keep my sanity, which means if keep this up. If I am going to live in this hell with Sonja, I won't let you dangle this love in my face."

Michael walked towards the bathroom.

"Baby, I can't do this..." He opened the door to the bathroom. "...I just can't do this anymore. Maybe you should leave, please, just leave."

He closed the door behind him.

****

The elevator rested at the first floor to the lobby. As the doors opened, Natalie slowly emerged not knowing what to think. Her mind was flood with thoughts.

What went on up there? What has changed all of sudden? One minute Michael and she were embroiled in their love for one another and now this.

I cannot believe this, she thought. *What did I do*?

However, she knew. She knew that once again she chose what is safe over what is unsure.

Of course, she was sure of Michael's love for her; that was not it. Her insecurities were that she has never had to make a decision to throw her life to the wind before. To just pick up and start anew; the uncertainty of things has never been Natalie best forte. So he made the choice for her.

She slowly moved through the lobby of the hotel as she considered her options. She could go back upstairs to the room, sit down, and try to reconnect deeper with Michael, to try to reach some kind of compromise, but to what use?

He asked her, no he begged her to be gone when he returned from taking a shower. She heard his plead in his voice, the hurt. That's why she obeyed him; she heard it and it crushed her. She thought he would make love to her again, but it was not to be.

He was wonderful she agreed and he adores, no, he worships her. Though she did not purposely take advantage of what he felt for her, she did feel herself, sometimes doing just that.

Was it because she knew that he would always be there? Did he really know how much she loved him? Did she really ever get that across to him? What if he was gone, would she feel any different? Would it affect her? Did she really have to ask that question? Of course, it would affect her. How much, she did not want to think about that. What if she, just went home? What will be tomorrow?

Natalie sat down on the sofa in the lobby near the huge canvas picture window. She had looked at this furniture every time she came here with him. However, it only became scenery to her, on her way to her true destiny with Michael. She never imagined that she would one day just stop and take in the surroundings or that it would be a comfort for her.

She decided she would wait here for him to come down and then they would talk again, here, about their future. She was not sure, but to Natalie, she had an awful feeling that she has thrown away her chance with him. Well at least, she has caused a little friction.

Why was she resisting what she felt? Why would it be so hard for her to just up and leave? Isn't that what she felt like doing for years, many, many years?

Reality is that she has married to a cynical fool and that will be her pain for the rest of her life. At least until she runs out of things to keep her busy from him and putting off divorce will not be an option.

Why all of a sudden when the choice is, given to her, it suddenly became one of the highest hurdles of her life. She had decided long ago that if she ever got a chance with Michael again, she would seize it.

She no longer was in love her husband, fact one. She was no longer threatened by Sonja, fact two. It was the kids that she thought about, but even that could be, worked out. They were already used to their father not being there and who knows he may have an entirely new family elsewhere. She has thought that before, even confronted him.

It was not the kids and all the other things that she kept using as excuses to not make her decision, it was, her. She was the one stalling all because she was too afraid to make a choice that she felt was too soon, too hard. But why was it too soon? Why did it feel like this was too hard?

Natalie felt the weight of all this and relaxed further into the comfort of the sofa. As she directed her attentions to the outside of the streets through the picture window, she saw Michael. He was waiting on the curb, about to cross the street. How did he get there? When did he pass by me? She wondered.

She was transfixed as she stood up and went to the window. He was crossing the street by now and all she could do was watch him. What was he doing?

He, had to be going to his car but why?

She didn't want to let in the thought that was bursting to get out at her. He was leaving. That would be the only reason why he would be going to his car. What was he thinking?

She moved closer to the window almost attempting to walk threw it. Michael opened his car door, she saw him do that and then he got in and drove away. It was like slow motion.

She felt the shock from what she was seeing and knew what it meant. She knew that a change had occurred between the time she spoke her last words to him and now. He has removed her options. She no longer had that power to keep him waiting while she wrestled with whatever morals or decisions she could throw at him.

Almost in a panic, Natalie quickly went backward, almost stumbling, almost staggering, to sit back down on the sofa. It was too overwhelming to think about the possibility of what was happening; Natalie almost fainted.

Simultaneously her cell phone rang wildly and she immediately thought it was Michael. She knew she had hurt him when she chose her current life over him. Kimberly had hurt him, so did Sonja and now today she has joined these women and he was gone. He was gone and he did not even bother to say goodbye...

"Hello...yes Dr. Austin, I'm glad you could return my call..."

She hadn't been feeling quite herself lately since leaving the hospital. So she had a physical to make sure that she was okay and not seriously damaged by her recent trauma.

As the doctor spoke to her, she was so shocked that she couldn't speak, as she listened intensely.

****

Much later that night when Michael arrived home, he hesitated going inside. He had been driving around for hours after leaving the hotel with Natalie, thinking.

He placed his key into the first lock and he felt the tear fall on his hand, as thought about Natalie and their last conversation together.

What did she expect him to do this time, wait around for her to lock his heart down again for another ten years? He would be as he was for so many years, never quite able to love freely and totally giving some other woman her fair chance.

In no way did he doubt Natalie's love for him, not even once. He knew she was very much in love with him; but she would not take the risk to be with him. That realization hurt Michael deeply. Why wouldn't she?

There was no turning back now so what does he do? He cannot go back to before Natalie, because if anything she has awakened in him, something that has been dead a long time. He cannot stay where he is with Sonja, because that's where he died.

He had to move on possibly. He had to create a common ground with Sonja, for Tiffany's sake, if he decides to leave and he can never revisit anything with Natalie again. He placed his key in the second lock he felt another tear and thought how easy it was to think. The real deal is he loves Natalie with his very breath. He could say that forever.

Yes, it was wrong because she belongs to another man, but it was wrong for the fates to play this trick on him. Why can't a man have the woman that he loves and that loves him? What could possibly be, accomplished by having to struggle through, a relationship that only fueled by despair?

He was sure that he never really loved Sonja. Sonja was somebody that he had settled on. No, that's not right he thought, Sonja has good qualities that drawn him to her.

He had loved her once because she was focused, a great mother and for a time she seemed interested in what he was interested in. It was just a simply thing of the two of them growing apart.

That could have easily happen if Natalie and he had been married, no guarantees. However deep in his heart, Michael knew that he would have gladly taken the chance with Natalie, but given the choice to renew with Sonja again, he wouldn't do it.

He made his way into the kitchen and sat down on one of the stools that surrounded the large kitchen island. This was the thinking tank, this spot right here, he thought.

Earlier, some months ago, Sonja was sitting in this exact same place staring off into a void trying, he guessed, to understand what was happening to her. He had asked her why she hadn't just gone to bed and slept on it, but now he understood the comfort this spot must have been to her. It just seemed like the ideal spot to be.

He saw mail on the baker's rack and retrieved it. Flipping through it he saw a letter address to him marked, urgent. He opened the envelope and inside was what looked like two birth certificates. He pulled them out.

The first one had the name Kimberly Stanford on it and the typical stuff you see on certificates. The second had Kimberly Prentiss. What was this about Michael thought to himself? So Kimberly had an alias, why would someone send him this?

He went to set the envelope down on the kitchen island. Another document fell out on the surface. Michael picked it up and read it. It was a marriage license. The names on the license were Kimberly Stanford and Everett Edwards.

What's this all about? Kimberly is married to a man who's last name is Edwards. Strange, that's Natalie's friend's last name,

Janice Edwards. Kimberly said she didn't get married. He didn't get it.

Nothing that made any sense, made any sense to Michael. He had too much on his mind for puzzles. For the first time in his life, he had no direction, no ideas and no means of escape, from this crisis that was before him; a no win situation.

Some married men that leave their wives, kids and home lives make it seem so easy. They make the new life that they get as a trade, seems like something made for the history books. All that Michael felt right now was pain. Mostly because, when he had asked Natalie to leave, her married life, she didn't agree to do it.

The nerve of him he realized now. How selfish of him, to ask her to do something that was clearly tearing him up to do. Then it hit him, that feeling of awareness, awakening. He had asked Natalie to do what he knew that ultimately she would not be able to do.

Could it be that he too didn't have the guts to take them to the next level? Subconsciously did he try to leave it in Natalie's hands, knowing she wouldn't do it? Why was it so important that she made the total commitment when he hasn't left home?

It wasn't in her nature to take something for herself and run with it. He knew that she has always, even when they were not together, chosen sacrifice over personal gain. Now she has children. Both of her parents raised her and so will her children be raised; no matter what.

Maybe he was wrong, Michael thought. Maybe it was just as simple as she always had a sanctuary with him, within him and keeping it open would keep the hope of love alive. Michael felt even more longing for Natalie because to him she never has lived her potential in love.

What they had, have, had together is a once in a lifetime thing. This is his view. He wanted them to be together now and knew it would not be like before. But it would be love with his woman.

Natalie may not have wanted this dream, or may not have known that even she disserved to be as happy as she was with him. She was always on a technical mission. Doing what others thought was the right thing for her.

****

What will he say to her, he thought as he got up from the stool and made his way to the stairs? What could he say? What does he say to eyes that have been eluding him for all these years?

Since the last time they really talked about their marriage, he has seen a change; but is that enough. It may just be too late to accept the change now. Would Sonja settle on being second best, her words, not his? He still loved her, but there was the matter of being in love with his soul mate, Natalie.

He will always be in love with Natalie; he has accepted this. God has chosen this journey for Michael, he was sure, but he didn't understand it.

Could he actually make the efforts and make it appear effortless, because Sonja will be watching. He had said too much, she had said this and that, but no one is the victor. What was he going to do, make amends? Could they...no time for indecisions, he thought as he opened their bedroom door.

"Sonja, are you up, I'm home, and it's time we talked..."

****

Natalie pulled up in front of Michael's house and parked her car. She wasn't sure if this was something that she should do but she had to tell him and Sonja.

Was this vengeance? She thought for hours what to do but he has to know that she is pregnant. What were they thinking sleeping around like a couple of college lovers? Why was it always coming down to them being apart, with the chance to be together?

Will Michael still want to be with her or will he just choose his hell with Sonja, in the presence of lies? What will Sonja and Christopher do with the news? What will happen with her girls and his daughter? These are all question that they never thought about and now there really is no turning back.

She picked up her cell phone and dialed his.

Inside the house Michael has Sonja's attention and is about to tell her...he saw Natalie's number as he looked down at his cell phone and thought how bad her timing is. Even though tonight's event made little sense to him, he knew he could never deny her his attention. He would never deny her, ever and so he chose to answers the call.

"Hello." He said softly.

"Michael, I've got to talk to you before you talk to Sonja."

"Well that's a little beside the point now isn't it?"

"Michael, who is that calling this late?" Sonja screamed from the bed.

She was not as convincing as she would have like to have been. She knew it was Natalie and Michael knew she knew, but he listened intently to the woman he loves.

As Natalie told him the reason for her call, Sonja called Michael's name repeatedly. It was like a distant voice, trying to lure him away from paradise.

"Michael, answer me. Who is that? Michael! Michael!"

He clasped on the side of the bed and grabbed his forehead. He started to laugh himself and then loudly. It was going to be a long night.

****

In the late hours of the night, Dr. Edwards walked through the door of Chicago Mental Hospital. The electronic doors slid open to accommodate her. She was in fairly good spirits as she glided across the lobby floors on her way to the elevators.

She walked in the elevator slowly as the elevator door closed behind her and she pushed the number five on the floor selector. She busily hummed to herself to pass the time on ride up and then the doors let open to the floor she chose.

She exited the elevator and started down the long white, sterile hallway. She showed her ID badge to the security officer that guarded this section of the hospital. She stopped at the last door of the hallway, took out a key and unlocked the small window to the room inside. Nonchalantly, she peered into the window to the view the female occupant who was sitting on the floor strapped in a strait jacket.

"She's a nutty one Dr. Edwards," a doctor standing beside her said, jarring her from her thoughts. "Dr. Boggs left here earlier commenting on how many personalities this patient has."

"Nutty, doctor, isn't that a little insensitive?"

"Tell that to the poor guard she murdered. The poor girl she shot and the others that she stalked for years. No I think it's right on it. The latest personality started to surface just recently. She claims to be a psychiatrist."

"Really a psychiatrist eh? Well I guess imitation is the best form of flattery."

"I guess if you think having a mentally disturb woman as a fan is flattering; sounds dangerous."

"Only, if you don't handle it right. Doctor, I think I'll spend some time with her and maybe she will manifest this psychiatrist for me."

Dr. Edwards watched as the doctor slowly walked down the hall away from her. She turned and slowly opened the door to the hospital room. Once inside the room she walked up to the patient who was still sitting on floor leaning against the wall in a strait jacket Dr. Edwards insist they put on her. She smoothed her skirt as she knelt down beside the subdued woman.

"Hello Kimberly," she said aloud as if she thought someone was listening. "I came by to see how you were doing. I know it's been awhile but I've been busy since you ran rampant. I had a lot of inquiries to fulfill and of course the other thing."

She looked up at Dr. Edwards with contempt in her eyes. She was barely able to form thoughts and her mouth was very dry.

"You will never get away with this..." She hissed at the doctor.

She was weak from the medication the hospital staff kept pumping into her veins. Dr. Edwards insured that a heavy rotation of meds was kept in her system.

"Me?" she said in sing-song voice and then lowered her voice. "I had nothing to do with this. You stop taking the meds. You let yourself get caught."

"But you were the one all along; you're Kimberly, not me...I'm Dr. Janice Edwards."

"Are you sure dear?"

"You know I'm sure, Kimberly."

"Well it's your own fault. Maybe you should not have had so many personalities."

"Those were personalities that you created."

"Yes I did, but apparently they were too much for you. The plan was so perfect, well thought out. You were going to kill all my enemies for me, dear. Then you were going to kill yourself and I would be left with your life and your career. When that idiot Jackson came into the picture with the scheme to steal samples and documents from Mona was the perfect idea to ruin her and bring pain to her. I made you into Désiree, because that perverted JC consumed exotic dancers daily. I had those personalities so well in hand that you really thought you were me."

"He loved you, did you know that? You shouldn't have kill him or any of the others."

"What the hell? Where did that come from? Of course I didn't know. And what does it matter? He didn't love me enough to save me from his lecherous friend. He just sat there watching, helpless as I was tortured, high on his drugs. Once I told him the truth, he had to die anyway. He became a loose end, just like Jackson. I would never allow anyone to be a loose end. I just got back from California. It was a wonderful little trip. I wanted my revenge and a new life, your life, the life of Dr. Janice Edwards, psychologist and I have it, I will have it. No one is going to stop me. I won't have to be poor Kimberly anymore. I'll continue to act on your behalf from now on. I'll have your inheritance and your career. You let yourself be overtaken because it was too much for you to handle, your life and all of this. You don't think that I knew that you were trying to break free of my hold. You were trying to confess instead of shooting them all when you had the chance, the nerve. Shooting them would have been the right thing to do. I'm not going to take responsibility for your mistakes. I had this all planned dear cousin Janice for too long and you like the weakling that you've always been, you go and mess it up."

"But I'm innocent." Janice said as her mind began to clear up a little. "You had me drugged and under suggestive hypnosis for years. I was only doing what you made me do; made me think. I tried to tell them the truth."

"What truth, who do you think is going to believe that?"

"I'll tell them that we're related. That you made me believe that I was you, to get me to commit murder."

"Too bad for you, that we look so much alike that I could easily take your place and especially with a bit of plastic surgery to augment the switch. You now look like I use to and I look like you. You see what a little hair color, a mold here, a mold there, eye color and always the glasses can do to change a person. I'm glad that Natalie didn't get a chance to see you clearly. That's why I instructed you to keep those glasses on at all times. No one is going to hear that wild story because once I inject you with what's in this vial you won't be able to tell anyone your name. I guess I do have to share some of the blame, though. You can't send a self-righteous girl to do an avenging woman's job. I'll just chock this one up as an opening scene and I'm the grand finale. They really won't see me coming. I will kill Sebastian; he will be my first target."

"You won't get away with murdering me. It's all down on paper and I gave it Michael. He won't be fooled by you."

"Janice, don't anger me. What did you do? When did you give Michael a letter?"

"I gave him something he'll be opening real soon. As you already know dear cousin, not all of the time I was under your control; lithium has a way of clashing with hypnosis, you know. You would know that if you didn't flunk medical school. So you can do whatever you want to me, *dear cousin* because soon it will be all over for you."

"I knew enough to carry on my mission and I know enough to be you." She said panicky.

"You think you can pose as me, by wearing that wig and glasses. You won't fool Natalie much longer."

Anger swelled in Kimberly almost like a bomb imploding from the inside out. So much anger she has not been allow or she has not allowed herself to experience in fear that she would not be able to keep up the Janice guise.

"I—hate---you---witch." She said forcefully as she grabbed Janice's head and started to bang it against the wall, she was leaning against. "I've *always* hated you. You have *always* tried to outdo me as the do-gooder you are. I hate you. I hate YOU. I HATE YOU."

She fell silent abruptly and stop the assault. She altered her mood back to calm.

"No matter at first you don't succeed, try and try again. No matter about Natalie either. It's a shame that she dodged the first bullet, but she will not be as fortunate the next time. This time she will be facing the real Kimberly. It's a shame really because I really liked Natalie and valued her friendships. But like all things sometimes, some friendships have to end."

It wasn't that she held a grudge against her because they were vying for the same man, she thought now silently to herself. Kimberly has finally given up on that pursuit because Michael has made his choice. If he wants to be with Natalie then he can be with her forever, rest in peace.

Silently, with hate in her eyes and a snarl, she injected the needle she told Janice would silence her. She injected it into Janice as painfully as she could, almost breaking the needle point off in the soft part of her shoulder. Janice simply turned her head. She knew that at this point there was nothing that Kimberly wouldn't do and she couldn't stop her.

She slowly began to feel the effects of the injection and was flooded with memories, dark memories. She remembered when she had to comfort Kimberly, the night of the attack and spent many a weeks trying to help her cousin through it. This was right after she had stolen drugs from the medical department at school, trying to kill herself. Janice was almost expelled by taking the rap for it and she swore she would never help her again.

She guessed she felt sorry for Kimberly because during her college years she was able to focus. She was not thinking of her horrible past and finally it seemed as if she was allowing her life to start anew. She was allowing herself to feel like a real woman with real triumphs.

After a fail relationship with Michael Montgomery and realizing that she was wrong, a chance to make up with him came by. Sebastian Black halted all of that and reverted Kimberly back to the basket case that she had been practically all their lives. Janice honestly felt like killing him herself for what he had so callously done. That's how much control Kimberly gained over her.

Kimberly came to her again a few months after the raped and begged her to help her because she was pregnant. The two women decided that Kimberly would get an abortion. She didn't want her high society world to find out about this. They turned to Janice's boyfriend at the time, med student Everett Edwards. Everett was too green, too distracted to carry out a procedure as delicate as an abortion, but he performed it anyway. No wonder Kimberly was left barren, unable to bear children and she eventually punished him for that.

After the abortion, Kimberly left school and her plans took years to manifest, but they came to light. Years later she had an ongoing affair with Everett. He completely abandoned Janice who he was then married to, so he could be with Kimberly. The two of them were caught by Janice one night in his office. That nearly drove her insane. The image of their sexual embrace, forever etched in her mind. She divorced him shortly afterwards.

She had him hypnotized. Janice couldn't really blame him, she fell under her spell as well. He thought he loved her and couldn't see that she only stole his heart from Janice to punish him for the botched surgery. That was Kimberly's way. She expected everyone around her to be perfect and that is probably how she drove Michael away.

After they were married, Kimberly eventually turned on Everett in the long run. She killed him. Though Janice thinks she always planned to do it, which was also her way, advance planning. She bashed his head in with a heavy statuette and lied to say he fell down the stairs.

Janice was stupid to come running when Kimberly called her. She had her husband, what more did she need? She rang the doorbell and Everett was coming downstairs to answer the door. The door was unlocked and she opened it. She saw Kimberly hit him at the top of the stairs and pushed him down the full flight. When Janice ran to help him, Kimberly explained to her what she was going to say when the police came. In her story she implicated Janice. She would be accused of the assisting with the murder if she told. A crime of passion Kimberly said.

She made sure that Janice's would not be able to tell anyone of her dirty little secrets this time. No one suspected a thing, a clean murder. She was in control then and that's when the evil within Kimberly eventually took over, totally.

Five years of being under this woman's control and now this. Slowly she had drugged Janice daily, to the point that she would be so easily taken over by hypnosis. So quickly that Janice doesn't even remember if it was her suggestion or Kimberly's to commit these heinous acts.

Now she will be punished for these deeds, an innocent among a malevolent goddess, whose powers are as invisible as the air itself. All that anyone is going to remember is that 'Kimberly' died the death of a murderous evil disserving. God how can this be...

Janice dreamed as she seemed to fade away, of the memories of things she witnessed and things told to her by Kimberly. She felt sorry for what Kimberly had become and what she had endured in her young life. The rape just opened up all the old wounds she had helped her seal when they were young girls.

The years of abuse from her psychotic father who took pleasure in watching his pervert gentlemen's club friends fondle and molest his daughter as he watched. He was nothing like Janice's father who was almost like a saint.

A few years later, as Kimberly got a little older she would share hysterically the horrors of the attacks with her and Janice would try to console her. It was through this that she chose psychiatry as her profession because she wanted to help others. But Janice couldn't carry the secret any longer, she couldn't handle the guilt of hiding it and she eventually told her father.

After telling him things moved in Kimberly's favor quickly. Her father was jailed. Kimberly's mother having divorced him remarried a very well to do man, Harmon Stanford, one that genuinely loved both her mother and Kimberly. So much that he adopted Kimberly as his own child.

She had a chance to move forward. But this never came to light. Instead of thanking her, Kimberly accused Janice of betrayal and never forgave her for what she thought was disclosure of her embarrassing past.

She just simply wanted to forget and Janice knew she envied her life. She just couldn't see that Janice had saved her. The only thing that she seemed to care about was revenge. Something Kimberly said she felt in her soul was all that she had. The cold calculated desire of paying back anyone who stood in her way and who hurt her in any way.

Kimberly walked out of Chicago Mental Hospital pleased with herself. Her Dr. Janice Edwards, persona intact. She was ready to begin again. Begin her revenge. But this time it will be quick.

Carry it on like she began those years ago, her attack on those who started this defile of her life. Like she did on those perverted, deprived friends of her father at that gentlemen's club he attended when she was a young girl. It took years to do it but she did.

Oh how she made their deaths an agonizing one.

Even when she was a little girl she liked to dress up and play act. She dressed in a wig and became this sexy bartender. Serving drinks to all the gentlemen's club members that day. Of course they were so far into their lust that they didn't even recognize she was there. They were too comfortable because they never had to fear persecution.

She poured them each a glass of Cognac brandy. She poured one for herself. They told her she wasn't going to leave the room without providing each of them with what she had best to offer. In her disgust she went into her act coercing them to first toast to her.

They all greedily, guzzled down their drinks. Anticipating an exotic evening as she accidently dropped her glass, spilling the contents. She bent down to clean up the spillage. She deviously and satisfyingly watched them all writhing in pain. The cyanide that she had mixed in with the brandy had begun to take quick effect.

She smiled cunningly at that memory. Those deaths were never solved. The police knew that there was a murder.

No one had paid any attention to her. They never mention a female bartender that mysteriously vanished.

No one knew she was there and most importantly they all died in agony of her vengeance.

It will be the same way now; punishing those who hurt her with their lies hidden in darkness.

All involved will die; Sebastian, Mona and many, many, more.

THE END

Additional works

Wrong Woman at the Wrong Time

Author's website
www.dharveyrawlings.com

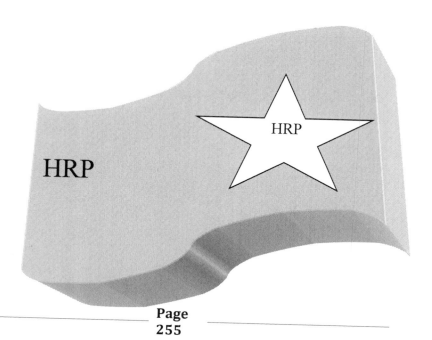

28576377R00145

Made in the USA
Charleston, SC
16 April 2014